Books by T.J. Mindancer

Tales of Emoria

Jame and Tigh Saga
Book 1: Future Dreams
Book 2: Present Paths
Book 3: Past Echoes
Book 4: Fall Time

Hekolatis' Promise

Emoran Campfire Tales

Other Books

The Queen's Sister

Novellas

Bountiful Glen

Tales of Emoria
Book 2

Present Paths

T.J. Mindancer

Mindancer Press
Bedazzled Ink Publishing Company • Fairfield, California

978-0-9886061-3-5 paperback

Cover Design
by

First published 2002
Renaissance Alliance Publishing
4th revised edition 2022

Mindancer Press
a division of
Bedazzled Ink Publishing, LLC
Fairfield, California
http://www.bedazzledink.com

The Saga of Jame and Tigh, Book 2

Note on Pronunciation

Jame is one syllable with a long "a." Rhymes with "fame." Tigh is pronounced "Tig." Rhymes with "twig." The spelling of her name follows the Ingoran rules of grammar where the "h" indicates the eldest daughter of the House of Tigis.

Chapter 1

FOG HAS THE ability to make the landscape disappear. The words of the Master Warrior ran through Jame's head as she squinted into the cloud world that held the young forest hostage. Fog also made sounds clearer and louder, and she winced at the thunderous noise coming from her own traitorous boots. She spun around at a rustle and caught the dusky figure of an indignant egret beating slow shadows into the fog.

She shook her head and continued on the rambling path. She opened up her senses and tried to keep her footfalls quiet against the leafy path, working to achieve total awareness of everything around her. Emoran scouts had the ability to ghost through a forest fog without even rippling the vapors or casting shadows on the impenetrable white. But she wasn't dealing with an Emoran scout . . .

She spun around at a snapped twig about ten paces away—*Ah ha, got you*—only to find her hands pinned to her back. "Aagghh."

"Want to try it again?" Tigh breathed in her ear and released her hands. Jame turned around and put her hands on her hips. "How did you do that?"

Tigh raised an eyebrow. "I didn't do anything because," she pounced into the dense fog and reappeared with a girl clutched in her hand, "someone else made that noise." She presented the wide-eyed girl to Jame.

The girl shivered. "Don't hurt me."

"We're not going to hurt you," Jame said. "What are you doing out here?"

"I'm practicing my tracking skills." The girl straightened. She didn't look more than thirteen or fourteen.

"Must be contagious," Tigh muttered.

Jame narrowed her eyes at Tigh, who answered with an innocent expression.

"So, you stalk unsuspecting travelers?" Jame took in the girl's poorly dyed black leathers and black wooden sword peeking over one shoulder.

"My friends and I are having a war tomorrow, and my side lost the last time," the girl said, turning shyly to Tigh. "I was practicing."

"War?" Tigh stepped around the girl and stood next to Jame.

The girl looked up at Tigh in awe. "Did you fight in the Wars? Were you a Guard? Bal's Children. That's a black-bladed sword. I've never seen one in person before. Can I look at it? My friends will never believe this."

Tigh rolled her eyes and raised a meaningful eyebrow at Jame.

"My name is Jame, and this is Tigh," Jame said.

She never imagined the Guards would ever be objects of hero worship among young girls. But girls tended not to look much beyond the battle skills and the weapons in choosing their heroes.

"Tigh?"

Jame realized her mistake as the girl's attention focused on a startled Tigh. "Uh, what's your name?"

"You're Tigh the Terrible?" The girl was in some kind of hero worship haze because she fell to her knees and bent down to kiss the boots of a very alarmed Tigh.

"Jame?" Tigh gave her a pleading look.

Jame sighed and pulled the reluctant girl up and away from Tigh. "Is your village up ahead? Our horse needs a new shoe."

The girl looked around, confused. Tigh rolled her eyes and sounded a low whistle. A large pale horse trotted out of the fog.

"Gessen was that close, too?" Jame rounded on Tigh, who struggled to keep an amused look off her face.

"Maybe you should have spent a couple more seasons in Emoria before you decided to put all that warrior stuff behind you," Tigh said.

"You're Emoran?" The girl looked as if she was about to faint from excitement. Jame and Tigh rolled their eyes together.

"If you take us to your village, we'll tell you all about it," Jame said in resignation.

"I can't believe this is happening," the girl gushed. "My friends are going to just die." "Now there's a thought," Tigh mumbled as she grabbed Gessen's reins and followed

Jame and the Guard-worshipping girl down the foggy trail.

TIGH SHIFTED THE saddle bags hanging off her shoulders and wondered if Jame had gotten a little carried away when selecting cooking ware from the kitchens of the House of Tigis. Of course, the scroll of instructions on preparing Ingoran food weighed at least as much as the frying pan. *Maybe Jame'll have it memorized by the time we return to Ynit so we can leave the scroll at home.*

She lazily snatched an arrow out of the air before it grazed her ear. She studied the construction of the shaft and had to admit it was nicely made. A flourish of whispers from the three girls hiding behind a row of fat oil jars outside the spice shop told Tigh they were impressed by her skill at catching arrows.

What's this? They think they can sneak up on me after making all that noise? She grinned in amusement. This was kind of fun as long as they didn't start yakking at her.

Tigh landed from a flip several paces in front of the three puzzled girls sprawled on the spot she'd just occupied. She ignored the sounds of admiration rising up behind her and continued walking.

"Now they're going to be practicing flips all winter," a woman said from an open doorway. She was of medium height with a streak of gray through her dark hair.

Tigh paused and glanced at the Peacekeeper sign hanging over the door. She shrugged. "They'll outgrow it."

"I'm Kandar, peacekeeper." The woman held out her arm.

"Tigh, peace warrior." Tigh grasped Kandar's forearm.

"Your companion has gone to the Inn." Kandar nodded at a two-story building across the road. "We have a couple of cases for her. Nothing terribly exciting—just a property dispute and a damages suit. Unless you want to bring charges against those girls for assault." She glanced at Tigh, amused.

Tigh grinned. "I have to admit, it's an unusual way of making strangers feel welcome."

Kandar snorted a laugh. "Come on. Let me buy you a drink." She led the way across the road into the inn. "It all started when a storyteller came through last spring. He told story after story about how the Guards won the Wars. About their bravery and skill as fighters, leaving out the ruthless gutting of cities and how the Federation kept complete control over you."

Tigh nodded as they sat at the end of a long wooden table in the tavern room of the inn. "Usually storytellers like to exaggerate the more gruesome parts of war."

"I had a little chat with him about that," Kandar said as an older man put two tankards of dark ale on the table. "Thank you, Rewer." She smiled at the man.

"Anything else you need, just give a holler." Rewer grinned back.

Tigh hid her amusement by taking a sip from the tankard.

"The storyteller said he'd been hired by the Federation Council to tell those particular stories," Kandar said.

Tigh was stunned by this revelation. The storyteller had passed through the village in the spring—around the time she'd been finally captured and taken back to Ynit to be cleansed. So, the Federation Council was already trying to remove the more undesirable aspects of the Guard enhancement program from the oral history of the ordinary people.

She frowned. "Surely the people berated him for telling false tales."

"That's the funny thing," Kandar said. "We're in the middle of nowhere, really. The Wars had been little more than rumors and whispers. The skills of the Guards kept us from having to give up our daughters to replenish their armies. Don't get me wrong, we heard dark rumors about the Guards, but we'd much rather believe the heroic tales of the storytellers."

Tigh stared at the dark ale for a few heartbeats. "They wouldn't be able to tell these stories in the larger towns and cities. It's interesting the Federation Council decided to spread these tales in the places untouched by the Wars."

"Maybe they were trying to create safe places where the Guards could go and live," Kandar said. "I find the stories of cruelty hard to believe if you're an example of a former Guard."

Tigh sighed and took another sip of ale. "The storytellers wouldn't be able to find words horrific enough to describe our cruelty and ruthless disregard for life and property. We've been cleansed of that, but it's hard for people who witnessed us when we were Guards to accept that we've changed. Most people would be telling you to flee for your life if they saw you with me."

Kandar gazed at Tigh with speculative eyes. "I didn't get to be a peacekeeper without learning to be a good judge of character. You're about as ruthless as my two-moon-old niece. If I hadn't witnessed your brief display of skills, I might have had problems believing you had it in you to be a warrior, much less a former Guard."

"I have it in me to protect Jame and anyone else who needs protection," Tigh said. "Everything else had been cleansed out of me and I had to relearn it."

"Really," Kandar said. Her attention was captured by something at the back of the chamber.

Tigh turned to see Jame exchanging a few words with Rewer. "She's probably asking about a meal because she's starving."

A grinning Jame approached the table. "I just ordered some food. I'm starving. What are you laughing at?" She made Tigh scoot over on the bench and took a sip from the tankard before pushing it in front of Tigh. "I made arrangements to hear the cases tomorrow."

"Good." Kandar nodded. "We don't get arbiters through here very often, and sometimes we have to wait several moons to settle these things. It doesn't help the general climate of the village, if you know what I mean, when people are at odds for too long."

"I'll let them know back in Ynit this region could use another arbiter," Jame said.

The smell of food was followed by bowls of Ingoran stew placed in front of her and Tigh by Rewer.

"Thank you." She grinned and picked up a fork.

"I'll have my niece fill the tub while you're eating," Rewer said.

"Tub?" Tigh asked around a mouthful of stew.

"I thought a hot bath would be nice for a change," Jame said.

Tigh lifted a rakish brow, and Kandar hid her amusement behind her tankard of ale.

"TOO BAD GESSEN can't carry around a tub." Jame sighed as she sank into the steaming water and leaned back against a relaxed Tigh.

"Gessen has enough to carry with half my parents' kitchen ware on her back." Tigh ran the scented soap over Jame's shoulders.

"A frying pan, a pot for water, and three plates," Jame said. "You'll be thanking Bal we have them the first night we're not near a village."

"I'll be sure to find easy to cook plants until you have that cooking scroll memorized." Tigh got her hands in place to stop a well-aimed splash.

Jame turned and got her hand into position to make the splash. "Are you saying my cooking may possibly be less than appetizing?"

Tigh pulled their bodies together and whispered, "Everything about you is appetizing."

Jame grinned, and Tigh didn't have a chance to defend herself from the ensuing assault.

Jame was surprised that a full sandmark passed before they managed to finish their bath and get out of the cooled water.

"Brrr." Jame shivered as Tigh wrapped a large linen cloth around her and gently rubbed her dry. "Winter will be here soon."

"We need to be back in Ynit in a fortnight," Tigh said as Jame returned the favor and rubbed the moisture off her. "Maybe after that we should keep to the southern coast where it's warmer."

"I've always heard the Maymi Peninsula is an interesting place," Jame said.

Tigh shook her head. "It's too far from Ynit. We'll go there next year when I don't have to report home once a moon."

"I still don't understand why they feel they have to treat you differently from the other Guards," Jame said as she pulled on her leathers.

"Because I *am* different," Tigh said. "If this is what it takes to put their minds at ease, then I'll gladly do it. It's only for a year."

"It could have been worse, I guess." Jame ran a hand through her damp short hair.

The sound of several scampering footfalls and excited high voices in the corridor brought a profound look of resignation to Tigh's face. She pulled on her leathers and pressed an ear against the door.

Jame looked on in amusement. She loved to watch Tigh play.

Several dramatic shushing sounds took the place of the footfalls. Tigh pulled the door open, revealing four startled girls staring at Jame. A grinning Tigh remained hidden behind the door.

"May I help you?" Jame asked.

"We were just, uh . . ." a slender girl stammered. She was of medium height and wearing beat up black leathers and a wooden sword strapped to her back.

"Looking for Tigh?" Jame raised an amused eyebrow as Tigh rolled her eyes. "Come in. Don't be shy."

The four girls took a few steps into the room, and Tigh closed the door behind them. Startled, they turned to find a grinning Tigh standing in front of the door with arms crossed.

"Are you really Tigh the Terrible?" the girl asked.

Tigh nodded. "Yes."

The girl glanced at her friends. "You led the last campaigns that ended the Wars?"

"Yes," Tigh said, arching an eyebrow.

The girl frowned. "What are you doing here, then? I mean, you're a hero."

Tigh exchanged glances with Jame. "I'm serving the Southern Territories as a peacetime warrior."

"Peacetime warrior." The girl nodded as the other three nudged her. "We'd like to know more about that."

Tigh gave her a puzzled look. "Being a peacetime warrior?"

"We want to be warriors. But we aren't at war," the girl said.

Tigh nodded. "You want to be able to defend your village."

"We were hit by raiders last fall," the girl said. "Kandar did her best to muster a defense, but it wasn't enough. The raiders got our grain and made off with half our sheep."

"You've never had problems with raiders before?" Jame asked.

"Not for as long as anyone can remember," the girl said. "We've never had any trouble from outsiders. Right after the raiders hit, a storyteller came through telling tales about the heroic Guards during the Wars. We got the idea of starting our own militia to help defend the village."

"But you realized there's more to it than being able to swing a sword or shoot an arrow," Jame said.

"Yeah," the girl said, disheartened.

"What are your names?" Jame asked.

"I'm Magit and this is Trics, Emlid, and Steph." Magit pointed to each girl.

"Did you shoot the arrow?" Tigh stepped up behind Steph and pulled an arrow from the quiver on the girl's back.

Steph backed away from Tigh. "I wasn't trying to really hurt you or anything."

"Nicely made arrows," Tigh said. "And not a bad shot."

Steph relaxed, looking both proud and embarrassed by the compliment.

"So, Tigh," Jame tried to maintain a solemn expression, "do you think you could help these girls out?"

Tigh made a show of looking the girls up and down. "I guess I could work with them while you're taking care of business."

"Really?" Steph squeaked and the girls bounced with excitement.

"Warriors don't bounce." Tigh crossed her arms and leveled a stern look at them.

The girls stopped bouncing and focused all their attention on Tigh.

"We'll meet tomorrow after the morning meal. Find an open area suitable for sparring."

"Yes, Commander." The girls snapped to attention.

Jame hid her amusement behind a hand.

IT WAS AMAZING how the sounds and activities of a village could go from the occasional "gotcha," screams, yells, clattering of wood against wood, and groans, to well- coordinated shouts, foot stomps, and clashes of wood. Tigh knew, within a sandmark, these girls were serious about forming a defense militia for their village. The ones who weren't serious had quit the game long before she and Jame walked into the village.

"Is it true your friend is an Emoran?" Emlid asked as the girls took a break after two sandmarks of intense drills.

"Yes." Tigh nodded, a little uncomfortable about the way several of the girls were eyeing her. She needed to ask Jame about the crushes of teenage girls.

"What's Emoria like?" Emlid asked as several girls gathered around.

"I've never been there," Tigh said, staring at the edge of the forest that stretched away from the patch of field they were in.

"Then how'd you meet?" Trics asked.

"We met in Ynit," Tigh said.

The girls gave her uncomprehending looks.

"That's where the military compound is. That's also where the arbiters' school is."

"So, she was there to become an arbiter, and you were there as a warrior." Emlid jumped with enthusiasm. "And in the middle of that, you met and fell in love. That's so romantic."

The girls sighed, and Tigh sent a beseeching appeal to the impish deity who oversaw her destiny.

"But Emorans are fierce warriors," Magit said with a frown. "She doesn't seem very fierce to me."

Tigh grinned. "Trust me. She possesses every bit of the legendary fierceness of an Emoran warrior."

"Have you ever fought her?" Trics asked, as eager faces turned to Tigh.

Tigh tried to keep down the trepidation that still surfaced at the thought of engaging in even a bit of friendly sparring. "Jame chooses words as her weapons. I wouldn't have a chance on such a field of battle."

"But that's not the same as fighting with a sword." Magit swung her black painted wooden sword in one of the newly learned formations.

"You're right," Tigh said. "Words are much more powerful weapons."

The girls stared at Tigh with profoundly confused expressions.

"How can you say that?" Magit asked. "Skill with a sword commands respect and forces people to listen."

"But words can turn the dreams of village girls away from having their own farm or shop someday to becoming warriors skilled enough to defend those farms and shops." Tigh smiled at their startled expressions. "You're in this field because of the words of a storyteller."

The girls jumped a little at a nearby crunch of autumn dried grass. Jame was almost next to them before they were aware of her. So much for the summer-long wars to improve their warrior skills.

Jame's attention was focused on Tigh, who grinned at her. "Actually, the sword was never my weapon of choice. I always preferred the staff."

"Staff?" Magit scrunched her face. "What good is that against a sword?"

Jame lifted an eyebrow. "In the hands of an Emoran warrior, all weapons are equally lethal."

"Wood against metal?" Emlid shook her head.

Jame turned to Tigh and gave her a questioning look.

Tigh, startled, raised her eyebrows. "We don't have a staff."

"I just passed a pile of cleaned wood pikes." Jame nodded to the line of trees.

"They're used to repair the outer walls," Trics said.

"Do you think we could give them a little demonstration?" Jame's eyes asked more than that simple question. It was a challenge and a personal request for Jame to tap into her warrior side with Tigh.

Tigh straightened and took a deep breath. "If you're not too worn out from throwing words around all morning."

Jame held Tigh's eyes for several heartbeats then smiled. "I think I can muster up a little energy to knock some of the arrogance out of a certain warrior." She raised her chin in a teasing challenge.

"The only thing more arrogant than a warrior," Tigh said with a mocking grin, "is an Emoran word-slinger who thinks she can beat that warrior."

"Is that a challenge?" Jame sauntered up to Tigh.

"Yep." Tigh put her hands on her hips and looked down at Jame.

"I'll be back in a heartbeat." Jame grinned and trotted down the path to the cache of spare pikes.

Tigh strode to the middle of the field. She pulled her sword from the scabbard, and the girls gasped in admiration of the black blade. Tigh whipped the sword through a series of smooth maneuvers. Jame, holding a staff about her height in length, strolled onto the field. The wood seemed to flip and turn on its own in her facile hands.

Tigh laid her sword on her shoulder and admired Jame's handling of the staff.

"Taking a rest?" Jame asked. She whipped the wood near the ground, causing Tigh to jump to avoid a nasty blow to the shins. "I thought warriors didn't bounce."

Tigh hit the ground and neatly flipped over Jame. "We don't bounce. We flip." Jame turned and swept her staff at Tigh, who stopped it with the sword.

"These girls seem to think I can't disarm you," Jame said as they backed away from each other.

Tigh grinned. "You always disarm me." She whipped the staff from Jame's hands.

"That was unfair." Jame retrieved her staff.

Before Tigh recovered from her amusement, she was on the ground with her sword several paces away. The girls gasped at the speed with which Jame moved.

Tigh was frankly stunned. Her reflexes and speed were legendary. Had the cleansing taken that much edge off of her skills? Jame seemed to be just as stunned. This was something they needed to work on. Together.

"Nice move," Tigh said as she climbed to her feet.

"It's something I used against Argis," Jame said. "I guess it still works."

Tigh picked up her sword and slipped it into the sheath. She wrapped an arm around the still bemused Jame and turned to the dumbfounded girls.

"Always remember," she gave Jame's shoulder a squeeze, "never judge your opponents by their size or their weapons. Jame was trained to be an Emoran warrior. They practice hard and have standards that all warriors must live up to."

The girls, having gotten over their shock, gathered around Jame. Tigh shook her head in amusement as their curiosity about the staff increased, and Jame answered their endless questions.

Chapter 2

"I'M GOING TO be sore tomorrow, aren't I?" Jame asked as Tigh refilled her mug with tea.

"Probably." Tigh took Jame's hands and gently rubbed her thumbs over the wood roughened palms. "No blisters, though. Just a little chaffing."

Jame sighed. "I really should keep up my skills. For exercise, if nothing else."

"I need to work on my skills, too." Tigh took a sip of tea. "It's strange. I didn't feel any different than when I sparred with the other peace warriors. But they don't possess the skill of warriors trained to fight in battle." She raised sad eyes to Jame. "I never thought I'd lose that ability."

"That's the one thing that can't be cleansed from you." Jame grasped Tigh's arm across the table. "You're just a little rusty. It's been nearly three years since you last fought in battle."

Tigh stared out at the crowded tavern and nodded. "The only way to know for sure is to practice." She smiled. "That's something we can do together."

Jame mirrored Tigh's smile. She never stopped being amazed at how their lives meshed so seamlessly together.

Tigh picked up a fork to sample the cook's latest attempt to please his Ingoran visitor. "Not bad." Jame chewed on a mouthful of greens. Like all eager converts, she had quickly developed an expertise in the subtleties of Ingoran cuisine. "It needs less lemon juice and more ground mustard to be perfect."

Tigh grinned at Jame and then looked toward the door on the other side of the room. "We have a visitor," she muttered as she scooped up a forkful of sprouts in a poppy seed sauce.

"What?" Jame frowned at Tigh and then looked behind her. A small, slender woman wearing a cloak of the colors of Artocia, the city-state that oversaw the village, conferred with Rewer. The animated innkeeper kept flashing a look in their direction.

The woman nodded and approached their table. She was thin to the point of being birdlike, with light brown hair piled neatly under an embroidered cap. The clothing peeking out from under the cloak was what the villagers called city-weave—expensive and beautifully dyed.

"Jamelin Ketlas?" The woman's precise voice held a bit of a question in it as she took in Jame's plain brown leathers.

"Yes," Jame said, her curiosity ablaze.

"May I sit?" The woman indicated an empty chair at the table.

"Yes, of course." Jame smiled, put down her fork, and exchanged glances with Tigh.

"I'm Lavkin Tanerdon," the woman said as she settled into the chair. "I'm a representative for Jande and Rend. Are you familiar with us?"

"The House of Scrolls." Jame's curiosity turned to intrigue. "This is my peace warrior and life companion, Tigh."

Lavkin looked at Tigh, who continued with her meal. "How nice to have a peace warrior who's also your life companion. I couldn't help but notice your choice of food—"

"Tigh is Ingoran," Jame said. "And I became Ingoran when we were joined."

"Ah." Lavkin nodded. "You're probably wondering what I'm doing here, in this village."

"It seems a little small for a Jande and Rend Scroll Shop," Jame said.

Lavkin emitted a laugh. "Yes, you're right. I'm actually here because we heard that Ynit had finally assigned another peace arbiter-at-large for the Southern Districts. The moment we heard you were in Artocian territory, Jande sent me out to find you. Jande and Rend have shops all over the Southern Territories, and it has always been a tradition to extend a personal welcome to our legal representatives."

"Thank you." Jame sifted through Lavkin's words. "I find it hard to believe you came all the way here just to say hello from Jande and Rend."

"Most merchants and affluent citizens send letters of welcome to the new arbiters. But Jande and Rend prides itself on the personal touch. And Jande wanted to make sure you received this." Lavkin removed a soft cloth bundle from her belt pouch and laid it on the table. She pulled back the top folds of the cloth and revealed a silver scroll marker. The long flanges that gently slipped onto a scroll to mark a passage in the text were in the shape of arbiters' mallets. The Jande and Rend insignia was prominently engraved on the upper tab.

Jame stared at the scroll marker. Ingel had neglected to tell her about some aspects of her new job. "Please thank Jande for the gift, but I'll have to decline it."

"Decline?" Lavkin raised startled eyes. "It's a simple token of welcome."

Jame captured her eyes. "If the House of Jande and Rend doesn't understand why I'm declining this gift, then I don't doubt someday it'll be needing my arbiter services. I suggest your employers brush up on the law in case I happen to cross paths with them before a Tribunal."

Lavkin responded with a nervous laugh. "You're new to being an arbiter-at-large. There are little traditions that have developed over the years. Small gifts of this sort are simply tokens of appreciation for the hard work you arbiters do for—let's face it—very little pay. We feel we help our community by giving gifts you can exchange for lodging or supplies, if need be."

And spreading the name of Jande and Rend each time the marker changed hands. Jame could handle this several ways, but there was one way that hopefully would be repeated through the network of merchants and individuals who were most inclined to need the services of an arbiter-at-large.

"If that's your worry, then let me put your mind at ease." Jame smiled. "I'm fortunate that I am joined with a member of the House of Tigis."

Lavkin shifted her startled gaze to Tigh, who was dissecting a potato. "House of Tigis?"

"The eldest daughter of the House of Tigis," Jame said.

Tigh gave a stunned Lavkin a brief smile before returning to her meal.

"Eldest daughter?" Lavkin asked.

"Tigh's parents surprised us with a generous joining gift," Jame said. "Between that and the help of my Emoran sisters—"

"Emoran sisters?" The color in Lavkin's face drained away.

"I'm Emoran," Jame said. "Anyway, we always look out for one another. Although, we tend to be a little more violent than some—"

Lavkin shot to her feet, then recovered some dignity. "Please excuse the shortness of our visit. I need to get back to the city tonight. It's been a pleasure meeting both of you. Please visit us the next time you're in Artocia."

"The pleasure has been ours." Jame flashed her a disarming smile. "Don't forget this." She re-wrapped the scroll marker and pressed it into the flustered Lavkin's hand.

Jame and Tigh watched as the representative of Jande and Rend fled the tavern.

Tigh grinned. "You are so bad."

"Yeah." Jame investigated a reddish sauce. "But it was so much fun."

IT TOOK SEVERAL heartbeats for Jame to connect the strange groans and garbled utterances with Tigh lying next to her. She turned over and squinted through the darkness at Tigh, who was valiantly struggling against a dream.

"Tigh," she whispered, knowing better than to touch her. "Tigh, it's Jame. Whatever you're fighting can't hurt you."

Tigh, as if reacting to this foreign intrusion into her dream, struggled harder until her eyes popped open, and she bolted up and sat looking dazed.

Jame sat up and put a soothing hand on Tigh's heaving back. "You were having a bad dream."

"Dream." Tigh frowned. "There was a battle. I was doing everything I could to join in the fighting, but something was holding me back. The more I struggled against it, the tighter the hold."

Jame nodded and pulled Tigh into her arms. "I think your mind is trying to deal with the fact that your skills aren't what they used to be."

"I enjoyed being a warrior," Tigh mumbled against Jame's shoulder. "I loved the way my sword felt like it was a part of my soul. How every muscle, every move was focused on the opponent. It was taken from me against my will, and I want it back."

"Maybe we can find some former Guards who will spar with you," Jame said.

Tigh lifted her head and gazed at Jame with astonished wonderment. "Have I told you lately how much I love you?" She captured Jame's lips with her own.

"I guess that was a good idea," Jame said.

"I think that will help regain my skills and take away my uncertainties about them." Tigh wrapped her arms around Jame and settled them back down in the bed.

"I wonder why Ingel didn't tell me about the practice of bribing arbiters-at-large." Jame lifted her head and gazed down at Tigh.

Tigh smiled. "Maybe she knew you wouldn't be tempted by it."

"I can't believe my predecessors accepted gifts like that." Her career had just begun, and she already faced disillusionment.

"If one arbiter accepted a gift, then that's enough for a merchant to claim it's common practice," Tigh said. "Exaggeration is a finely crafted art for most merchants. The actual product is usually half of what a merchant boasts it is and a quarter of the asking price."

"No wonder she blanched when she found out you were a member of the House of Tigis." Jame grinned, feeling much better.

"Let's just say the House of Tigis wouldn't be as successful as it is without being masters at the art of winning favor of anyone with the power to sway an election or a Tribunal," Tigh said.

"Hmmm," Jame responded. "I wonder if they'll think you're the ultimate bribe from the House of Tigis."

Tigh's expression was worth several pounds of silver. She lifted her head and dropped it back down, forcing the air to hiss through the feathers in the pillow. "My parents are going to kill me."

"Why?" Jame couldn't keep from laughing at Tigh's theatrical sigh of resignation.

"The people who want to win your favor will try to go through the House of Tigis," Tigh said. "Let's just say, my family's going to become extremely popular throughout the territories."

"Maybe I shouldn't have mentioned your background then." Jame put her head on Tigh's shoulder. "It seemed like the best solution to stop people from thinking I'd take a bribe because I needed the money."

"It was a good solution." Tigh pulled her close. "I just need to send a message of warning to my parents. They'll be able to take care of it. Knowing them—after they let me have an earful about it—they'll probably think it a fun diversion."

Jame looked up at Tigh. "So, your strange sense of fun is hereditary?"

"Oh, yeah," Tigh muttered as they drifted back to sleep.

"UGH. YOU'RE DOING it again." Jame trotted past a bored Gessen to the casually striding Tigh.

Tigh slowed down. "Sorry."

"Not that I'm complaining too much about your long legs," Jame said. "They've come in handy a time or two."

Tigh flashed Jame an amused look. "Glad you appreciate them."

"That, too," Jame said with an impish grin.

They made the effort to match paces on the dusty expanse of the great road that followed the Nirlion Sea.

"I'm glad we decided to spend a few extra days working with those girls," Jame said.

"Their parents were relieved you introduced them to cheaper, less lethal weapons than swords," Tigh said. "Although several of the girls wanted me to tell them where the closest battlefield was so they could look for swords."

"They'll probably be the ones who end up in Ynit wanting to join the regulars," Jame said.

Tigh's attention was on the sliver of road rolling over the next rise of land. "A coach is headed this way." She steered Gessen to the side of the road to give the vehicle room to pass.

"It looks like it's slowing down." Jame frowned as Tigh warily watched the coach lurch to a stop about twenty paces in front of them. The splash of deep brown and blue across the vehicle's body indicated a coach-for-hire from Ynit.

"And I thought we were doing a good job of staying out of trouble," Tigh said as they approached the coach.

The side door popped open, and a wiry man of middle years jumped to the road.

"We heard you were near Artocia," he greeted as he took a moment to steady his legs. "I'm Sonder, special courier for the Federation Council. A case has been submitted to the Arbiters' Council that has need of the arbiter-at-large for the Southern Districts."

"So soon?" Jame asked. "I mean, all right. What is it and where is it?"

Sonder pulled a small scroll from a shoulder pouch and gave it to Jame. She held the document so Tigh could also read it, and two things immediately caught her attention.

"Jande and Rend. Why am I not surprised? It says that the trial will be held in Maymi." She looked up at Sonder. "Tigh has to return to Ynit every two fortnights as a part of her condition of release from the Guards. Maymi is too far away to make that possible."

"You're to go to Ynit first," Sonder said, motioning to the coach. "There's a time constraint on this case. If a decision isn't made by the winter solstice, then Jande and Rend lose their right to protest the building of a rival scroll shop in Maymi."

Jame's mind raced. They had only two reasons to return to Ynit. One was to get permission for Tigh to miss her meeting with Pendon Larke and the other was to assign her a new peace warrior for this case. They had to know she wouldn't stand for that happening.

"I'll follow on Gessen," Tigh said.

Jame nodded, pushing down her reluctance to be separated from Tigh on the long journey back to Ynit. But this was her job, and she had to separate her personal feelings from her professional duties.

"Be careful," she said.

Tigh raised an amused eyebrow but softened her expression from a tease to an affectionate look. "Always. Let's get some of this stuff off Gessen."

Sonder helped them put the saddlebags in the coach, and then disappeared into the vehicle to wait for Jame.

It hit Jame that this was the first time they were to be separated for more than a few sandmarks since they left Ynit. The first of many times, to be sure, but it was still difficult to leave her, and Tigh seemed to feel the same way.

"I'll be close behind you." Tigh wrapped her arms around Jame. "You can have the fire burning and a meal from the kitchens ready."

Jame tightened her hold as she nodded against Tigh's shoulder. She finally pulled back and looked into tender blue eyes that shimmered with an undercurrent of reluctance.

"I'll make sure they prepare your favorite dishes," Jame said, surprised at the urge to cry. They were traveling the same road a few sandmarks apart from each other, for Laur's sake. Nothing to get choked up about. But she saw in Tigh's eyes the same struggle to keep away the tears.

Tigh pulled Jame into a gentle kiss.

"I'll see you in Ynit," she whispered against Jame's ear.

"Love you," Jame said as she pressed her lips against Tigh's cheek.

"Love you, too," Tigh said.

JAME TOOK ONE last glance back at Tigh and climbed into the coach. Tigh stood unmoving until she realized she was in the way for the coach to turn around.

Tigh mounted Gessen and by the time the coach rolled back toward Ynit, she was a good distance ahead of them, determined not to spend a heartbeat more than she had to away from Jame.

JAME BLINKED HER eyes open. After a few disoriented heartbeats, she sat up from being sprawled on the uncomfortable coach seat. The coaches hired by the military were more utilitarian than the plush transports that catered to the well to do travelers.

She rubbed her eyes and noted that Sonder dozed sitting up with arms loosely crossed. Couriers learned to sleep under any conditions. An energetic drumming on the roof alerted her to what woke her up. *Rain. Tigh's out there miserable and cold while I'm in a dry coach.*

Jame's guilt turned to worry at a flash of lightning. The autumn storms could be treacherous as they blew winter-touched cold from the north into the southern warmth. She squinted at the thick quartz windows and determined that night had passed, and day was gallantly trying to assert its light through the heavy storm.

That meant they were close to Ynit. She prayed to Laur that Tigh had found a nice dry barn or building to sit out the storm. She reexamined that thought. The idea wouldn't even occur to Tigh.

Three soggy sandmarks later, the coach slowed, and Jame greeted the clatter of the wheels against hardened adobe brick with relief. It took a full day to Ynit from the road south of Artocia. Too long to be in a bumpy coach with only a few short stops and too long to be away from Tigh.

Sonder awoke and, after taking a moment to assess where they were, smiled at Jame. "We're here." Then he frowned at the roof. "Is that rain?"

Jame shook her head in disbelief that he could sleep through the insistent patter. She shouldered the pair of saddlebags just as the coach jolted to a stop.

"Thank you, Sonder," she said, then flung open the door and jumped into a puddle. The main fortress, brooding in the thick ribbons of rain, stood in front of her. "Good. It'll save me a trip." She ran up the steps and through the opened doors.

Jame shook off the raindrops and pushed wet hair out of her eyes as she strode to the office of Pendon Larke. She paused at the door that always stood open and rapped on the frame. A thin, elderly man with a wisp of white hair and a face wrinkled more often than not with a smile, looked up. His expression radiated a genuine joy at seeing her.

"Jame. Come in." He grinned as he waved her in. "Sit. You're soaked. What are you doing here? I thought you were out arbitrating. Where's Tigh?"

For the first time in a day, Jame relaxed and laughed at Pendon's exuberance. She put down the saddlebags and sat in the visitor's chair. "We've been called back to arbitrate a cross jurisdiction case. Time is tight on this case, so I was brought back on a coach and Tigh is riding Gessen in."

Pendon frowned. "In this weather?"

"We were south of Artocia when we were found," Jame said. "It wasn't raining there."

"I'm sure she has enough sense to take care of herself." Pendon nodded. "She's strong and healthy at any rate. She spent a good portion of the Wars up north in snow and ice."

"That's good because I want her with me on this case," Jame said.

Pendon smiled. "Of course, she'll be with you. A few sniffles wouldn't be enough to take her away from your side."

"Maybe not a few sniffles, but the Tribunal can," Jame said.

"What do you mean? I haven't heard of any trouble," Pendon said.

"The case is going to be heard in Maymi," Jame said. "It's too far away for her to be back in Ynit for her meeting with you."

"When that condition had been set, the Tribunal had no idea she'd become a peace warrior." Pendon gave her a sly grin. "They only had to ask anyone in the compound. It was the only logical thing she could do as your life companion."

Jame laughed. "We had planned it ever since Glaus."

"Do you have your argument prepared?" Pendon asked.

"Yes," Jame said, having spent most of the day, after the rain woke her, working out her strategy.

"Go get dry and get some rest," Pendon said. "I'll see what I can do to schedule a hearing with the Tribunal tomorrow."

"Thank you." Jame jumped out of the chair and grasped Pendon's hand across the table.

"I'm one of those around here who thinks Tigh the Terrible is long dead," Pendon said.

"Unlike the other Guards, there'll never be a chance your Tigh will revert back."

"Unfortunately, our convictions mean nothing," Jame said. "Only time will prove us

right."

JAME STOOD IN the open doorway and stared at the slashing rain. Four miserable sandmarks was too long to wait for the only person she wanted to see more than anything. The fire chattered away and several Ingoran dishes sat warming on a shelf in the fireplace. A clean, dry sleep shirt was laid out on the bed. All that was needed was one cold, soaked, hungry, exhausted warrior.

An agonizing quarter sandmark later, Jame let the tension that had seeped into every muscle of her body flow out as a bedraggled figure turned the corner into the little lane they lived on. Tigh seemed to be concentrating on just walking as she made her way to the small adobe house.

Before Tigh cleared the threshold, Jame grabbed her hand and pulled her into the bedroom.

"Clothes. Off," Jame said.

Tigh managed a sheepish grin as she complied with Jame's help.

"Nice weather," Tigh said as Jame rubbed her body and hair dry with a large cloth. "I hope Gessen is getting a good rub down."

"They took good care of Gessen for over two years," Jame said. "She'll be fine. Now put this on." She pulled the shirt over Tigh's head and led her back into the front room.

Jame fetched the dishes from the warming shelf and placed them on the table. She was stopped by the sight of Tigh slumped on the bench. Damp tousled hair fell into her unfocused eyes as her body shouted its need for rest. Yet she had a happy, contented expression on her face.

"What?" Tigh asked.

For an answer, Jame threw her arms around the befuddled Tigh and hugged her. She then sat next to her and pulled the lids off the dishes. "Sometimes I can't believe how lucky I am to have found you."

Tigh put down her fork and gazed at Jame with adoration. "I pray to Bal every night before I fall asleep that you're not a dream that will be gone when I wake in the morning."

A stunned Jame wrapped her arms around Tigh's neck. "I'm not a dream and I'll always be by your side."

"My mind knows that, but my battered psyche needs to be reminded on occasion," Tigh said with a weak smile.

"I've dedicated my life to mending that old psyche of yours." Jame brushed her knuckles against Tigh's cheek.

"It's in good hands," Tigh whispered.

Chapter 3

IF JAME DIDN'T learn anything else from this brief detour back to Ynit, she learned that arbiters-at-large with a pending case received preferential treatment. The Tribunal shuffled their hearing schedule so they could meet with her before the first regular case of the day.

The somber-faced keeper of the bench led them to a small room down the corridor from the main hearing chamber. Jame kept darting glances at Tigh who was trying not to sniffle. She'd already planned a nice quiet afternoon at home pampering Tigh. She grinned with anticipation as the keeper of the bench opened a door and nodded them into the chamber.

The seven members of the Tribunal sat behind a long thin table in front of a row of plain wooden chairs. Appeals were meant to be brief and to the point, so not much attention went into the comfort of the furniture.

"Come in. Sit." Acran, a heavy woman with a mild demeanor, waved to the chairs.

Jame and Tigh sat and waited as Acran studied a sheet of paper. Tigh interrupted the silence with a powerful sneeze, and she focused on the hands in her lap as the Tribunal stared at her.

"Bal bless you," Acran murmured. She shuffled the parchments and turned her attention to Jame and Tigh. "You're here to appeal one of the conditions for Paldar Tigis's release from the Guards. She is most fortunate to have someone who has been deemed skilled enough to become an arbiter-at-large to represent her."

Jame shifted at the compliment and glanced at Tigh, who grinned in agreement.

Jame cleared her throat. "Thank you, Tribune Acran. I feel fortunate to have Tigh as my companion and my peace warrior, which is why we're here today."

Acran nodded. "You may proceed with your argument, arbiter."

"Thank you." Jame had to keep from standing. She preferred to be on her feet, putting her whole body into her words. "I'm requesting that the conditions for Tigh's release into society be reduced to the standard agreement given to the other rehabilitated Guards. I'm not asking this as a special privilege for her but as a consideration that her circumstances have changed since those conditions were issued."

"Circumstances," Onderal said. He was a small man with a perpetual frown creasing his forehead. "She's still the same person she was a moon ago when we set those conditions."

"The circumstances aren't about who she is but what she is." Jame held up a scroll. "This is Tigh's separation document. It says that upon her release from the Guards and from the state she must meet with a healer here in Ynit once every two fortnights. And if she ever exhibits any sign at any time during her life that the cleansing process has been reversed, she must be taken into custody."

She paused to gauge the reaction of the Tribunal. Besides Onderal's scowl, they seemed to be open and interested in her presentation.

"Tigh may no longer be a part of the Guards, but, as a peace warrior, she's still employed by the state," Jame said. "The condition of regular meetings with a healer in Ynit was made as a precaution so you could keep track of her for the first year after her rehabilitation and is no longer valid because she works for the state. Not only that, she was given the position of peace warrior-at-large for the Southern Districts. Hardly a position for someone the state doesn't trust."

"She was given that position because of your special relationship," Acran said.

"Exactly," Jame said. "So, you don't have to worry about losing track of her because of her position, and she's in a stable relationship, so you don't have to worry about her mental or emotional well-being. Also, we've made Ynit our home, and we'll be back quite regularly. If Pendon feels he wants to meet with Tigh, he can do so at that time. All that I'm asking is for Tigh's conditions of release be the same as all the other Guards, so she can pursue her job without restriction."

"You have a case in Maymi?" Acran glanced down at her notes.

"Yes," Jame said. "And we all know if you don't allow Tigh to go with me, she'll break her conditions to follow me. Then we'd have to go through the whole rehabilitation process again, and I'm sure you don't want to do that."

The Tribunes stared at Jame with alarmed expressions.

"The latest you can afford to leave is the day after tomorrow?" Acran asked.

"Yes," Jame said, as the apprehension tightened in her chest.

"This must go through the Federation Council. Fortunately, they're convened in Balderon right now, a half day by coach," Acran said. "We'll let you know our decision before daybreak two days from now."

"Thank you." Jame took a deep breath and wondered if a time would come when she no longer had to defend Tigh—a time when Tigh was finally completely free.

JAME STIRRED A sauce in a small dish on the warming shelf above the fire, and Tigh sliced up various vegetables on a slab of stone on the table.

Jame looked up at the knock on the opened door and let out an excited yelp. She went to the door and pulled Ingel into a hug.

"Ingel. Come in," Jame said. "You're just in time for the mid-day meal."

Laughing at Jame's cheerful exuberance, Ingel allowed herself to be pulled to the table, where she sat next to a standing Tigh, who flashed her a grin.

"I just stopped by to say hello and ask if you have any questions concerning your new case," Ingel said as she watched Tigh chop through celery, cucumbers, spinach, and carrots, and then scoop each up and dump them into separate small bowls. Tigh pinched spices from several jars into each of the bowls.

"I have one question," Jame said, as she brought several small dishes of pale sauces from the warming shelf to the table. "Why didn't you tell me about the habit of bribing arbiters?"

"You've already been approached?" Ingel asked. "You've only been on the road a few weeks."

"A representative of Jande and Rend tracked us to a tiny out-of-the-way village just to welcome us to the neighborhood and give us a small gift," Jame said.

Ingel arched an eyebrow. "And your response?"

Tigh smothered a chuckle as she cast amused eyes at Jame.

"I told her if they don't know the law enough to know why I couldn't accept the gift, then they'd certainly be needing my services someday," Jame said.

Ingel snorted a laugh. "I bet that went over well."

"Not quite as well as when I mentioned that Tigh was a member of the House of Tigis, and I was Emoran." Jame grinned. "She seemed to think arbiters didn't make enough money to live on and these small gifts were to help out in a pinch. Of course, that was before I knew they were bringing suit against the House of Cadryn in Maymi."

Tigh pulled a pot of boiled potatoes off the fire, fished them out of the water into a larger dish, and brought it to the table. She and Jame then added the final spices and sauces to the different vegetables.

"Jande and Rend are used to getting their way, so they may make things unpleasant for you," Ingel said as Tigh put a plate and utensils in front of her and then sat across the table with Jame.

"I'm hoping the comment about my Emoran sisters always being ready to help out will deter some of that," Jame said. "Help yourself. I've taken quite a liking to Ingoran food."

"I've heard there are interesting rituals for eating Ingoran meals," Ingel said.

Tigh nodded. "If you're interested I'll explain as we eat."

"If you don't mind," Ingel said.

"There's one thing I learned about Ingorans," Jame said. "They love to talk about their food."

Tigh shrugged. "Food is an important part of the merchant culture." She pointed to a small bowl of greens in a light sauce. "The first course is green beans simmered in what we call a clear sauce . . ."

"Thank you for the meal," Ingel said as they sat back and washed down the last of the food with spiced tea. "I'll have to try Ingoran cuisine more often. I have a class in a quarter sandmark, so I'd better get going, but I want to see you both again before you leave."

"You seem confident that both of us are going," Jame said.

Ingel smiled. "Let me put it this way. If the Federation Council is foolish enough not to give in to this minor alteration in Tigh's conditions for release, they'll be faced with enough appeals from everyone in this compound who were involved in Tigh's rehabilitation to make them wish they'd never heard of Tigh or the Guards."

"Really?" Jame asked.

"You two have touched a lot of lives here. Almost forgot." Ingel pulled from her belt pouch a small cloth bag tightly closed with a string. "A courier delivered this to me for safe keeping."

Jame took the small bundle. "Thank you, and we'll come by to see you before we leave." Jame closed the door behind Ingel and gave the bundle a couple of speculative tosses.

"I think I know what that is," Tigh said as she snatched the bag out of the air.

She took a curious Jame by the hand and led her out the opened rear door into their small back yard. The usually dusty air was temporarily clear from the storms the day before and the sand crystals in the surrounding adobe walls sparkled in the overhead sunlight.

Tigh emptied the contents of the bag into her hand and turned to Jame. "My parents were appalled that we were willing to wait until we could afford these, and my father wheedled the sizes out of me before we left Ingor. He said for us to think of them as a joining gift."

Tigh raised Jame's hand and slipped a simple ring on her finger. Jame stared at the band of silver dancing in the sun, lost for words to express the wondrous feeling flowing through her. She opened Tigh's hand, took the other ring, and slipped it onto her finger.

Jame intertwined her fingers with Tigh's, and they gazed at the rings. Something about them made their joining feel real and permanent, and she could hardly breathe from the profound joy surging through her.

"That was a wonderful thing for your parents to do," Jame said. "I think we can forgive them for going against our wishes to wait until we could afford these."

Tigh answered with a happy grin as she enveloped Jame in her arms.

"HOW IS IT you were sneezing this morning and now you're not even sniffling?" Jame settled back into Tigh's arms as they sat on cushions in front of the fire in their bedroom after the evening meal.

Tigh shrugged as she wrapped her arms tighter around Jame. "I seem to be able to fight off things like that."

Jame was torn between being glad Tigh wasn't sick and disappointed she'd been denied the opportunity to pamper her. She studied the silver peeking through their intertwined fingers. That alone should make the Federation Council think twice about denying their appeal. Because it wasn't just an appeal for Tigh, it was an appeal for both of them.

"Do you think what Ingel said about everyone petitioning the Federation Council if they deny our appeal is true?" Jame asked as she polished Tigh's ring with her finger.

"When you were in Glaus and I was really missing you," Tigh murmured in her ear, "everyone seemed to be bringing me food and making me take a nap. Bede let me work in the children's ward, and no one said anything when I fell asleep at my desk in the archives."

Jame grinned. "I got a lot of ribbing about that from the other arbiters. They thought you were so helplessly cute."

"Cute? I was miserable," Tigh said. "I missed you so much I couldn't think of anything else."

"Pendon came up with the theory that your extreme reaction to our separation was tied to your emotional recovery from being a Guard," Jame said as she relaxed against Tigh's strong body. "I was miserable without you, too. The difference was, I had something to concentrate on. All I could think about was finishing the case as fast as possible so I could get back to you. Now I have rather fond memories of Glaus."

"So do I," Tigh mumbled against Jame's hair. "What will you do if the Federation Council denies the appeal?"

"I'll resign and take one of the regular arbiter positions," Jame said.

Tigh sucked in her breath and Jame waited for her to respond.

"We'd both have to resign—at least for a while—until all the petitions and subsequent appeals put enough pressure on the Council to see things our way," Tigh said. "You've always wanted to be an arbiter-at-large. Don't compromise that dream for what's only a temporary setback."

"I'm not going anywhere without you by my side," Jame said. "So, they'll have the choice of having to find a new arbiter for the Southern Districts or let both of us go to Maymi."

Tigh grinned. "I think you just found that nice, cozy spot between a rock and a hard place the Federation will find themselves in if they turn down our appeal."

Jame gazed at Tigh. "You're right. They have to give in."

"Or spend many moons dealing with a feisty Emoran arbiter who won't rest until they see what a big mistake it was to have gone against her wishes."

"Feisty, huh?" Jame descended on Tigh's surrendering lips.

"Did I mention I like feisty?" Tigh mumbled when Jame pulled back to catch her breath.

"If you didn't, I was ready to work with you on it until you did," Jame breathed into Tigh's ear.

"I could always stand to be convinced some more," Tigh said.

"I think I can do that," Jame murmured, and she did her best to cover all the finer points of feistiness and then some.

THE SHOUTS CAME closer, followed by hard-soled shoes clattering on the adobe brick. Unheeding invaders to her peacetime world, bursting through the quiet crooked lanes, scattering the raked sand and artfully placed rocks of her yard, pounding on her door demanding entrance . . .

Tigh sat upright on the bed before sleep had released its hold on her. She sucked in air and willed her brain to turn on all her senses. She picked up noises that didn't belong in the Ynit that she shared with Jame. They were sounds from her life before.

"What?" Jame's sleep-confused voice penetrated Tigh's scattered focus.

"Something's going on," Tigh muttered as she tossed back the covers and vaulted off of the bed.

Jame sat up and frowned for a few heartbeats. "They're rallying all fighters, regulars, reserves, retired . . ."

She jumped out of bed and pulled on her clothes alongside Tigh.

"Never thought I'd have to wear armor in Ynit again," Tigh mumbled as she buckled the sections of molded metal to her leathers and clipped her sword sheath to her back.

"Maybe it's a drill," Jame said.

"They wouldn't dare tick off a compound full of well-armed warriors like that." Tigh waited for Jame to finish pulling on her boots.

"I see your point." Jame grabbed the neglected Emoran staff decorating the corner of the chamber. Tigh stopped in mid-stride and stared uncomprehending at her. "In case I have to defend myself."

Tigh nodded as Jame rushed past her and pulled open the front door first. She stopped and stared at the chaotic and foreign sight. Tigh guided her through the door into their front yard.

A cacophony of shouting and running sounded from the unseen warren of lanes around them. Everyone, warriors and civilians alike, were stumbling out of their houses, pulling on clothes, armor, weapons, and rushing to the main square.

Tigh and Jame jogged past their bleary-eyed neighbors of arbiters and their families. None seemed to know why they were out in the cold dawn air instead of warm and asleep. Many faces wore the same grim mask as Tigh knew she wore, as if they were collectively flashing back to when this kind of alarm was almost as regular as meal call during the Grappian Wars.

They burst from the narrow confines of the lane onto the vast plaza that had once been the reviewing grounds for the armies of the Guard. Tigh was blinded by a horrific blow to all her senses. She stopped so suddenly, she stumbled to the rough adobe brick.

"Tigh." Jame dropped down next to the sprawled Tigh and pulled her to her feet.

Tigh could only stare spellbound at the hundreds of soldiers falling into their regimented lines as the civilians huddled near the edges of the square.

"Tigh. Look at me," Jame said.

Tigh trembled as Jame turned her head away from the plaza and pressed her palms against her cheeks. She sucked in air and worked to relax the paralyzing grip too many vivid remnants of her past still had on her soul. Only the intent gaze of green eyes on hers was strong enough to pull her away from the nightmare visions flashing through her mind.

"I'm all right," she said.

Jame slid her hands down Tigh's face and neck onto her heaving shoulders. "Are you sure?" She searched Tigh's face.

Tigh nodded, forcing her mind into a meditative calm. It wasn't a matter of whether she was all right, it was a matter of pushing it aside to deal with later. "Remind me to talk to Pendon about this."

Jame relaxed and nodded. "Let's see what's going on."

With eyes on the adobe brick ground, Tigh turned back to the plaza and allowed Jame to pull her along until she had calmed her mind enough to raise her eyes.

"Where's your place?" Jame held onto Tigh as they walked through the forming lines of soldiers.

"Huh?" Tigh blinked at Jame. "Over here."

She led Jame to the front of the lines where harried-looking officers were engaged in an animated discussion.

A medium-height woman, in full armor with a long bow arching over her shoulder, broke from the small group and hurried to intercept Jame and Tigh.

"Commander," she said. "We need your help."

Tigh exchanged mystified glances with Jame as they followed the master archer.

"Tigh. Thank Bal." Commander Maure, a striking woman with thick gray hair and an impressive scar across her face, grasped Tigh's forearm in greeting.

"We'd heard rumors for about a year now of bands of raiders hitting outlying villages," Kare, the master archer, said. "It sounded like the usual post-War chaos and the raids were too sporadic to appear organized. It looks like we should have been paying more attention to them."

"What happened?" Tigh asked.

"We think they've been pressing in on Ynit from all directions for several weeks now because all of a sudden there's a ring of them about a sandmark's walk out in every direction," Maure said. "Several thousand of them."

Tigh frowned. She had just ridden a horse through those invisible raider lines. The severe storm probably saved her from a nasty encounter.

"They're probably after the weapons in the armory," Jame said.

Maure rested curious eyes on Jame. "That and to rid the Southern Territories of its defense force."

"Several thousand?" Tigh asked. "Do they have siege engines?"

"So far we've counted six," Maure said.

"Is that wizard still here?" Tigh asked and blinked at the half-dozen eyes riveted on her.

"Wizard?" Kare asked.

"We have a few hundred peacetime soldiers. Most have never seen a battle much less fought in one," Tigh said. "They have several thousand fighters plus, at least, six siege engines. I was just thinking of a way to even up the odds."

"Do you think the wizard will help us?" Jame asked.

Tigh shrugged. "She will if she wants to make it back to wherever she comes from. Anyway, I think she's as interested in the survival of a peacetime force as the rest of the Southern Territories."

"But a wizard." Maure shook her head. "They've always refused to help us during the Wars."

"Allow me to suggest that Jame talk to her," Tigh said. "If anyone can persuade her to help us stop these raiders before they get close enough to use those siege engines, Jame can." She turned to Jame, who looked embarrassed by the compliment.

"We can't refuse any options at this point," Maure said, gaining Tigh's respect as a thoughtful leader. "We'll bolster the defenses within the city, and you have a talk with the wizard. And let us all pray to Bal that we succeed in stopping them."

Chapter 4

MAURE BARELY HAD a chance to open her mouth, much less utter a command to the lines of troops, when shouts rose up from the guard towers perched on the outer walls.

"Now what," she muttered as a soldier ran down the wall steps and across the plaza to her.

"Commander," the young woman panted, "they're within sight. Closing in."

"I thought you said they were a sandmark's walk away." Tigh scowled as she strode toward the wall with Jame, Kare, and Maure hurrying after her.

"They were—three sand marks ago," Maure said as she caught up to Tigh.

Tigh bounded up the steps. She stared across the arid land that stretched to rolling hills closer to the sea and studied the line of what appeared to be an organized army. Dust clouds indicated that trenches were being dug and tents dotted the desert with shimmering earth colors.

"Raiders," Tigh muttered as she squinted at a line of banners fluttering in front of the rapidly assembling camp. The low sun stretched the shadows of the poles into thin sharp lines. "They aren't raiders."

Maure gave Tigh a startled look. "What?"

"Look at those banners." Tigh had read everything she could when she had worked in the military archive during her rehabilitation. She'd been especially fascinated by the stories about peoples from across the seas, living on lands as vast as their own.

"I can't make out the design," Maure said. "I don't have Guard enhancements."

"It's a silver dragon," Tigh said. "They're from across the seas."

"Across the seas?" Jame asked.

"How could an army of that size land here without being seen?" Kare asked.

"As you said, there have been seemingly random raids for the past year or so," Tigh said. "We went through a village in Artocia that had been raided. They took only food and supplies and left the villagers unharmed.

They could have landed at various remote harbors and made their way across country in small bands."

"So, you're saying this is an invasion force?" Jame shaded her eyes and stared as more tents, undulating in the breeze, rose up from the sandy ground.

Tigh shrugged. "That would be my guess."

Maure ran a shaky hand through her hair. "They're not giving us much of a chance to prepare."

"I think that's the idea," Tigh said. "We don't have time to recruit more troops. We'll just have to work with what we have."

"Which isn't much against an obviously well-organized army," Maure said. "I have no battle experience. I want you to lead us."

Tigh gazed at Maure. "I'll advise but you must lead. Otherwise, you'll never learn."

"Going from complacent peace keeping to all-out war like this has frightened me more than the worse nightmare, I'm not ashamed to admit," Maure said. "But it's not a nightmare. It's real and something has to be done about it. And you're right. It's my responsibility even though I want to hand it over to the warrior who led the victorious campaign that ended the Wars." She straightened and faced Tigh. "I accept your counsel in this matter."

Tigh unsheathed her sword and saluted Maure. "I'll serve your command as you see fit."

"Uh," Jame gasped in a strangled voice as she grabbed Tigh's sleeve. Her attention was riveted on the desert plain. "I think we need to come up with something fast."

Huge clouds of sand billowed toward them. Tigh's keen eyesight caught the fierce morning sun striking long flanks of metal crawling across the sands.

Kare gasped. "What are they?"

Tigh draped an arm over Jame's shoulder and pulled her close. "Something we have no defense against. Our only hope is that wizard."

JAME WAS RELIEVED the heavy wooden doors were opened at the end of the corridor because she would have slid right into them as she tried to stop running on the age- smoothed stone floors of the old fortress building. One of the original structures in the compound, the ancient building resembled the stone temple monuments that rose from the thick forests in the eastern wilderness.

Jame slid to a stop right inside the reverberant six-sided chamber. Long wooden tables were draped with oversized sheets of parchment covered with thickly inked gibberish to her eyes, and a strange structure fashioned from sticks and twine sat in the middle of the floor like the skeletal remains of an eccentric animal.

"Yes?" came a friendly, if somewhat preoccupied voice.

Jame frowned as she determined the source of the voice in the echoing chamber and focused on a mound of finely spun cloth piled on the floor near a window. As she approached, she saw the wizard cross-legged and facing the wall while flipping through the pages of a small bound journal.

"Minchof?" Jame asked.

Friendly, watery, blue eyes blinked up at her. "Yes." Using the wall to support her ample body, Minchof stood and faced Jame.

"My name is Jame," Jame said. "We've been caught by surprise by an invasion force from across the seas. They have the city surrounded with several thousand troops and weapons that can cause much destruction from a distance."

"Oh my." Minchof put her hands to her cheeks. "I'm glad I sent my apprentices home already. My work is almost done here."

"We need your help," Jame said.

"Wizards don't participate in armed conflicts unless it's against the actions of another wizard," Minchof said.

"We're not asking you to participate in an armed conflict," Jame said. "We're asking you to save a city, possibly the entire Southern Territories."

"And how do you propose I do one without the other?" Minchof asked.

"Work with us to devise a way," Jame said. "I'll be honest with you. We have no time. They're moving in swiftly to catch us off guard. We need either a miracle or a wizard. Fortunately for us, we have both." She smiled at Minchof's puzzled expression. "We have you and we have my partner, Tigh—the former Supreme Commander of the armies for the Southern Territories."

"Ah." Minchof nodded. "The one Guard who's been rehabilitated without any troublesome complications." She slipped the journal into the multi-layered folds of her filmy long tunic. "I'll help as much as I can. But unless that other army has a wizard, I'm limited in what I can do."

"They've been moving through our land undetected, they must have a wizard helping them," Jame said as they strode from the chamber.

"Then it's a very clever wizard or else I'd have felt the use of magic," Minchof said. "But I'll do what I can."

"That's all we ask for," Jame said as they hurried down the corridor.

MINCHOF BLINKED IN the bright morning sun. "Oh my."

Every inhabitant within the military compound was in the plaza. The soldiers were lined up listening as Commander Maure, atop a reviewing stand, issued detailed orders. The civilians were gathered in impromptu huddles and looked as if they were forming plans of their own.

"This way." Jame led Minchof to Tigh, who was still on the wall.

The portly Minchof paused to catch her breath at the top of the steps and followed Jame along the parapet.

Tigh cast a thankful glance at Jame then turned her attention to Minchof, who stared wide-eyed at the sandy plains.

"Oh my," Minchof breathed.

Two dozen wooden catapults, holding thick metal shafts, stood just out of arrow range.

"See the sticky substance on the metal?" Jame asked. "Tigh thinks it's flammable and they set those giant spears on fire before catapulting them."

"What can you do?" Tigh asked.

"I can't do anything directly to the weapons or those who wield them," Minchof said. "I *can* extend the walls of the city upward to stop the spears."

"That'll, at least, break their advantage of a surprise attack," Tigh said. "How fast can you cast the spell?"

"Working on it now." Minchof grasped her tiger's head amulet and muttered a few words. "Reach out your hand."

Tigh extended her arm over the parapet until she poked at an invisible barrier. "How high does it go?"

Minchof grinned. "Twice the height of the actual wall."

Jame breathed out in relief. "That ought to do it."

"Not a heartbeat too soon," Tigh muttered.

Fires flared on the ends of long staffs, and the breeze picked up barked commands. The staff bearers marched into position and, in response to a sharp order, lowered the flaming tips to the metal points of the shafts. Jame heard the roar of the flames engulfing the spear points. Within heartbeats, the flaming projectiles hurtled toward them. Tigh pulled Jame into her arms and crouched under the lip of the lookout.

Minchof was about ready to follow suit but stopped and gave the air above the wall a puzzled look.

"Get down," Tigh said. "The impact could still cause damage."

"Something's wrong," Minchof muttered. "Bits of the spell are unraveling for no reason I can detect. I have to hold the wall together from the impacts."

Jame peeked back at the plaza. The people stared in shocked surprise as flames burst over the walls and fell away. She was grateful they didn't panic and more than a few glanced at Tigh, as if waiting for her to give a signal as to what they should do.

The bursts of flames stopped, and Jame looked up at Minchof. "I think you did it."

Tigh released Jame and they looked down at the still flaming spears lying in the sand outside the wall.

Tigh surveyed the wall in both directions and looked back at the plaza. "I don't think any spears got through. What happened?"

"You say they're from across the seas?" Minchof rubbed the perspiration from her forehead. "I think they have a wizard with them. One who practices an ancient and very difficult kind of magic. We've heard rumors of a wizard cult in the realm of the Silver Dragon who practice this magic."

"I guess I should have mentioned their banners have a silver dragon on them," Jame said.

"It wouldn't have mattered," Minchof said. "I wouldn't have believed it before."

"But now?" Tigh asked.

"Now I can help you as much as my ability allows." Minchof straightened. "It's our duty to stop a wizard who uses magic for war instead of peace."

"Thank Laur." Jame raised her eyes to the patron deity of the Emoran people.

Tigh turned to the watching crowds. "Clear the plaza and stay under cover as much as possible. Dowse the rooftops with water."

"THIS INVISIBLE WALL'S like a dam with too many leaks in it," Minchof said to the small group gathered in an old war room. "One leak gets plugged and another opens up. That foreign wizard's trying to keep me from sending out probes to find the source of the magic. The problem is, she's learned to weave wards that make the practice of magic almost undetectable."

"Almost," Tigh said.

"The practice of magic is always detectable," Minchof said as she wandered the chamber, occasionally batting a hand as if to wave away a pesky insect. "The first thing we need to do is gather all the practitioners of magic within these walls and concentrate their efforts on keeping the invisible barrier in place. Of course, that won't stop the wizard from making the projectiles go higher, but that kind of spell takes time to weave, and I don't think they're prepared for this kind of opposition."

Jame frowned. "The wizard didn't know you were here?"

"It's a possibility, since I haven't cast any large spells in a fortnight, just small experimental weaves," Minchof said.

Maure looked up from studying the scaled detailed replica of Ynit and the surrounding countryside on an octagonal platform. "So, we get the healers and the assorted weavers of magic together to keep the barrier in place and then what?"

"Then I'll do my magic," Minchof said with a grim smile and a flourish of hands.

Tigh snorted at Maure and Kare's wide-eyed expressions. "I think we bought a little time by catching them off guard. We've evacuated the civilians to the shelters, and we've posted soldiers all along the wall. We'll know if they try another attack. In the meantime, we let Minchof instruct all the magic-weavers on how to keep the invisible wall in place so she can find that wizard."

"Then what?" Maure stalked the chamber in frustration. "We're going to have to face that army at some point. I just can't see any way around it."

"You forget you have a former member of the Elite Guard right here," Jame said. "Tigh routinely led her army against forces many times its size. You fought in those armies."

Maure grimaced. "Mind games."

"You have to let her do what she does best," Jame said. "It's our only hope."

Maure turned to Tigh, who stood passively, waiting for her orders.

Maure straightened and strode up to her former Commander. "Your assignment is to work out a strategy to stop that invasion force with as little bloodshed as possible."

"Yes, Commander." Tigh whipped her sword into a salute.

Maure gazed at Tigh for a few heartbeats. "You have a plan?"

"Yes," Tigh said.

Maure cocked her head. "Care to enlighten us?"

"Are the caches of weapons we put outside the walls still there?" Tigh asked.

Maure strode to the scale model of Ynit. "How could I have forgotten? We put those out there in case Ynit was attacked. But how do we get to them? They're behind the enemy line."

Tigh turned to Minchof. "What's so special about a silver dragon?"

Minchof blinked at her then flashed a truly wicked smile. "You're good. No wonder we won the war."

"What?" Jame looked between the two.

"If your society was based on aggression and invasion, what kind of symbol would you use to represent you?" Tigh asked.

"If it were me," Jame sauntered up to Tigh, "I'd use to most vicious creature I knew of."

"That's the silver dragon in the lands across the western sea," Tigh said. "At one time during the Wars, the Federation Council feared the Northern Territories would enlist peoples from other lands to help in their defense. So, we received instruction on everything known about them just in case."

"But the silver dragon isn't a real creature," Jame said. "Is it?"

"As far as we know it's not real," Tigh said. "But that doesn't make it any less real or feared in their hearts. It's difficult to be rational when faced with a vision of what's been used to frighten people for generations."

Kare studied the positioning of the caches of weapons. "That'll only stop them for a little while, until their wizard convinces them our conjured silver dragon is only an illusion."

"It'll give us the distraction we need to get to those caches of weapons," Tigh said. "Under cover of an illusion."

"That'll leave less troops in the city." Maure creased her brows into a worried frown.

Tigh rubbed her chin as she studied the miniature city. "Can you protect us if we pull those metal spears inside the gates?" she asked Minchof.

Minchof beamed at Tigh. "I've extended the barrier around them already. I thought they might come in handy."

"But we don't have anything to catapult them with," Kare said.

"One step at a time." Tigh scanned the others as if to challenge them to make any more protest. She smiled and gazed at the model of the city she had made her home and was going to save—no matter what it took.

TIGH CROUCHED NEXT to a thick metal shaft. "Nice design and craftsmanship."

They'd been dowsed with water and dragged into the compound with nets of thickly twined hemp. Now the weapons of terror glistened benignly in the soft autumn sun.

"How'd they ever move something like this across the country without anyone seeing them?" Jame asked as she knelt next to Tigh.

"Hidden in merchant caravans probably." Tigh looked from the shafts to the top of the wall and back to the shafts again. "I wonder how many of these there are."

She stood, pulling Jame up with her, and led the way through the city gate. The citizens of Ynit, prepared from birth for the possibility of an invasion because of their proximity to the military compound, were busy securing their homes and shops. Cellars, concealed with cleverly devised trap doors, were beneath nearly every building and residence in the city. Ideally they were used to store personal treasures and foodstuffs that attracted ransacking invaders, and the people evacuated to main shelters so they could be accounted for and protected.

Jame scampered after Tigh, taking in the grim preparations for invasion and Tigh's calm determination. A disquieting feeling gripped Jame as she watched the passive Tigh sink into a role that was as natural to her as breathing. "Tigh."

Tigh turned around and blinked at Jame. "Sorry." She slowed her pace.

"Who's going to lead the group to the outer caches of weapons?" Jame asked.

Tigh stopped and stared at her.

"You're out of practice," Jame said. "You haven't had a chance to even test the extent of your skills yet."

Tigh cocked her head. "How'd you know I was thinking of leading them?"

"I know you." Jame smiled as they continued their trek to the eastern gate.

The crowds were heavy in that section of the city and a little more chaotic in the reality of a true crisis than they'd been in their orderly drills during the Grappian Wars.

"I also know you won't be doing anyone any good if you get hurt trying to pull off a heroic stunt. Besides, remember your reaction to seeing the troops lined up. Is this the right time and place for you to face an enemy in battle? When you're needed for your strategic skills rather than your ability to fight?" Jame allowed Tigh to think about this reminder that she no longer possessed all the skills of Tigh the Terrible. She had too many unhealed wounds, and the closer they came to anything that had to do with combat, the more serious the wound.

Tigh's expression relaxed a bit.

"Trust Maure's judgment in choosing the best warrior for the job," Jame said.

"We have no choice," Tigh said as they turned into a wide road and faced the eastern gate.

Dozens of soldiers and civilians had dragged thirty or so of the metal shafts into the city.

"Who's in charge?" Tigh asked as they approached a knot of soldiers studying the projectiles.

"I am." A soldier with short red hair stepped forward.

"Do you think you can haul these up to the top of the wall and place them, pointed side up and leaning outward, every five to ten paces?" Tigh asked.

"They're hollow, so they're not too heavy," the soldier said. "It shouldn't be difficult."

Tigh nodded. "Good. Send someone to the other three gates and instruct them to do the same thing."

"Most of them seem to be burned out," the soldier said. "I don't think we'll be able to re- light them."

"First rule of the Elite Guards. Never use an enemy's weapon the same way it was used on you." Tigh grinned. "With the size of that army out there, catching them off-guard will be as powerful a weapon as any sword."

"We'll get right on it." The redhead saluted, even though she outranked Tigh.

"What do you have in mind for those shafts?" Jame asked as they picked their way back through the city. Soldiers were now scrambling to build barricades around the evacuation shelters.

"Nothing yet." Tigh cast a sheepish glance at Jame. "But I can't think of any better place for them strategically, and it'd be a waste not to have them where they might possibly be useful. Second rule of the Elite Guards is to be as prepared as possible using everything at hand."

Jame nodded. "That explains those weapons hidden out there."

Deafening booms coming from all directions rocked the structures around them. Tigh was wrapped around Jame before either had a chance to think as a second and third round of heart-stopping explosions shook even the brick in the street. Panicked voices rose from the people still rushing to the shelters and they increased their pace.

"There goes the idea they wouldn't try anything until they penetrated our invisible wall," Jame said as they dashed back to the compound.

They ran across the plaza, up the steps on the wall, and stared out over the desert, seeing nothing but thick smoke.

"What do you think that was all about?" Maure asked as she and Kare hurried to them.

Tigh gazed over the sand and the billows of smoke about a thousand paces from the wall.

"I think they're moving closer."

Chapter 5

MINCHOF INSTRUCTED THE two dozen magic weavers residing in Ynit on how to keep the invisible wall intact, then turned her attention to the four score archers who were ready to run through the enemy lines to the weapons caches.

"This is the way the amulets work." She raised her voice as the archers studied their ceramic eagle's heads. "When each of you is in position, rub the amulet until it turns green. When all the amulets in a group have been rubbed, your leader's amulet will flare red. The leaders will then rub their amulets until they flare yellow. When all the leaders' amulets are rubbed, Kare's amulet will turn blue. Then Kare waits for her amulet to turn gold. This will be the signal from Maure to start the attack. Kare rubs her amulet. When your amulets flare gold, that is your signal to attack."

Tigh marveled at the ingenuity of the simple signal system and half-wished they'd had a wizard during the Wars. But she knew of only one wizard who'd been willing to use her skills in war, and she was long dead.

As the four groups of archers set off for each of the city gates, Minchof, head bent in thought, walked to Tigh and Jamc, who were tying up loose ends of the strategy with Maure.

"I've put together a spell that will tie the dragons and runners together," Minchof said. "Hopefully, we'll create enough distraction for their wizard that she'll focus on the big illusions that will bring strong reactions from her troops and miss the mice slipping through."

"It's a good strategy." Maure nodded then turned to Tigh. "This morning I thought we were trapped with no chance of facing such an army without being crushed. Now I have glimmers of hope. I want to thank you for reminding me the greatest weapon in battle is the imagination."

"Maybe you should hire a former Elite Guard to teach you their approach to strategy," Jame said.

"Not a bad idea." Maure gave Tigh a speculative look.

Tigh looked from Jame to Maure and sighed. "I'll think about it."

A soldier shouted from the wall.

"Ready to show the people of the Silver Dragon why we won the Grappian Wars?" Tigh asked.

Maure straightened and met Tigh's steady confident eyes. "Let's show them what we're made of."

The smoke from the fireballs had cleared enough to reveal that the foreign army had advanced closer, tightening the circle around the city.

"Is everyone in place?" Tigh felt a long missing thrill that she had experienced when she was about to engage the enemy.

Maure looked at her amulet. "Not yet . . . wait . . . yes, everyone's ready."

Tigh turned to Minchof. "Are your dragons ready?"

Minchof grinned. "In all their horrific ugliness."

"Commander Maure, the campaign is yours." Tigh saluted with her belt knife.

"Thank you, soldier." Maure unsheathed her sword. She took one last look at the score of archers waiting at the compound gate and whipped the blade in the sunlight.

A soldier shot a flare straight up from the middle of the plaza, and the ropes used to raise the gate squeaked and groaned as they slid the heavy gate upward.

A dozen dragons with glistening silver scales and eyes the color of crimson death materialized in front of the archers. They had sharp claws the size of a person's arm, sticking out from thick feet, and tails tapered into long sinewy whips. Teeth, that looked more like knife blades, were revealed as the dragons' long narrow muzzles dropped open in hideous grins.

"Laur's waterfalls," Jame breathed, "that's incredible."

"Thank you," Minchof said, looking on her handiwork with pride. "I tried to make them as close to the drawings of silver dragons as possible."

"The gate is open," Maure said.

Minchof smiled at her dragons, and they lumbered out of the gate. Even the ground trembled against their spell-driven weight.

"Good touch." Jame grabbed the railing as the wall quaked from the army of the scaled beasts.

The enemy camp was suddenly alive with shouts of dismay and calls for order. The remnants of smoke whirled as the enemy troops became a maze of chaotic movement.

Maure rubbed her amulet, and the archers ran through the gate in the dragons' wake. She looked over the wall to outside the gate. "I can't see them. That's amazing."

"I'll keep them hidden for as long as they're out there," Minchof said.

"How long do you think it'll take their wizard to convince them the dragons are an illusion?" Jame nudged Tigh as they stared at beasts so realistic they left deep squashing footprints in the rain-soaked desert sand.

"As long as it takes for the dragons to reach them," Tigh said, then turned to Minchof. "Slow their pace and let them engage in some menacing activity. Create a barrier of dragons between us and them." She looked around at the metal shafts propped against the upper wall with the points hovering over the outside ground. "If we set these on fire, can you propel them to just beyond the dragons?"

"Yes, but how can we set them on fire? There isn't enough time to cast a spell that will put a flame on all of them." Minchof scratched her head as she studied the closest shaft.

"Maure is going to order her soldiers to go to the compound storage and fill small jars with lamp oil. Then they're going to douse the points of these projectiles with the oil, light them on command, and use the ropes to jump the wall while you set the projectiles off. Right, Maure?" Tigh arched an eyebrow.

"Jame," Maure said, "you're a very lucky woman."

Jame beamed at Tigh as Maure rushed down the wall steps, barking orders before her feet hit the adobe brick ground.

"I could have told her that." Jame shrugged as they watched the silver dragons frolic in the morning sun.

KARE AND HER small band of archers had to fight the feeling of being exposed to the enemy as they squashed across the wet desert sand. It helped that the troops, dressed in sleek silver and bronze-colored tunics and leggings, were focused on the mythical beasts dancing grotesque quadrilles. Illusion or not, the dragons commanded attention and from the sound of it, the leaders of the invading army were having a difficult time bringing their troops to order.

Kare wondered at this as she padded between the legs of a dragon posed in a menacing stance. She couldn't believe an army, that could creep unseen over the countryside and surround Ynit without setting off an alarm until it was too late, would lack basic discipline. Unless Tigh was right, and the silver dragon was the ultimate terror in their society.

"Wish we could have done this during the war," Claudi, a small woman with an eagle eye, said as she caught up to Kare.

They hopped over the ropy end of a scaly tail, even though Kare knew they could have run right through it. "But the enemy would have had the ability to do it, too." She glanced back at her best archer. "Like now. We must keep alert to any tricks their wizard may play. Hope the other groups remember this."

"After dodging around big ugly dragons, I don't think you have to worry about the others panicking over what is obviously an illusion," Claudi said.

When the score of archers cleared the dragons, Kare signaled them to halt while she assessed the best path through the deep lines of silver and bronze as the enemy soldiers swallowed their fear and assembled back into formation.

"Don't you think it's kind of strange that only some of the soldiers seem to be overcome with panic?" She squinted at the faces of the enemy. "Look at them. Some of them can't take their eyes off the dragons, and others are just standing there not paying attention to anything."

"You're right," Claudi said. "I've never seen anything like it."

Kare bit her lip and remembered Minchof's parting words to her. If it didn't ring true then it was most likely an illusion. "By the Children of Bal. That explains how they were able to cross the country and sneak up on us."

"What are you talking about?" Claudi asked.

"Most of the army is an illusion," Kare said. "This is going to make our job much easier.

Let's go."

Walking amongst the enemy was disconcerting until Kare and her archers relaxed enough to trust Minchof's blanket of invisibility. Kare brushed past uniforms of silver and bronze and the counterfeit warriors were so apparent it was a wonder they looked real from a distance. The wizard seemed to be going for the effect of thousands of soldiers rather than detailing each one.

The weapons cache was a thousand paces beyond the soldiers who were pitching large tents behind the line of troops. Kare was impressed with how quickly they could pull down and set up camp through a clever use of poles and ropes. She diverted her attention to a gathering of women in finely cut uniforms outside a half-standing tent.

Kare signaled the others to continue across the sands to a small clump of boulders barely seen from that distance. She then trotted around the scurrying soldiers who were too intent on putting up the tents to notice the sudden appearance of footprints in the wet sand.

"You said you could detect the presence of wizards," a woman said. She had a strong jaw and the steady confidence of someone used to being in command.

"I can detect them if they are practicing magic," a small, thin woman said. A light brown cloth wound around rather than draped her body and her voice was almost magic in itself, with a timbre that seemed to sooth and caress the soul.

"And how did they know enough about our culture to choose the dragon to menace us with?" another woman asked. "Dragons that look like our own depictions of them."

"They probably know of our world in the same way we know about theirs," the small woman said, seemingly unperturbed by the agitated commanders. "They can create as many illusions as they want. As long as they think we're capable of crushing them, they'll run out of tricks and surrender to our siege. It's worked countless times before. There isn't any reason why it shouldn't work this time."

"She's right," a sharp-cheeked woman said. "We're masters of the siege. We win because we have the discipline to patiently wear down the enemy."

"Let the dragons dance." The strong-jawed woman's face creased in an evil grin. "It'll make the tale all the more interesting when we bring our victory home."

Unable to stop from chuckling, Kare sprinted across the desert to the special surprise that Tigh the Terrible, herself, had prepared for anyone foolish enough to challenge her title as the supreme master of the siege.

"I CAN'T BELIEVE we had enough time to douse all the shafts with this oil, not to mention get the safety ropes in place before they tried something," Maure said. "What are they up to?"

Tigh, who was studying the construction of a nearby metal shaft, looked up at Maure and then out over the desert at the now calm lines of enemy troops. "They're calling our bluff— except they don't know we're not bluffing."

Maure frowned. "An army that large could just storm this city."

Tigh shrugged. "They'd rather bring us down with a siege. They're far away from home and can't replenish their ranks and have to rely on what they find to keep their armory well stocked and their bellies full. A siege is the best strategy. They know that this is the only full garrison in the Southern Territories and all the high commanders are here. It'd take time to muster a counter force from the pockets of soldiers scattered through our lands."

Maure stared at Tigh. "Did you know they were going to do this, instead of invade?"

Tigh rubbed her chin as her mind journeyed to a time when every decision she made hinged upon her ability to properly read the enemy's intent.

Jame wrapped a supportive arm around Tigh who smiled down at her and gave her shoulder a squeeze.

"That's what I'd do. That's what I did." Tigh gazed at the dragons, now stomping in a menacing way as they patrolled the desert. "At the Siege of Operal."

Maure sucked in a sharp breath and nodded. "I was there. It was war."

Jame removed her arms from Tigh's waist, held her face between her hands, and gently pulled it down until she could look into Tigh's eyes. After several heartbeats, Tigh lifted herself from the darkness her soul was plummeting into and took a deep breath. She turned her head and brushed her lips against Jame's palm then took the hands in her own and pulled them to her heart.

"I'd be lost without you," Tigh whispered. "You're my salvation from the past."

"And you're our salvation at the present," Jame said in a soft voice. "Those memories can be used for good now."

Tigh swallowed hard, trying to glean any good from the most horrific episode of the Grappian Wars. She'd found good only a few heartbeats earlier, coupled with a confidence in her ability to read the enemy and confidence in their strategy. Why was it all suddenly streaked in black?

"Tigh?"

The deep concern in Jame's voice sliced through the darkness. She saw the visible relief in Jame's eyes and was struck by a heart-stopping panic that she hadn't been cleansed. That she was capable of relapsing back into being a Guard. That everything that meant more to her than her life would be torn away from her.

Jame wrapped her arms around Tigh as if trying to physically catch her as her world plunged into the abyss of her deepest despair.

"Should I send for a healer?" Maure asked in a tight voice.

Jame shook her head. "No. She has to work through it on her own. We discovered that the memories recede when she's allowed to face them."

Jame led Tigh to a bit of wall that protruded enough to create a place for soldiers to sit. She knelt in front of Tigh, and Tigh could feel her closeness and comfort through her agony.

"THEY'RE READY," MAURE said in a hoarse voice as she stared out over the desert.

Jame looked at Maure and saw the amulet blaze green. Maure seemed to be struggling with her own panic. *Laur's waterfalls*, what did she ever do to receive the bitter gift of two warriors downed by their own worst enemy at the most inopportune time?

"We need to get off the wall so you can give the signal," Jame said as she pulled Tigh to her feet. "The plan will only work if we take them by surprise, so we must be quick about it."

Maure tore her eyes from the desert and helped Jame maneuver Tigh down the narrow wall steps. They sat her down on an upturned wooden box.

Jame released Tigh's arm and watched as Tigh blinked away the faraway haunted look in her eyes. It was if the black shadow that Jame knew draped over Tigh's mind was gone— like an echo on the wind.

Tigh clenched her fists and jumped to her feet. Jame grabbed her shoulders and looked into her eyes, relieved to see the heart-breaking sadness gone.

Tigh took Jame's hand. "When we get this bothersome army off our doorstep, we're going to see Pendon."

"Before we leave for Maymi," Jame said.

"Light the tapers," Maure yelled.

The hiss of fire coming to life was all that was heard as a hush enveloped the plaza. Tigh savored the almost magical moments of peace that happened before the air was ripped with the violence of an attack. She watched with satisfaction as Maure raised her sword and, after making eye contact with a single soldier holding a flaming taper, lowered the blade.

CLAUDI STOOD ALERT as she clutched a palm-sized ball of fire dust wrapped in thick parchment in one hand and a small covered metal lamp in the other. She thought it amazing that she stood out in the open holding a lamp with a flame blazing in it with the enemy only a hundred paces away. She glanced around and could just make out a comrade on either side of her as they stood in an arc around the camp and toward the city.

A hissing noise, unlike any she had heard before, came from the enemy camp in front of her. Missiles of fire hurtled over the oblivious dragons and slammed into the wet sand with a sickening thud in front of the first line of soldiers. The fire jumped from the shafts before impact and danced on the sand until it found something to burn.

Claudi held the fireball and the lamp in front of her, careful to keep the short stiff fuse away from the flame, and waited for what felt like sandmarks rather than a few heartbeats. She had to watch the amulet around her neck and couldn't give in to her curiosity to see what was causing all the shouts and shuffles in the camp.

Her amulet flared gold. She assessed the chaotic scrambling of the enemy troops and latched onto a billowing half-pitched tent as her target. She thrust the stiff wick into the flame, ran several paces, and hurled the ball. Within a heartbeat, she dug another ball out of a shoulder pouch and lobbed it into a tableau of swirling smoke and shocked panic as fireballs from the archers all around her sailed into the camp.

Her wild grin faltered when a small slender figure wrapped in brown cloth emerged from the thick clouds of sand and smoke. The woman walked a few paces then stopped. She glanced around and then lifted her arm and pointed at Claudi. The woman waved her other hand, and a slow feral smile creased her face as she met Claudi's eyes.

By the Children of Bal, the spell of invisibility has been broken. Claudi ignited a fireball and heaved it at the woman. She ran as hard as she could in the wet sand. She glanced back. The slender woman watched the fireball hurtle at her and flicked a finger at it.

"Oh no," Claudi gasped as the ball flew back toward her.

She dove into a puddle of wet sand, hoping it contained more water than sand. She rolled over in time to see the wad of fire bounce off a wall that wasn't there and shoot back at the woman.

The woman—shock barely described her expression—didn't have time to avoid the blazing ball and was consumed in flame.

Kare and several of the other archers squashed across the sand to the stunned Claudi, who sat dumbly in the puddle staring at the pillar of flame that had been a woman just a heartbeat before.

"You destroyed the wizard." Kare pulled Claudi to her feet and wrapped powerful arms around her.

"That wasn't me," Claudi muttered.

"It was your fireball that allowed Minchof to do her magic," Kare said.

"They're retreating," Hoglan, a tall archer, said.

"I don't think we're invisible anymore," Claudi said.

"I wonder if the invisible wall will stop . . ." Kare began.

The soldiers of the Silver Dragon, in their hurried retreat, hit something invisible.

Kare grinned. "I guess it will."

Claudi and the other archers shaded their eyes against the glaring sun and watched a greatly diminished army of the Silver Dragon crash against the invisible wall.

"The magical soldiers are gone," Claudi said. "They vanished when the wizard died."

Caught up against the barrier, the invading troops, too puzzled and perplexed to be frightened, turned their backs on the archers and faced Ynit.

Several heartbeats passed as the smoke and the dust settled. The dragons, obedient to the end, stopped their patrol and lumbered back to the city gates that creaked open for them. Claudi thought it interesting that their wizard didn't break the illusion. Any lingering fear in the enemies' minds was a weapon in itself.

The abandoned banners of the Silver Dragon cracked in a gust of wind, heralding an approaching storm. The last dragon stomped through the gate and the enemy waited.

Thunder, not from the thickening gray clouds in the distance, broke through the voice of the wind. The city of Ynit created its own storm as hundreds of soldiers on horseback in full battle gear galloped out of the gates and formed a circle around their city.

A single rider on a white horse adorned with a simple saddle emerged from the compound gate and cantered through the line of horses into the abandoned enemy camp. Claudi shaded her eyes and saw that it was Commander Maure. She pulled her horse to a stop fifty paces from the cluster of agitated battle leaders.

"We give you a choice," Maure said in a strong voice. "Surrender or fight. It matters not to us, which you choose. We enjoy a good fight."

The battle leaders muttered agitated words to each other.

The sharp-cheeked commander of the forces of the Silver Dragon strode to the commander of the Southern Territories Reserves. The rumbling in the distance was real thunder and the sky crackled in flashes of light.

Claudi watched in fascination as the woman in silver and bronze studied the woman in simple utilitarian leather and armor. She realized that Maure didn't need a fancy uniform to exude the confidence of a battle leader.

"We lay down our swords to you," the woman shouted against the spirited weather. "I take the shame of my people into my hands."

Maure, expression unchanging, nodded back. She danced her horse around and faced the city. She slipped her sword from its sheath and pointed it to the clouds.

"People of Ynit. Victory is ours," she shouted as magic picked up her voice and carried it around the perimeter of the city. Cheers rose up from behind the city walls.

Claudi exchanged grins with her comrades as they savored their first battle victory.

Chapter 6

"THIS HAS GOT to be the most unbelievable day I've ever witnessed," Jame said as she and Tigh lounged near the entrance of the warren of lanes that led to their home.

The six hundred or so prisoners were lined up in the plaza surrounded by the proud soldiers of the Southern Territories. Curious inhabitants of the compound and citizens of Ynit crowded the plaza's perimeter. The quick storm had already swept over the city, and the adobe glistened as the sun erupted from behind the scattered clouds, illuminating the rain-cleared air.

"Yeah," Tigh said in a subdued voice.

Tigh had been withdrawn since the memories of the Siege of Operal had flooded her psyche, and Jame was more than a little concerned about it.

"Is it something we can talk through?" Jame placed a hand on Tigh's arm.

Tigh turned to her, and she was relieved to see a sad thoughtfulness rather than the anguish from some kind of inner pain.

"It's . . ." Tigh looked at the commanders from both armies huddled on the other side of the plaza. "I miss all this. I want to be able to fight again."

Jame, feeling deep pangs of sympathy, pulled Tigh into her arms. "We'll do everything we can to get that back for you."

"What if—?"

Jame stopped Tigh's words with a gentle kiss.

"We've proven you can overcome these demons from your past," Jame said. "We just need to concentrate on finding that wonderful warrior again."

"It's not going to be easy." Tigh sighed and gazed at the armies.

"But it'll be worth the effort." Jame smiled as Tigh gave her a puzzled look. "It'll bring me great joy to see Tigh the warrior."

Tigh wrapped her arms around Jame. "You're the source of all my strength."

They stood arm in arm as they waited for the commanders to make a decision about what to do with the unexpected company of an invading army.

A young soldier trotted toward them from the group of commanders.

"Now what?" Tigh muttered.

The young soldier stopped in front of them. "Commander Maure would like to see you, uh, Commander."

"Thank you," Tigh said.

They followed the young soldier around the lines of silver and bronze uniforms and large puddles of water from the storm.

"Wonder what Maure wants," Jame said.

"Hard to tell," Tigh said.

The leaders of the Silver Dragon turned to them. Jame was surprised to see a mixture of curiosity and fear in their eyes as they watched Tigh. So, they knew of Tigh the Terrible across the seas.

"Tigh, Jame," Maure said. "This is Commander Druthe."

Tigh faced the woman with high sharp cheeks, deep black hair, and proud dark eyes.

Druthe straightened to her full height, which was a finger's length shorter than Tigh. "You're the one they call Tigh the Terrible. We've heard of you. Many soldiers of the Silver Dragon fought as mercenaries on the side of the Northern Territories. They returned to our lands with stories of a superior siege master, even greater than ourselves. We only considered it to be true because we had heard that you'd been enhanced by magic to possess these skills. Later we heard that all of the enhanced soldiers had been rounded up like animals and cleansed of these enhancements."

Tigh nodded. "That's true. We were. My cleansing had a fault in it, and I retained everything about being a warrior, except the will to fight."

"Interesting." Druthe cast intrigued eyes over Tigh. "We've been defeated by a siege master possessing skills far beyond our own. That, coupled with the lesson we've learned on this day, is enough to prevent us from facing dishonor in our own country. We're only an advance army for a much larger force preparing to invade your land. If we're allowed to return to our home, we'll have a convincing enough tale to tell, about how the armies of the Southern Territories are still invincible because Tigh the Terrible lives."

"Maure is the commander of the army of the Southern Territories," Tigh said. "Today was her victory."

"Of course," Druthe bowed her head, "we simply honor her ability to seek the best counsel. Your quickness and efficiency are truly inspiring. In our lands we'd say you had a touch of the dragon in you."

Jame couldn't help but grin at the description. It fit Tigh very well.

"Your fate is in the hands of Commander Maure," Tigh said.

Maure straightened and turned to the row of silver and bronze clad warriors. "We accept your word that you'll do everything in your power to keep your invasion force from our shores. Keep in mind, I may be the commander of the peacetime force, but in time of war we call upon all battle commanders who are still in the reserves to resume their ranks. And Tigh, as a peace warrior, is still a soldier of the state."

Commander Druthe nodded in acknowledgement of the warning and took another look at Tigh. "We accept your terms of surrender."

TIGH COULDN'T HELP the affectionate grin as a happy Jame skipped down the outside steps of the Tribunal Hall.

"If I had known that all we needed was a little war to convince the Federation Council you're no longer a threat to society, I would have arranged a skirmish between Emoria and Lukria." Jame laughed. "Defeating an invading army in a single day. They'll be talking about it for years."

Tigh caught up with the exuberant Jame and wrapped an arm around her shoulder as they strolled across the plaza. "I was inspired."

Jame cocked her head at Tigh. "Inspired?"

"I wasn't happy with our home being threatened like that," Tigh said.

Jame tightened her one arm hold around Tigh. "I guess there are disadvantages to calling Ynit home."

"I think we just faced the worse of it." Tigh blinked at a knot of grinning soldiers passing by and saluting her.

"They'll get over it," Jame said. "They're just happy you were around to help out."

Tigh sighed. "That was too much luck for my taste. I'm going to have to find the time to mentor Maure before something like this happens again."

"It'll be deep winter by the time we're finished at Maymi," Jame said. "I wouldn't be averse to spending the rainy season close to home."

"We could always head further north and tromp through the snow and ice instead," Tigh said.

"I've had my share of snow and ice living in Emoria, thank you very much," Jame said. "I've learned to appreciate the warmer climate."

They entered the brooding fortress and pushed around the knots of people who didn't seem to have anything better to do than to talk about the events of the previous day.

Pendon lounged outside Patch Lachlan's old office as he chatted with several assistant healers about the one-day war. He grinned as Tigh and Jame came into sight. "Ah, there's the dragon herself."

Jame stifled a laugh. Tigh rolled her eyes.

"I'd appreciate it if that doesn't get around," Tigh muttered.

"But it fits you so well," Jame said.

"I take it everything went well with the Federation Council," Pendon said.

"Lucky for you," Tigh said. "You won't have to see my face every two fortnights."

"I could think of worse things to look at." Pendon grinned. "Come in. I've got tea brewing in the back room."

When they were settled in the small parlor with a window that overlooked the plaza, Tigh couldn't muster the words to voice her fears and uncertainties. She finally turned beseeching eyes to Jame.

Jame put a reassuring hand on Tigh's arm and turned to Pendon. "Tigh's been having flashbacks and episodes of panic when faced with situations that remind her of when she was a Guard. She experienced two rather major attacks yesterday, one of which disabled her ability to help Maure. Fortunately, the strategy in place stopped the invaders."

"Was it a flashback?" Pendon asked.

"Yes, of the Siege of Operal," Jame said.

Pendon took a deep breath and turned to Tigh. "You say there have been other flashbacks. Are they recurring?"

"Not yet," Tigh said. "Something happens that reminds me of an event or a feeling while I was a Guard, then Jame always works miracles by finding the right words to help me through it."

Pendon nodded. "As far as I know, the other Guards aren't plagued with flashbacks, but they also don't want to be warriors. Only their need to fight forces them to retain that aspect of their lives as Guards. You, on the other hand, want to be a warrior. It's something that's been woven into your psyche. Unfortunately, you have to separate the warrior you want to be from the one you were during the Wars."

"I can't keep being blindsided by these attacks each time something reminds me of what happened when I was a Guard," Tigh said. "We got lucky yesterday that the invading force was as much illusion as real."

"The only thing you can do is the most painful for both of you," Pendon said. "You have to face who you were as a Guard. Only then will you be able to put it behind you and become a whole warrior."

Even the idea seemed to suck the air out of the chamber for Tigh. She gasped for air, and her mind filled with panic.

Jame took Tigh's cheeks into her hands and whispered soothing words. She kept her eyes on Tigh's face as if willing her to come back to her. Unable to resist Jame's compelling voice or her soft touch, Tigh fell into Jame's eyes and released her panic.

"I'm all right," Tigh said.

Jame nodded, took Tigh's hand, and returned her attention to Pendon.

"I know it'll be painful and that it seems hopeless right now," Pendon said. "But, believe it or not, I think you'll find your own way of dealing with this. I don't think you'll have to relive every single moment of your life as a Guard. You just have to figure out how to discard those parts of Tigh the Terrible you don't want. The only way you can do this is to focus on who you want to become, instead of how much it reminds you of who you were."

Tigh nodded at the reasonable logic of this, but didn't believe it was really possible to achieve.

Pendon smiled. "If it means anything, I have every confidence that you can do it. It doesn't always require a healer to stitch up a wound. Sometimes it just needs a proper salve to ease the pain."

AFTER TWO LONG days on a coach, the only thing that saved Jame from exploding from the infernal vehicle and running the rest of the way to Maymi was the enforced opportunity for her to learn Guard meditation techniques.

Tigh's more placid personality was better suited to relaxing the mind and body into a state of floating tranquility, but Jame possessed a strong capacity for concentration and focus, so she wasn't a difficult student to teach. Just a harder one to get to relax. She just couldn't keep her mind from its usual chatter of activity long enough to allow for the effortless passage of time.

Well into the second day of travel, they gave up on the meditation. Jame spent the sandmarks spinning out tales about Emoria, her childhood, and her student days.

"Laur's waterfalls." Jame interrupted her description of Regir's Theory on judging cases between two parties of equal guilt when the open-topped coach rounded the last break in the southern foothills of the Phytian Mountains. A vista of thick, green forest stretched before them. The odor of rich organic decay made her nose twitch even from that distance, and moisture seemed to paint everything a sparkling haze including the air.

Tigh, sitting with her back to the front of the coach, twisted around to see what caught Jame's attention. "Maymi Peninsula. Forests of rain. Insects the size of household cats. Flesh eating plants and snakes filled with deadly poison."

"Thank you very much." Jame glared at Tigh in mock exasperation. "Is there anything nice about the place?"

"It rarely gets cold, and it never snows." Tigh put a finger to her chin. "The humidity is supposed to be good for your skin."

"That's why we have sweat huts in Emoria," Jame said.

Tigh grinned. "Just think of Maymi as one big sweat hut."

"Great," Jame said. She hated being inactive, and the long coach ride was hard on her patience.

"I hear they have oils and mineral waters that are very soothing when slowly massaged into the skin," Tigh said.

"Massage?" Jame grinned. The assault to her senses of the imagined feel of Tigh's strong fingers working fragrant oils into her skin made her lightheaded.

"We don't want you tense after two long days in a coach, do we?" Tigh asked in a low voice that vibrated against Jame's soul. The emphasis on the word "tense" alone was enough for Jame to find the increasingly humid air difficult to breathe.

"It's not good for a judging arbiter to be tense," Jame said.

"Then I'd say the first thing we do when we get to Maymi is to go oil and mineral water shopping." Tigh's voice held a tenor of seduction that turned the ordinary words into a strong warm embrace.

"Without delay," Jame said in a husky voice.

By the time the coach clattered down a palm tree-lined road on a narrow built-up strip of land surrounded by brooding swamps, they were more than ready to be alone in a room with several bottles of massage oil and each other.

The trees in the swamps before them thinned to almost nothing, setting off the city rising from what looked like a tenuous island on a sea of cypress knees and duck weed. The contrast between the moisture-darkened greens and browns of the surrounding swamp and the garish colors of the wooden structures that comprised the city of Maymi was startling.

To Jame, who was used to a more harmonious blending of humans and nature, it was not particularly attractive. "It's different looking."

"Enough to scare off the rodent-size insects, not to mention the poisonous snakes," Tigh muttered as she sat next to Jame to get a better look at the odd structures spiraling up from the swamp.

"It's different, but interesting." Jame gave Tigh a sidelong glance.

"I wonder what kinds of plants produce colors like that," Tigh said. "Why would anyone want to build a city in the middle of a swamp?"

"I bet it floods," Jame said as the coach rattled to the impressive but closed gate.

The noises coming from the city sounded too loud for everyday activity, and music was easily discernible, adding to the already alien feel of the place.

"The city is full to capacity. There are no more rooms left to stay," a man said in a bored voice from the porch of the rambling guard hut to one side of the gate. He had leathery sun- darkened skin and was clothed in a light-colored thin shirt and leggings.

Jame and Tigh exchanged bewildered glances.

"I'm Jamelin Ketlas, arbiter-at-large for the Southern Districts. I'm here to try a case and a room has been reserved at the Emoran safe house."

"In that case, you may enter." The man yawned as he waved a hand at someone on the palisades.

As the gate rose to knee height, Jame understood what the guard meant. Crowds of feet and legs surged close to the gate. The sounds of laughter and chatter blended into a loud rumble as the city was revealed.

"I have the feeling, this isn't the best time to be in Maymi," Jame said.

Never had she seen such elaborate costumes draping the people tightly packed in the wide street that ran all the way to the middle of the city. As the coach lurched through the oblivious revelers, all she and Tigh could do was stare dumbfounded at the endless sea of masks of fantastical birds and whimsical creatures. The feathers and dyes on the light filmy material of the equally creative costumes exploded with garish hues.

On thin, bent, wood balconies overlooking the street were people throwing coins and strands of bright-colored beads into the crowd. Tigh caught a strand of beads and looked up to see a woman, wearing only a wrapping of transparent material around her middle and several strands of beads around her neck, gazing at her with seductive interest.

Jame, following Tigh's stare, was even more riveted than Tigh. "She was practically naked," she squeaked as the coach lurched away.

Tigh fingered the strand of beads. "This is Carnival."

Jame cocked her head. "Carnival?"

"A time of abandoned revelry before the rainy season," Tigh said. "Several Guards were from Maymi. They used to talk about how wild it was."

"I believe that." Jame watched a pair of tall exotic bird masks surge by. "But it looks like fun."

Tigh turned to Jame in astonishment. "Do I have to keep you out of trouble here?"

Jame laughed. "I'll try to be good."

EXHAUSTION FROM TWO days of enduring a bumpy coach hit Jame the moment she saw the bed in the airy room at the top of the rambling Emoran safe house. Tigh knew she had only a couple of sandmarks to learn more about Maymi before Jame awoke from her nap. Her job, both personally and professionally, was to protect Jame, and she had heard enough about Carnival to know there was a fine line between harmless good fun and reckless behavior.

She slipped out the kitchen door of the safe house with hopes that the alley would have less people than the packed streets. Several drunken exotic birds stumbled by, using the alley as a shortcut between streets, and a few huddled laughing groups were taking refuge from the crowds. All and all, Tigh was satisfied that it remained relatively free of people. Now the challenge was to find the best route to the Tribunal Hall.

Emoran safe houses were usually located in the middle of cities, tucked between shops and government buildings with a door bearing a simple crossed bow and sword design. Lucky for Tigh, the safe house was only a block and a half from the Tribunal Hall—a block and a half of the greatest concentration of Carnival celebrants in the city.

Tigh sighed and studied the building across the alley with its opened back doors to narrow shops. She grinned as she ducked through a door near the end of the alley.

Tigh gave the airy wood frame structure of the shop a nervous glance. It felt even more unstable than the safe house. How could anyone feel secure in such flimsy buildings? The creatures, sporting feathers and whimsical ungainly masks, poking around the islands of brightly colored jars didn't help her unease. The floorboards bounced and shifted every time anyone moved.

Tigh wandered around, trying to make sense of the endless varieties of oils. She realized she didn't even know if Jame had a favorite or if there was a scent she intensely disliked. Maybe surprising her with the oil wasn't such a good idea.

"You look like you need help, good warrior," a small man dressed in simple light clothing said from a stool near the front door.

"I'm looking for massage oil," Tigh said.

"Hmmm." The man gave Tigh an appraising look. "For yourself or a special someone?"

"For my life companion," Tigh said. "She likes flowers."

"Our flower-scented oils are over here." He hopped off the stool and guided Tigh around several islands of jars. "As you can see we have many different kinds of flowers, scents, and blends."

Tigh blinked at all the jars. It sounded so simple when they had discussed it on the coach. "She's from the mountains."

"Ah, then she would love this particular blend." The shopkeeper lifted a jar that was splashed with every possible hue. "It's a special combination of the spring flowers that grow in the upper valleys of the Phytian Mountains." He released the metal clamp, raised the ceramic lid from the jar, and held it out for Tigh to sniff.

The aroma was pleasant, not as overpowering as Tigh was afraid it would be. It held the scent of the field flowers Jame couldn't resist passing by without taking a sniff. "I'll take three jars."

The little man raised an eyebrow before graciously smiling. "Three jars it is. Two pieces of silver."

"How early are you open in the morning?" Tigh asked as she dug into her belt pouch for the coins.

"During Carnival we never close," the man said as he accepted the silver. "Hmmm, Ynit. Don't see many of these coins around here." Then his face reflected enlightenment. "The bookseller's case."

"My partner's here to judge it," Tigh said.

The shopkeeper glanced around at the surrounding bobbing masks. "Step this way. I'd like to show you a nice soap that complements this oil."

Tigh followed the man through an opening on the side of the shop, covered by long hanging strands of gaudy beads that clattered together.

"A word of caution to you," the shopkeeper said in a low voice as he sorted through a pile of fresh cut soaps. "There's something about this situation that's making us humble shopkeepers nervous. It's not anything we've been able to put a name to. Just a feeling."

"Feeling," Tigh said.

"These booksellers, the ones from Artocia, keep strange company." The shopkeeper picked up a cake of soap, put it to his nose, and breathed in its essence. "We're afraid if they get a foothold in our city, it'll impact on the rest of us trying to make an honest living."

"This strange company doesn't appear to be the bookish type?" Tigh asked, raising an eyebrow.

The shopkeeper turned to Tigh. "I think you've grasped the situation. Here. On the house." He handed Tigh the soap and walked back into the main room.

Tigh sniffed the soap and wondered if there was such a thing as a simple case when Jame was involved.

Chapter 7

JAME'S SENSE OF smell woke up before the rest of her, and her languid dreams were filled with offerings of delicately spiced greens and tubers. She opened her eyes, and her stomach, reacting to the real aromas, growled.

"Dinner," she mumbled as she lifted her head and glanced around the large chamber.

Tigh was taking dishes off a large tray and placing them on a small table near the window.

Jame slipped off the bed and stretched her stiff muscles, vowing never to spend more than a few sandmarks on a coach again. "I thought they didn't serve Ingoran food here." She inspected the delicious looking offerings beneath the lids on the dishes.

"I found a small Ingoran establishment close by," Tigh said. "Run by Ingorans so the food ought to be fine."

Jame grinned. "No over-spiced potatoes?"

"I hope not," Tigh muttered. "From what I hear they use too many hot spices here. As if they didn't perspire enough."

"It doesn't smell over-spiced." Jame sat at the table and waited for Tigh to complete the ritual arrangement of the dishes.

Tigh dragged the chair opposite Jame around so she sat adjacent to her. Jame loved the fact that Tigh felt the other side of the table was too far away from her.

"I did some snooping around," Tigh said as they worked their way through the pleasantly prepared greens.

"And?"

Tigh sighed. "Things are not what they seem."

"Of course not." Jame speared a delicate piece of carrot with her fork. "That would make it too easy."

"I found out that the Jande and Rend Scroll Shop is into other things besides selling scrolls and books," Tigh said. "Their representatives are staying with a prominent Maymian family whose wealth comes as much from less respectable endeavors as respectable."

Jame stopped in mid-chew and gave Tigh a wondering look. "I was asleep, maybe two sandmarks. How did you learn all this in that short time?"

Tigh shrugged. "There's no discretion in large drunken crowds."

"So, what are Jande and Rend up to?" Jame asked.

"The local shopkeepers are nervous about something," Tigh said. "Jande and Rend are associating with individuals not known for their love of the written word."

"Besides the prominent local family?" Jame asked as she scooped up a small potato and dunked it in a clear sauce.

"Yes."

"Do you think this is just a matter of the locals being nervous about a foreign business moving in, possibly paving the way for other foreign businesses if Jande and Rend gets a foothold in Maymi?" Jame popped the potato into her mouth and sighed from the harmony of flavors assaulting her senses.

"Only partially, I think," Tigh said. "I got the idea that they're more concerned with some kind of underworld control on their businesses. The Maymians have had that problem before."

Jame nodded. "We covered Maymi's underworld activities in school. This could help the case in favor of the local Scroll Shop."

Tigh laid down her fork and put a hand on Jame's arm. "From what I've heard, these underworld people are dangerous and violent when they don't get their way. We have to be very careful about what we say and do."

Jame raised an eyebrow. "They can't be dangerous if they're brought to justice." A dozen emotions scuttled across Tigh's face. "I know you don't like it, but this is what my job is about."

"I'll not let you out of my sight for as long as we're here," Tigh said.

Jame pushed down her normal resistance to being treated as though she couldn't take care of herself and nodded. Tigh's job was to protect her. "We'll stick together as long as we're here."

Tigh relaxed and they finished their meal to the increasing sounds of revelers greeting the moon as it chased away the sun.

"I'm kind of glad we aren't out in all of that," Jame said as she stood and watched the activity in the street. "It could be fun if there weren't so many people."

"We'll just have to find our own fun," Tigh said.

Jame turned and squinted at an innocent-faced Tigh who had her hands clasped behind her back. Tigh grinned and held up a colorful jar.

"You didn't." Jame snatched the jar from Tigh and opened it. "It smells like my childhood."

"Really?" Tigh asked. "The shopkeeper said it's a special blend of mountain flowers. You mean it really is?"

"It is and it's wonderful," Jame said. "And you're wonderful."

"You haven't had one of my special massages yet." Tigh ran her fingers lightly down Jame's arm.

"Special massage, huh?" Jame murmured as she savored Tigh's touch. "How many people have you massaged?"

"Only one." Tigh leaned close to Jame's ear. "In my mind. Over and over again."

Jame grabbed her arm and dragged her to the bed.

JAME WOKE TO the lingering scent of wild, spring flowers and the warmth of love enveloping her body and soul. Tigh was wrapped around her, her steady breathing telling Jame she was still asleep. Unusual for Tigh.

Jame carefully rolled over, not wanting to wake Tigh. She wanted to savor the rare sight of Tigh in contented sleep. She'd better be content. She was amazed at how a little oil could heighten the senses to overload.

Tigh stirred and Jame knew she was close to waking as strong arms pulled her closer.

Not for the first time did Jame wonder how lucky she was to have found Tigh. At times like this, she thought about how different it would have been if she'd been joined with Argis instead. Argis didn't like to cuddle and simply revel in being close. *Warriors don't cuddle. Hah.* Jame grinned. The greatest warrior of them all was a wonderful cuddler.

"What are you grinning at?" Tigh mumbled, as she cracked her eyes open a bit.

"I was just thinking about how Argis used to declare that warriors don't cuddle," Jame said, snuggling closer to Tigh. "You don't seem to mind cuddling at all."

"You know it's not nice to think about other women when you're in bed with me," Tigh said, mimicking Jame's words from the first night they shared their love.

Jame snorted. "You were just waiting to get back at me for that comment." She breathed in Tigh's smooth skin and sighed in contentment. "Hmmm. I love that oil. Too bad we used the whole jar."

Tigh wrapped closer around Jame until her mouth was next to her ear. "I bought three jars."

Jame pulled back. "Have I told you lately how much I love you?"

"Last night. Several times," Tigh said. "Half of Maymi knows by now."

"What about the other half?" Jame found herself in a sweet kiss.

An insistent rapping on the door reached Jame's preoccupied senses.

She slipped out of Tigh's warm arms and into her neglected sleep shirt and padded to the door. She pushed her hair out of her eyes and pulled opened the door.

"Good morning, Resde," Jame said without enthusiasm to the proprietor of the safe house.

Resde straightened, her tall lean frame betraying her early years as a warrior. "Good morning, arbiter. I'm sorry to disturb you, but I was instructed to deliver this message to you right away." She held out a small scroll, which Jame accepted.

"Thank you, Resde."

Resde nodded. "The clothier is just across the street. Someone will meet you there to lead you to the meeting," she added then turned and strolled back down the corridor.

Jame broke the seal on the scroll and read as she wandered back to the bed and sat down on Tigh's side.

Tigh sat up to read the note over Jame's shoulder. "Looks like we have to continue our little discussion later."

Jame frowned. "Whatever's going on really has the merchants nervous."

"They think their livelihoods are being threatened," Tigh said.

Jame glanced over her shoulder. "I have the feeling your merchant background is going to come in handy on this trip."

"At least I understand what's going on in their minds." Tigh sighed. "Maybe that Ingoran place will deliver a morning meal while we're meeting with these people."

Jame arched an eyebrow. "Hungry?"

"I just don't want your growling stomach to drown out the discussions." Tigh moved fast enough to avoid Jame's playful slap to her arm.

"Actually, I am a little hungry," Jame said.

A grinning Tigh gathered Jame into her arms. "Then I'll make sure the Ingoran place delivers."

"Don't threaten them too much," Jame said. "We're at their mercy for meals while we're here."

"Threaten? Me?" Tigh blinked innocently.

Jame laughed and jumped off the bed, pulling Tigh with her. She had no doubt she was the luckiest woman in the world. All because of a certain warrior in her life.

GETTING ACROSS THE street in Maymi in the middle of Carnival at that early morning time was tricky even for a master strategist such as Tigh. Tradition was that each Guild sponsored a procession that wound through every street in the city. Since Maymi boasted two score Guilds, processions were nearly continual, day and night. Only the banners and distinct change in costumes and pageantry marked one Guild's efforts from another's.

For all the Maymian's deliberate attempts at abandoned and shocking revelry, there were still rules no one dared to break. One such rule was not being allowed to cross a street as a procession passed by. The result was a crush of people on the street at the end of one procession, halting the progress of the processions behind it. This in turn caused pockets of people to temporarily take over the streets from the Guilds, leaving the marchers and garish coaches stationary.

To Jame's well-ordered mind, the result reflected a chaotic and dysfunctional society, but also one with a strange sense of fairness. The processions prevented the people from crossing the street, so it was only fair the people prevented the processions from progressing. If she was to pass judgment in this city, she had to understand how Maymians thought.

"We'll just have to wait until this procession passes by," she said.

"How did the merchants get to the clothier's shop?" Tigh asked.

Jame shrugged. "I'm sure they waited for their chance to cross the street."

Tigh looked at the next door down from them. "Follow me." She slipped her hand into Jame's, and they edged their way to the narrow shop.

Jame took in the fruit and vegetable shop and cast a curious look at Tigh. "Need a snack?"

"Actually, while we're here," Tigh muttered, picking out an assortment of vegetables.

"Why are we here?" Jame asked, as she added some small oranges to Tigh's pile of food.

"Notice how fresh everything is in here?" Tigh delivered the food to the bench in front of the dozing merchant.

"Yes," Jame said.

"How did all this and all the other fresh food get through to the merchants and eating establishments in the city if the streets are constantly clogged with people and processions?"

Jame shrugged. "The same way we got through."

"We were one small coach, and we made it here before the first procession. We got lucky that yesterday was the first day of Carnival," Tigh said. "That's why they wanted you here as early as possible. To get you into town before Carnival began."

"They'll have to send their complaints to the people of the Silver Dragon." Jame grabbed an intriguing looking green fruit out of a nearby bin and put it on the bench.

"I suspect the merchants in town make most of their income during Carnival time, so they must have figured out a way to bring in merchandise to keep their shelves stocked without having to deal with the crowds and the processions," Tigh said.

"If this were Emor, I'd guess a system of caves," Jame said. "But this city is built on a swamp."

"Things are not always what they appear to be," a light sleepy voice said. The small woman behind the bench straightened and stretched. She took a closer look at her visitors. "I'm going to guess you're not here for the Carnival. That you're here for the hearing between Cadryn's House of Scrolls and those thieving out-of-towners."

"Yes, I'm Jamelin Ketlas, arbiter-at-large for the Southern Districts," Jame said. "This is Tigh, my peace warrior."

"Let me guess." The pixie-like merchant put a finger to her lips. "You're trying to figure out a way of getting to the small gathering of anxious merchants across the street." She squinted in amusement at Tigh and Jame's startled expressions. "What happens in this case will impact on all of us trying to make a living in Maymi. It's not the first-time outsiders have tried to move in on our businesses, and we'll not allow it to happen again. All the merchants are standing as one behind Cadryn."

"We need to get to that meeting, so we can hear all sides of the case," Jame said.

The woman sorted through the vegetables and fruit on the bench. "We've heard you're fair because you keep truth as a companion." She flicked a glance at Tigh. "We know Guards can detect falsehood in others. You see, Jande and Rend have been able to get their way in other cities because they had the previous arbiters-at-large in their belt pouches, so to speak. I know it's difficult to imagine arbiters giving in to corruption, but being an arbiter-at-large is a difficult job from what I've observed."

"It's a sad fact that I find hard to accept," Jame said.

"When we learned you were appointed arbiter-at-large, it was as if Bal finally took pity on us and presented us with a miracle." The woman grinned at an astonished Jame. "Even though you're just out of school, you've already made a name as a clever, but just, arbiter. And rumor has it you'll not knowingly defend someone who is guilty and to make sure, your peace warrior is a former Guard. We knew you'd apply these same convictions when judging a case, so we pressed our case against Jande and Rend."

Jame shook her head in amazement. "I had no idea."

"Will you help us get to that meeting?" Tigh asked.

"Of course." The woman folded the vegetables and fruit into a thin sheet of paper. "Four copper pieces. I won't insult you with trying to give you this food as a gift."

"Thank you." Jame laid the coins on the bench.

"Anyone who turns down a generous gift from Jande and Rend wouldn't have a problem with paying for a few greens." The woman laughed. "Since the moment we petitioned for a hearing, we've kept a close eye on you."

"We didn't even know about the case then," Jame said. She obviously had a lot to learn about the complicated politics of at-large cases.

The merchant grinned. "We know. We were quite impressed with your convictions. Now, if you'll follow me, I'll get you to that meeting."

Jame and Tigh followed the tiny woman into the back room. She unlocked a door that opened onto another chamber filled with crates of vegetables and fruit. An opening on the side of the chamber had a slanted staircase leading downward. The scent of richly nourished soil and water permeated Jame's senses.

"This way." The woman led them down the staircase that extended possibly two stories below the shop into a chamber that opened onto a wooden tunnel with a river of dark water running through it. "Everything is brought in by ship from the Gulf and floated on small flat boats in these canals."

Tigh nodded. "Very efficient."

"Why weren't we told about this in the first place?" Jame asked. "We'd have gotten to the meeting much quicker if we'd known about it."

"I don't know what it's like up north," the woman cast kindly eyes at Jame, "but we're in the habit of testing the resourcefulness of others. Especially those who hold our fate in their hands. We had no doubt you'd discover the ways of our city in your quest to get to the truth."

Jame didn't know how to respond to this, but a single glance at Tigh told her that truth was all she sensed from the merchants of Maymi, and, at the moment, that was enough for her.

WITH SOME RELIEF, Jame climbed the steps leading up into the clothier shop. Tigh's discussion with the person steering the flatbed boat about whether the Carnival crowds had ever broken the supports above them didn't help the discomfort she felt on the underground river. Her reaction was strange, considering she grew up in a city of caverns but, in her mind, stone offered a lot more support than networks of wooden beams.

A fidgety bald man rushed to them as they stepped into a chamber filled with tables stacked with colorful filmy cloth.

"Arbiter. So glad you're here," he said. "I'm Sigtor, the owner of this humble establishment. Please come with me."

Jame and Tigh exchanged curious glances as Sigtor led them up a set of stairs to the floor about the shop. The large chamber was Sigtor's business office and was surprisingly attractive with several chairs and couches in the middle of the floor for casual consultations and dealings. Perhaps a dozen men and women were seated or wandering around the chamber. Their somber mood rang with sincerity to Jame's mind, and she was glad Tigh was there to put it into perspective. Jame was inclined to see the best rather than the worst in people.

Sigtor rattled off the names and occupations of each person, leaving for last a woman, standing apart, staring out the window at the swirling crowds below. "Cadryn."

Cadryn turned around, revealing a young serious-faced woman, probably not much older than Tigh. Jame realized why Jande and Rend thought they had a chance of winning this case. Cadryn was most likely just out of her apprenticeship and had no experience as a merchant. But the formidable Scroll Shop didn't take into consideration the solidarity of the Maymi merchants.

"I'm Jame and this is Tigh." Jame stepped forward and offered her forearm. Cadryn grasped Jame's arm. She appeared to be more cautious than wary.

"Welcome to Maymi and thank you for judging the case," Cadryn said in a pleasant resonant voice. Her brown eyes were filled with worry and her bearing was one of resignation and defeat. This was a woman who didn't believe Jande and Rend could be defeated and it tore at Jame's soft heart.

"Thank you," Jame said. "And it's my job to judge the case. Fairly."

"Please, sit down." Sigtor pointed to a small couch.

A SOUND, FOREIGN even to the strange assortment of noises from the surging crowds on the street, penetrated Tigh's consciousness. She saw a flash shoot through the window. In a split-heartbeat she side-tackled both Cadryn and Jame. Something clattered against the far wall.

After several heartbeats of stunned stillness, Tigh glanced around the chamber. The merchants were either on the floor or cowering behind the furniture.

"Stay down." She crept to the window. The projectile had to have come from across the street. She noted with relief that the building across the way was two doors down from the Emoran safe house. At least they didn't have to worry about anyone within those walls trying to get at Jame or Cadryn. She looked back at Sigtor. "Is there somewhere else we can go? Without windows?"

"Yes, yes." Sigtor nodded. "This way, quickly."

The shaky group scrambled down the back steps after him.

Tigh helped Jame and Cadryn up, while keeping them shielded from the window.

"Thank you." Cadryn's voice was tight with fear.

"Have you been receiving threats?" Tigh asked as she wrapped an arm around Jame.

"Small things," Cadryn said. "Like scary jokes and sick messages."

Tigh went to the wall, picked up the dart, and followed Jame and Cadryn down the stairs.

Jame frowned. "I didn't get the impression that kind of thing was Jande and Rend's style."

"No, but it's the style of the Dranderal clan," Cadryn said.

"The clan who's being hospitable to Jande and Rend," Jame said.

"This isn't just about a foreign scroll shop trying to move into Maymi." Cadryn stopped and turned to Jame and Tigh. "We're vulnerable to outside influences because of our isolation from the rest of the Southern Territories. And most of these outside influences are on the other side of the law, engaged in unspeakable trade. The combined forces of Jande and Rend along with their alliance with other powerful merchants and the Dranderal clan would bring disaster to Maymi."

Jame straightened. "Then we can't let that happen, can we?"

"No, we can't," Cadryn said, showing the backbone it had taken to defy Jande and Rend in the first place.

Tigh nodded, satisfied that the young merchant had it in her to face what would most likely be an increase in threats and, she somberly mused as she sniffed the dart, attempts on her young life.

Chapter 8

JAME ACTUALLY TREMBLED as she and Tigh climbed off the flat boat onto a rickety looking— in her mind at least—landing. The incessant creaking of the tangle of wood supports above them reminded her they were just below the middle of the city where the Carnival crowds were the thickest.

Tigh gave Jame a confused look as Jame muttered words about extra tributes to Laur and never cursing Bal's Children again.

"Constabulary is two doors down," the wiry woman called to them as she maneuvered the flat boat away from the landing.

"Kind of strange that only merchants have direct access to these underground rivers," Jame said as she scrambled up the stairs into the back room of an apothecary shop.

"The problem with this sort of thing is the easy access goes both ways," Tigh said. "I don't think the local law enforcement wants the possibility of infiltration from below."

Jame nodded as they stepped into the shop proper. The wrinkled woman seated behind the counter merely tilted her head at them in greeting before they exited the establishment through the front door. News certainly traveled fast in Maymi.

"Besides, the constabulary could use any of these shops to get underneath," Jame said. "Making their actions unpredictable."

The crowds surged in unheeding masses. Tigh glanced at the hanging signs over the doors on either side of them, then put Jame in front of her and guided her to a door on the street's corner.

They stepped into the cavernous main hall of the Constabulary. The press, of relatives there to bail family members out of jail, knots of people who looked as if they'd been hauled in for fighting, and an assortment of others who seemed far too intoxicated to care where they were, hit Jame with a blow that made her lightheaded. She shook her head and swallowed down the rise of bile at the stench of sweat and stale ale.

Tigh made a quick survey of the chamber. "This way."

Jame grimaced. "Uck. How can they stand it in here?"

"Humans were never meant to live in a humid climate," Tigh muttered as she steered Jame around the perimeter of people to a set of stairs rising to a second-floor overlook.

"We're here to see Chief Constable Bary," Jame said to the young man in a light-colored cotton tunic and leggings with the Maymi insignia—the head of a colorful large-beaked bird—embroidered across the chest. "I'm Arbiter Jamelin Ketlas."

The young guard grinned. "This way," he said in a somber voice before the grin threatened to envelop his face again.

Tigh cast a puzzled look at the young man.

They followed the guard into a nice-sized chamber, pleasantly decorated with subdued pastels. At the far side of the room was a large desk with a salt-and-pepper haired man seated behind it, bent over some papers.

When Jame and Tigh were halfway across the room, the man blinked up and grinned. Tigh's puzzled frown furrowed deeper into her brow. The man, maybe a finger length taller than Jame, pushed out of his chair and rushed around the desk to greet them.

"Ah, arbiter Jame." He captured Jame's hand in his. "We're so glad you're here. Thank you, Ahmin." The young man smartly saluted and walked out.

Jame exchanged confused glances with Tigh and focused on the man with sparkling brown eyes and a salt-and-pepper beard. "We're glad to be here. This is Tigh, my peace warrior."

"Ah yes, the former Guard." Bary turned his attention to Tigh. "Greetings, fine warrior. I'm Chief Constable Bary, with the accent on the 'y.' Come sit. Sit." He directed them to the guests' chairs as he sat in his own chair behind the desk. "Now, what can I do for you?" He sat forward and folded his hands together on the wooden desk.

"We're here out of concern for the safety of one of the parties involved in the scroll shop case," Jame said. "We believe an attempt was made on merchant Cadryn's life this morning."

Bary's eyebrows shot up. "An attempt?"

"We were talking with a few of the merchants, including Cadryn, and a dart flew in through the opened window," Jame said. "Fortunately, Tigh got her out of the way before it hit her. The dart had poison on it."

Tigh fished a soft cloth from her belt pouch and unfolded it on the desk, revealing the shaft of wood.

"How do you know it was meant for Cadryn?" Bary asked as he studied the discoloring at the end of the dart.

"There've been a number of malicious pranks and nasty threats against her," Jame said. "Enough to make her uncomfortable but nothing really overtly criminal."

"As you observed from the madhouse downstairs, we have our hands full with Carnival," Bary said. "Not only is our regular force on continual call, we have to take on temporary recruits for less skilled things such as crowd control."

"That explains the grinning guard," Tigh muttered.

"There's always someone who wants to be a Constable but just doesn't have the disposition for the job," Bary said. "Ahmin has served as a second-floor guard for the last four Carnivals. Sometimes I think it's the highlight of his year. Such a cheerful lad to come from such a sour family." He shook his head. "I'll see what I can do. But I think, until Carnival is over, the best thing for Cadryn is to keep out of sight. Preferably, where no one can find her."

Jame nodded, her heart sinking at the added burden of having to keep one of defendants alive long enough to bring the case to trial. "We'd be grateful for anything you can do for Cadryn. In the meantime, we'll follow your advice."

Bary rubbed his beard. "Maymi isn't the easiest town for certain aspects of law enforcement. There's an undercurrent of corruption that's been around for as long as the city itself. This is the first time in a long time anyone has tried to break this corruption legally. Unfortunately, there's always been an element of corruption in the Constabulary. We've never had a means of keeping it out, despite many efforts. So, take the advice of a weary but honest servant of the people. Trust no one."

"Thank you for the warning, Chief Constable, but I have a remedy to that little problem," Jame said with a smile. "Tigh knows if someone is being truthful or not."

Bary gazed in surprise at Tigh. "Hmmm," he put a finger to his lip, "that could be extremely useful. I'd like to learn more about this skill, if you don't mind."

TIGH WAS NOT happy about leaving Jame alone, even in the company of Cadryn in the Emoran safe house. She ran up the steps of one of the warehouses on the edge of where the swamp met an inlet to the Gulf of Oheria. She raised an eyebrow at the sounds of hard thumping against the solid wood above her and muffled voices and clashes of steel. Sounded like a full house.

The upper floor of the warehouse was a rougher version of the other floors, with a high ceiling and an area the size of a Glak field. But the timbers were only half finished, and the sun filtered through gaps between the beams in the walls and ceiling. Possibly thirty women, dressed in light leather armor, were sparring with swords and staffs, focused on the need to expel the building violence from their bodies.

Tigh had never imagined there were so many former Guards in Maymi. She squinted in the dim light and tried to pick out the one woman she knew to be from Maymi, surprised when she didn't see her.

One by one the pairs of women stopped sparring to stare at Tigh.

"Where's Meah?" she asked.

A stocky woman with dark close-cropped hair and brown eyes laid the blade of her sword on her shoulder and sauntered up to Tigh. "We haven't seen Meah. Has she been cleansed?"

"Yes." Tigh frowned in puzzlement. "She left the compound eight moons ago. She told me she was coming home."

The woman's brow furrowed. "We haven't seen her, and there isn't any way a former Guard can stay hidden. Not with the need to fight to keep our sanity."

"Not all of us have a cute Emoran arbiter as a sparring partner," a taller woman said. A scar sliced across the bridge of her nose.

Tigh shrugged. "I just got lucky, I guess. I need your help."

The stockier woman barked a laugh. "You were never one for small talk. Vorkin. I served under Ienor Quet." She grasped Tigh's arm. "We heard you don't have the urge to fight. Is that true?"

"Yes." Tigh looked down at the floorboards, unable to come to terms with the guilt she felt about that. "But I have the desire to fight."

"An interesting dilemma," Vorkin said. "We have the urge to fight but not the desire."

"I'm Iklas. Tell us what you need from us, Commander," the woman with the scar said.

"I need your ability to determine the truth," Tigh said. "My partner is here to judge a case that has deep roots in corruption."

A tall, muscular woman with sparkling gray eyes laughed. "Now there's an understatement."

"With that much corruption, it's not going to matter how my partner judges the case, the corruption will win," Tigh said. "The only way for justice to prevail is to get rid of those standing in its way."

Iklas grinned. "You have our attention."

CADRYN PACED AROUND Jame's room in the Emoran safe house. "I appreciate what you're trying to do, but those people are ruthless."

"Tigh thinks we can do it," Jame said.

"Not that I have any doubts about her abilities," Cadryn tossed her deep bronzed hands into the air, "but unlike an enemy on a battlefield, this enemy is woven into the fabric of our city."

"All it takes is pulling a few threads to unravel the entire cloth," Jame said. "And Tigh thinks she knows how to find those threads."

Cadryn shook her head. "Too many people are afraid to stand up against them."

"I'm here to conduct a just hearing. I can't do that until the circumstances surrounding the hearing are equally fair and within the law. If it takes ferreting out every corrupt citizen in Maymi, so be it, but I'm not the type of person who can do things halfway." Jame surprised herself with her own conviction. But it was true. She wouldn't be happy until she was positive her judgment held after she left Maymi.

Cadryn stopped pacing and gazed at Jame. "Maymi needs to learn what it's like to live without an undercurrent of fear. Something inside me hoped, when I challenged Jande and Rend, that it wouldn't come to this. But that was only a dream on the wind. I'll do everything I can to assist you."

"Thank you," Jame said. "Perhaps I can start by picking your brain about everything you know about who we're up against."

Cadryn grinned and sat at the small table with Jame and filled her ears with tales of the underworld in the city of Maymi.

VORKIN STUDIED TIGH as they skirted the thinning crowds. Most of the revelers were inside the many eating establishments for the evening meal and the processions stopped for two sandmarks during that time of day.

"You look like Tigh, but you don't act like her," she said.

Tigh shrugged. "I don't feel much like the old Tigh, either. But the more I get used to who I am now, the more I like it."

"What about fighting?" Vorkin asked.

"I'm working on that," Tigh said after they had walked for nearly a block.

"You passed the peace warrior training," Vorkin said.

"I have no problem protecting Jame," Tigh said.

Vorkin nodded as they turned down the alley that led to the back door of the Emoran safe house.

"The Emorans occasionally spar with us," Vorkin said, as she followed Tigh into the small corridor that passed by the large, noisy kitchen. "They're good enough warriors to give us a bit of a challenge."

"That's how I found out about you," Tigh said.

They padded up the steps to top floor. Tigh looked up and down the passageway for anything that seemed out of place. Safe house or not, the

Emorans weren't able to determine the loyalties of all the women who frequented the establishment.

Tigh pushed the door open and hid a smile at Jame and Cadryn seated at the little table. Both were talking with enthusiasm and scribbling notes. She glanced at Vorkin and her curiosity about why she quickly volunteered to be Cadryn's bodyguard was satisfied. Vorkin struggled to keep from staring at the young merchant.

Jame looked up and grinned. "Tigh."

"I found someone to protect Cadryn," Tigh said as she closed the door behind them. "This is Vorkin. She's an archivist at the University and because she's on holiday due to the Carnival, she volunteered for the job."

Cadryn twisted in her seat and stared at Vorkin in surprise. "We've met, I think." She stood. "Although I'd never guess a quiet unassuming archivist was a former Guard."

Vorkin nodded.

Tigh and Jame exchanged wry knowing looks.

"Thank you, Vorkin," Jame said as she stood. "I'm Jame, Tigh's partner."

"It's an honor to meet you, arbiter," Vorkin said. "I remember seeing you around during my rehabilitation. I was a part of the first group to go through the cleansing."

"Ah, yes. That was a busy time for us," Jame said. "We were all learning and doing at the same time."

"We Guards really appreciate your hard work. It couldn't have been easy." Vorkin looked at the floor.

"We did it willingly," Jame said with a smile. "You deserved to rejoin society again."

"Thank you." Vorkin looked up. "I hope society learns that someday."

"I hope as much as anyone," Jame said, glancing at Tigh. "I think we've done enough background work for today. Cadryn should get back home before nightfall and the Carnival crowds get too crazy."

"Good idea," Vorkin said.

Cadryn turned to Jame. "I don't know how to thank you for, at least, trying to help."

"I wouldn't be doing my job properly, if I couldn't ensure a just hearing," Jame said. "Keep yourself safe, and if you need any help, just send us word."

"I will. Thank you again." Cadryn flashed a smile at Tigh, then gave Vorkin an expectant look.

Vorkin straightened and pulled the door open for her.

"Thanks, Tigh," a grinning Vorkin murmured as she followed Cadryn out of the room.

Tigh and Jame looked at each other and laughed.

Jame went to a long wooden box on a side table. "I can tell you really had to convince Vorkin to take on the job of protecting Cadryn."

"Oh yeah. It took her a whole heartbeat before she stepped forward and volunteered." Tigh grinned as she gathered up the sheets of paper on the table to make room for the covered dishes Jame pulled out of the wooden box.

"I take it the Guards are going to cooperate." Jame paused in laying out the evening meal, wrapped her arms around Tigh, and gave her a proper kiss.

"They're eager to help," Tigh said as Jame's gentle warmth soothed her senses for a few heartbeats. "I wish the healers could come up with a way to cleanse them completely. I think it's more difficult to be a peaceful being with an insatiable urge to fight than being a warrior in every way except having the urge to fight."

"You have a chance to be what you want to be," Jame whispered. "We just have to break through a few more barriers. But they have an addiction that constantly threatens their chosen way of life."

"Maybe they'll have to find an acceptable compromise," Tigh said. "Like a scroll house guard."

"Only Maymi would need a guard for a scroll house." Jame laughed as she released Tigh and turned back to the table.

Tigh sat down. "The Guards will be gathering information tonight and give us a report in the morning."

"You do realize what we're trying to do is absolutely crazy." Jame put the last dishes on the table and sat down next to Tigh.

Tigh raised an eyebrow. "So was fighting off a foreign invasion force in one day."

"So, we do crazy rather well." Jame shrugged and dug into the evening meal.

THE SLOW STATELY procession passing below the small balcony off Jame and Tigh's room was a beautiful study in dignity. It contrasted so strongly with the colorful abandonment that had characterized the Carnival so far, that it drew their attention.

The chair of bent sticks and cloth proved to be perfect for Tigh to lean back with Jame lounging on top of her. The thick humid night cast an inert blanket over Tigh's mind and body as she watched the personified birds and creatures of the swamp saunter by in slow exaggerated steps.

"How come the rest of the world doesn't know about this?" Jame asked as a stunning person in a tall mask of a swamp lizard strolled by.

Tigh shrugged. "The city is full enough as it is. I think the Maymians decided early on to keep the Carnival quiet."

"On the one hand, it's really something to witness," Jame said. "But I can see how it wouldn't be possible to have any more visitors than are already here."

"I guess this is one of the blessings of being an arbiter-at-large," Tigh said. "You get to see things that most people only just hear about."

Jame smiled. "I think I like that."

"An Emoran with a curious mind," Tigh said. "Your ancestors must be turning in their graves."

"Very funny." Jame playfully swatted Tigh's arm then settled back against her. "So, what do you think about the invitation from Rend Fanders?"

"I think it's interesting that she chose the Ingoran establishment as the meeting place," Tigh said as a half dozen illuminator's balls whizzed up from the street, spun in place for several heartbeats before blinking out.

"Do you think she's going to try another bribe?" Jame asked.

"I don't think they'll try anything so obvious again." Tigh pulled Jame closer, breathing in the scent of her hair. "It's hard to tell what merchants are up to."

Jame laughed. "But you know most of the tricks, which makes me feel better."

The music reached Tigh's ears before the musicians were in sight. Drums beat a lazy rhythm as several wind instruments meandered around a tune. Her quick ear picked up the ancient air that was barely discernible by the teasing instruments. She hummed the melody in counterpoint to the band passing below the balcony.

Jame turned and stared at Tigh.

"What?" Tigh asked.

"You can sing?" Jame asked.

"I've been known to sing on occasion," Tigh said, puzzled by Jame's sudden intense interest.

"You really can sing?" Jame's face lit with a wonderful light.

Tigh shrugged. "I guess."

"I can't and I love music." Jame sighed as she put her head back on Tigh's shoulder. "Will you sing something for me?"

Tigh looked down into Jame's beseeching eyes and knew this was something important to her. "It's been a long time, I don't know if I can remember any words."

"Hum the parts you can't remember," Jame said. "I just want to hear your voice."

"All right." Tigh took a breath and sang the first song that popped into her head. A long-forgotten favorite about how rare it was to find true love. Only while she sang it did she realize how her present life meshed with the message of the song: to never let go of the precious gift of love.

When the breeze picked up the last whisper of the refrain, Jame buried her head into soft black leather. "That was beautiful," she whispered, with tears in her eyes. "You are truly a gift to me."

Tigh didn't understand Jame's emotional reaction to her singing but was glad it was one of happiness. "I'm the lucky one," she murmured as she let the languid tropical night and the subdued Carnival crowd envelop her in restful magic.

Chapter 9

JAME HADN'T ENVISIONED the nervous timidity that rolled off the woman seated across from her. Rend would never be mistaken for half of the team that put together the phenomenally successful Jande and Rend Scroll Shops.

"Thank you for coming," Rend stammered, nondescript brown eyes not quite making contact with Jame or Tigh. She wasn't young, probably well past forty summers, yet her behavior was more like a shy young girl hanging in her mother's shadow.

They were in a back section of the main room of the Ingoran eating establishment, hidden from the other tables by delicately carved and painted wooden panels. Jame and Tigh sat on a padded wooden bench facing Rend, who looked as if she was struggling just to be there, much less ready to engage in a discussion with her guests.

"Thank you for inviting us," Jame said.

A server placed a pot of spiced Ingoran tea and a trio of delicate cups on the table, along with a tray filled with dishes comprising the traditional Ingoran morning meal.

Rend blinked at the intricate arrangement of dishes, and panic overtook her features.

Tigh passed the empty plates around and set up the first serving for them.

Rend relaxed a little. "I, uh, I wanted to talk to you."

"And we appreciate you taking the time from your work to see us." Jame smiled then sampled the egg and potato mixture. "The food here is quite good."

Rend gathered a bit of the food onto her fork and nibbled it. "Yes, very good. I, uh, I need your help."

Jame and Tigh looked up.

"I mean, I'm, uh, I . . ."

Jame finished chewing her mouthful and put the fork down. "Do you need counsel?"

"Yes, I mean no." Rend looked as though she was ready to shatter from nervousness and embarrassment. "Yes."

Jame looked at Tigh, who shrugged. *Could this case get any stranger?*
"Why haven't you sought out one of the arbiters here in Maymi?"

"Trust," Rend muttered, lowering her eyes to her plate.

Jame's mind spun. What could be bad enough for Rend to risk her
partnership with Jande? Unless this was the latest tactic to put her off her
guard. She turned to Tigh.

"You could send for a special arbiter," Tigh said.

"No one must know," Rend said.

"Then meeting us in a public place may not have been such a good
idea," Jame said.

"No one," Rend stammered, then took a deep breath. "No one ever
pays any attention to me."

Jame frowned. "But you're half of Jande and Rend."

"Jande is the business half," Rend said.

Jame nodded as understanding dawned. "You know the inventory."

Tigh stopped chewing and stared at Rend who was concentrating on
gathering a bit of potato onto her fork. "You don't agree with how Jande
is handling the business here?"

"She's gone too far," Rend whispered to her plate.

Great, Jame sighed to herself. Now they had to protect Jande's own
business partner. They may as well bring in the Southern Territory
Reserves to keep everyone alive and well until the hearing took place.

"You want to dissolve your partnership with Jande?" Jame asked.

Fear-filled weak brown eyes flashed up. "It's not possible. I can't break
our contract."

"There's always a way if criminal activity is involved," Jame said. "I'll
find an arbiter to counsel you. How can we contact you without causing
suspicion?"

Rend stared at her food for several heartbeats. "I spend most of my
time in the Maymi Archives."

"We'll do what we can," Jame said, wondering what the next surprise
would be in this case.

OF ALL THE nights to be raining. Tigh splashed across a deserted
street near the edge of town that overlooked the dark waters of the Gulf of
Oheria. The steady drizzle had to be Bal's way of punishing her for going
out against Jame's wishes.

Tigh kicked at a bundle of firewood in frustration. She hated seeing
Jame upset, but she couldn't ignore the urgency in the note from Iklas.
She'd just have to think of a way to make it up to her. She stopped her

abuse of the hapless firewood at the thought. Finding a way to apologize to Jame could be fun.

Tigh looked around for a shingle with a quill and ink jar painted on it. The soaked wood darkened and subdued even the brightest colors, forcing her to use her feet as much as her keen eyes to search for her destination.

She spun around at a shuffling noise behind her and relaxed as a trio of exotic birds stumbled into the street from the corner doorway. The Maymians must take weeks to recover from Carnival, she mused as she trudged along the road, glancing at shingles as she passed by.

She saw the shingle she sought and walked past it to a shop two doors down, where she stopped to run a hand through her soaked hair and to shake off her leathers, while scanning the street for any hidden observers. Reasonably sure she was alone on the street, she strolled back to the other door and slipped inside.

Tigh adjusted her eyes to the dim light in the tiny establishment and determined it was a parchment and ink shop, most likely catering to the students at the nearby University of Maymi. A minute sound near the back of the shop told her she wasn't alone.

"Is it too late to purchase some writing supplies?" she asked.

Iklas stepped into the middle aisle. "I don't recommend carrying clean paper in this kind of weather."

"Makes it hard to write on." Tigh strolled to the slender dark-haired woman, the scar across her face somehow illuminated in the gray light. "This your shop?"

"Mine and Tret's," Iklas said as she turned and walked through the opening to the back room. Tigh followed her into a neat office illuminated by a single orange glow from an oil lamp on the wooden desk. A smaller woman with short brown hair and brown eyes sat at the desk, bent over a bound ledger.

"Tret, this is Tigh, my former Supreme Commander," Iklas said in a voice that bordered on reverence.

Tret looked up. "It's a pleasure to meet you, Tigh." She stood, revealing that she wasn't much taller than Jame.

Tigh studied Tret for a heartbeat, then nodded.

Iklas grinned. "Tigh was never one to waste words. Although, I hear she's loosened up a bit since taking up with her partner."

"You have information?" Tigh turned to Iklas and raised an eyebrow. The reminder that Jame was both unhappy and waiting for her pushed at the back of her mind.

"It's better if I show you," Iklas said.

"Be careful," Tret said.

Iklas shrugged. "We're just taking a walk along the causeway. Nothing suspicious about that."

Tret sighed. "In the middle of the night. In the rain."

"In the middle of Carnival. Everyone's a little crazy now, so it doesn't matter." Iklas leaned across the desk and kissed Tret's forehead. "We'll be careful."

The rain was, if anything, drilling harder against the wooden planks that bordered the back of the little shop. Tigh was surprised to see most of that part of the city gave up the pretense of being supported by land and was built on intricate supports of wood.

"She doesn't sound very happy with your involvement in this," she said as they strolled down the rain-slick boardwalk leading to a shadowed huddle of warehouses.

"It took her a long time to reconcile the woman she used to know, with the Guard I had become," Iklas said, staring into the bleak sleeting rain. "You're lucky your partner didn't know you before. It makes coming home a lot harder."

"It's difficult enough," Tigh muttered as she slouched against the breeze driven water.

"At least she's Emoran." Iklas shook the droplets from her hair. "She understands warriors."

They skirted the inner edge of the brooding warehouses to a pocket of open water with large piers jutting away from three-sided structures used to protect goods from the elements as they were loaded on and off of ships. Small craft from larger ships anchored offshore shuttled back and forth across the black waters. Workers unloaded crates and bundles of fresh foods onto the dock. The soul of the Carnival centered upon this quiet unseen activity.

"I was visiting the corner grocer earlier this evening while a delivery was being made." Iklas led the way past the piers to what looked like the edge of the boardwalk. "Tret had made a special order of fruits, and Quanar, the grocer, thought it was in the shipment being delivered. As I went downstairs to the underground dock, I overheard a couple of the stock deliverers talking. They seemed relieved the job they were on was just delivering foodstuff. I got the impression their boss is making them do things they aren't comfortable with. After I got Tret's package, I took a walk out here to look around."

Iklas sat down on the end of the boardwalk with legs dangling over the edge and motioned Tigh to do the same. Tigh was surprised to see a buildup of sand and crushed shell behind the wood supports of the boardwalk.

"I grew up here and spent my childhood haunting these docks." Iklas stared at the gently lapping water below her. "There used to be only water beneath here." She squinted into the darkness behind her, slid forward, and lowered herself until she clung to the wooden supports.

Tigh followed her actions.

Iklas slithered between two beams and jumped down with a crunch onto the solid sandbar beneath the boardwalk. Tigh landed lightly next to her.

"You did do some exploring," Tigh said.

Iklas shrugged. "I'm as anxious to get rid of the scum threatening Maymi as anyone. Besides, Cadryn is a good soul. She apprenticed to my mother, who ran a little scroll shop here for many years. Unfortunately, this isn't just about scrolls."

Iklas led Tigh through the dim underpinnings of the boardwalk. Tigh noticed it was free of cobwebs, and the sandbar was more packed down than it ought to be.

"It's right up here," Iklas whispered as she slowed her pace. The supporting beams were farther apart, creating a rough open area in front of them. A knee-high wall of brick, an expensive import in Maymi, circled the middle of the area. They cautiously approached it and peered into the circle. Tigh was surprised to find it protected a set of wooden steps leading downward.

Tigh found the idea of a livable chamber beneath the swamp unbelievable. "Jame's not going to like this," she muttered as she peered into the darkness.

They ducked away from the wall at the sound of a woman's voice slicing through the air below them. They took cover in the shadowed supports on the edge of the open area.

"Keep moving," the voice shouted as the first heads popped up from beneath the wall.

A handful of people in rags climbed clumsily over the wall and fell onto the packed sand. Three women with hard glints in their eyes and leather whips in their hands vaulted over the wall and wasted no time pulling the ragged group to its feet. The hapless people were shoved down the narrow passageway arching away from the direction that Tigh and Iklas had come.

After several heartbeats of silence, Tigh relaxed enough to sit back against a wood support. "Slaving," she breathed in disbelief. As far as the civilized world was concerned, that barbaric practice had been done away with centuries before. "For who?"

Iklas shrugged.

"Jame's really not going to like this," Tigh mumbled as she held her head in her hands.

TIGH HAD DIFFERENT levels of quiet and Jame had become adept at distinguishing between them. When the natural quiet deepened into a preoccupied stillness, Jame knew something was gnawing away at her. The quiet hanging over Tigh as she methodically stripped off her soaked armor and leathers and put them on wooden dryers near the fireplace went a level deeper than preoccupation and conversely raised Jame's level of concern.

Jame picked up their drying cloth and went to Tigh. She was surprised at how cold Tigh's skin was as she rubbed the moisture away.

"I hope you didn't catch a chill," she murmured as she concentrated on getting Tigh dry.

"Not from the rain," Tigh mumbled.

"Let's get you dried off and into the nice warm bed," Jame said. "Then you can tell me about it."

Tigh nodded, then wrapped her arms around Jame and held her close for several heartbeats. Jame, used to Tigh's impulsive acts of affection, brushed her lips against the arm she was drying and couldn't help but smile at the love that radiated from Tigh.

Jame pulled the sleep shirt over the Tigh's head and led her to the bed, making sure there was enough warmth, between the covers and her own body, to ease Tigh's chill.

"We have a big problem," Tigh said.

"I already knew that," Jame said.

"The illegal trading involves more than goods and services," Tigh said.

"What else is there?" Jame raised her head to look into Tigh's stark eyes. "Laur's waterfalls. You don't mean—?"

"Slaves," Tigh whispered.

"But owning slaves has been outlawed," Jame said.

"Here," Tigh said.

"There hasn't been trade with the rest of the world for centuries." Jame shook her head. "Not since we adopted the policy of isolationism."

"That seems to have changed when the Northern Territories tried to form their own sovereign nation," Tigh said. "They recruited mercenaries from the lands across the seas to help them fight against us. Then, all of a sudden, the people of the Silver Dragon thought they could invade our lands and defeat us. Obviously some network of communication and commerce has been set up with these foreigners."

"If we didn't have an isolation policy, there wouldn't be a reason for all the underground activity with foreigners." Jame sighed. "Sometimes what seems to be a solution to a problem, only makes the problem worse."

"Hmmm." Tigh got that look in her eyes. The one that usually preceded an impossibly outrageous idea that none-the-less was too irresistible not to consider.

"What are you thinking?" Jame couldn't help but grin at the first spark of optimism she'd seen since Tigh returned from the docks.

"I'm thinking that I'm joined with a very intelligent woman," Tigh said.

"What did I say?" Jame frowned, mentally scanned their conversation, and narrowed her eyes. "You want me to challenge the validity of the isolation policy?"

Tigh shrugged. "That's a part of an arbiter's job. To test the laws of the land."

"It'd only work if we can actually tie Jande and Rend to the underground commerce with foreign countries." Jame always loved a challenge.

"It's something to think about," Tigh murmured and then placed a gentle kiss on Jame's forehead. "It could be a way of neatly taking care of everyone's problems at once."

"It would really throw everyone off guard, too." Jame relaxed against Tigh as she latched onto the idea. She barely noticed when Tigh's breathing evened off into a contented sleep.

THE FIRST THING Tigh noticed when she woke up was the sound of water dripping off the eves onto the balcony. She focused her hearing to the street outside and heard . . . nothing. She carefully slid out from under the sleeping Jame, padded to the balcony, and stared into the shrouded dawn light. No one.

A sleepy shuffle from behind her was followed by a hand on her back. "Where'd everyone go?"

"This is the day for the ceremony to the swamp creatures." Tigh squinted as she remembered what their Emoran host had told her. "Maybe everyone is resting up for it."

It sounded like as good an explanation as any, and they decided to take advantage of the deserted streets and go to the Ingoran establishment for the morning meal instead of having it delivered.

They stepped away from the safe house door and saw a carriage across the street and a man watching the door. He smoothed down his thinning black hair, put both hands on an ample stomach, and bounded across the street to them.

"Arbiter Jamelin." His joyous gray eyes crinkled in greeting. "I'm Cipronis Tangigar."

"Cipronis." Tigh sighed but she wasn't surprised.

"Paldar Tigis." Cipronis grinned. "I remember when your mother took you everywhere in a baby sack on her back. Couldn't very well do that now, could she?" He laughed as he looked up at Tigh.

"What do you want?" Tigh asked.

"It just so happens I'll be arguing Jande and Rend's case." He flourished an outrageous comical bow.

"I thought Jande and Rend weren't going to hire an arbiter in deference to Cadryn's desire to argue her own case," Jame said.

"I was initially brought in as a legal consultant," Cipronis said. "But when we heard you'd put in a request for an assistant arbiter to be assigned to Cadryn, Jande and Rend took that to mean she changed her mind."

"Cadryn needs an arbiter for an entirely different reason," Jame said.

"You mean it has nothing to do with this case?" Cipronis asked.

"Only indirectly," Jame said.

"Indirectly. What—?"

"If it has nothing to do with the case, it's none of your business," Tigh said.

Cipronis reacted with several startled blinks before he recovered his good humor. "At any rate, that's not why I'm here. Jande would like to meet with you. As you see, she's sent a carriage."

"We're going for our morning meal." Tigh put an arm over Jame's shoulder.

"Would you care to join us?" Jame asked.

"Jande would be honored if you joined her for the morning meal," Cipronis said. "The Dranderal's cook makes excellent Ingoran food."

"In that case, we'd be honored to meet with Jande," Jame said.

Tigh struggled to control her scowl.

The open-topped carriage reflected the tastes of the opulent upper crust of Maymian society. The brightly painted paneling and gold and red silk cushions shouted prosperity in contrast to simple Ingoran understatement.

"Where is everyone?" Jame asked as they clattered down all but deserted streets.

"In the swamps." Cipronis wrinkled his nose in distaste.

"The swamps?"

"It's the most ancient tradition of the Carnival," Cipronis said without enthusiasm. "They take thousands of flat boats into the swamps and follow the hunt for the special ingredients of the Carnival stew."

"Hunt for ingredients?" Jame asked.

"Everything. The spices, the greens, the meats, all must come out of the swamp and be put in the giant cauldrons on the spit of land to the south of the city. They cook the stew, and everyone feasts on it well into the night." Cipronis wiped his hands together as if the very thought of the day's activity soiled them.

"Sounds . . . interesting," Jame said.

Cipronis grimaced. "If you like insects and reptiles and thousands of drunken Maymians splashing slimy water at you all day."

Much to Tigh's surprise, the carriage rattled away from the city onto a wide levee topped with a well-kept road. On one side lapped harbor waters and on the other side was the outer edge of the swamp. As they moved further from the city, the shouts and laughter and splashes cast ghostly echoes across the mist-shrouded, wetlands trees.

The carriage rounded a stand of trees, revealing a jumble of buildings about the size of a small village, and Tigh wished they were joining the swamp hunt rather than having to spend the morning in strained civility. But it was Jame's job to get to know all the sides in a case before she could fairly judge it.

"This is the largest estate in Maymi," Cipronis said as the main residence building came into view.

Unlike the gaudy buildings in Maymi, the Dranderal estate was painted white, creating a dramatic contrast with the dark swamp greens around it. The residence sprawled from what looked like generations of add-ons and renovations, and many sections reached three stories high. Wide balconies encircled each floor, allowing access to the outside from any point in the home. A necessity in the sticky heat of a Maymi summer.

The carriage pulled around an ample circle of cleared sandy land in front of the home.

The air filled with yodels and whoops coming from the surrounding swamp.

"Don't move," Cipronis said.

Scores of people in wild colored masks, many sloshing sweet wine down their throats, stumbled off flatbed boats that glided through the mists onto the wet sand.

Some staggered up the steps to the front door of the house and crawled onto the large porch, and some danced demented dances around the carriage, all screamed for the Dranderal clan to show itself.

A shout of triumph came from the porch as one of the besotted revelers gained enough control to open the door. A dozen feathered beasts rushed into the house as the rest continued to dance and shout outside. Heartbeats later, the dozen returned, dragging several members of the Dranderal clan onto the porch. A deafening cheer rose up in the swamps around them from the thousands of unseen onlookers.

One of the victims of the drunken raid was positioned at the top of the steps. The abductors pulled off the large yellow cloths that were tied around their waists and waved them until silence overtook the swamp.

A reveler with a mask of yellow and green feathers turned, with arms crossed in a menacing challenge, to the woman at the top of the steps.

"We're here for the tribute to save your house for one more year from the wrath of the swamp creatures," the reveler said to the accompaniment of rattles and whistles from his followers. "What do you have that will appease the swamp creatures?"

"That's for you to find out," the woman said in mocking challenge.

The head reveler growled in frustration and raised his bird's head staff. "We'll tear down this fine house and your fine buildings if you don't tell us where the tribute is." The rattles and whistles were louder.

The woman smirked and crossed her arms. "The answer is at the end of the riddle found behind the last built wing of the stable."

The revelers whooped and yodeled, hopped off the porch, stopped their dancing, stumbled back to their flat boats and guided them around the back of the house to the stable in question. The ensuing quiet was like the eye of a storm.

The woman walked down the steps to the carriage as if nothing outrageous had just happened. "Ah, arbiter Jamelin. Welcome."

Tigh and Jame exchanged glances as they climbed out of the carriage. No one was ever going to believe this story.

Chapter 10

FOR ALL THE elegant deep wood paneling and a decor that reflected an expensive, if not extravagant taste, the home of the Dranderal clan put Tigh on edge. Too many eyes watched from the upper landings and small doorways and niches. The home seemed to be full of too many curious people. At least Cipronis had other things to do. One less person to get on her nerves.

Ofnal Dranderal, the unflappable matriarch, led them down a wide corridor of galleries, as she chatted on inconsequential matters—the Maymian way of putting visitors at ease. The entire clan and then some seemed to be lounging in the galleries, watching the revelers' antics through large windows or chatting in small groups near the fireplaces.

Ofnal walked through opened double doors into a dark, paneled room dominated by a long oval table with an elaborate setting of Ingoran dishes laid out on it.

"Here are your visitors, Jande. If you'll excuse me, I have to appease the swamp creatures." Ofnal grinned then returned to the corridor and closed the doors behind her.

A rather heavyset woman of medium height stood from her seat at the far end of the table. Her angled face was hardened by the harsh work of running a successful business. Her eyes showed a forced patience for having to deal with the social aspects that came with the job. Tigh had seen this look many times in Ingor.

"Welcome, arbiter Jamelin," Jande greeted with a practiced smooth voice. "I'm Jande Fael. Please have a seat." She indicated a pair of seats next to her.

"Thank you, merchant Jande," Jame said as she and Tigh rounded the table to the chairs.

"Let me introduce my partner, Rend Fanders." Jande turned to Rend on her other side. "And this is Traq Nims, my head of sales. And Enoc Kimer, my head of marketing."

Jame and Tigh nodded to the thin gray-haired man next to Rend and to the boisterous-looking woman next to him. Both seemed to be more interested in what was on their plates than with them.

"It's a pleasure to meet all of you," Jame said, causing the silent three across from her to look up a little startled.

Tigh hid a smile by reaching for the tea decanter and pouring the spicy liquid into the cups in front of Jame and herself.

"This is my peace warrior and partner, Tigh."

"We're so happy both of you could join us this morning," Jande said. "Although, we might have been smarter to have picked a better day. I had no idea the citizens of Maymi would be so enthusiastic in scouring the swamps for their Carnival stew."

"Intriguing custom." Jame nodded. She flashed a grateful smile to Tigh, who filled her plate with food.

"We were thinking of putting out a line of scrolls devoted to the customs and folklore of this area," Jande said. "I've hired several artists to roam around the Carnival sketching impressions."

"Sounds like an interesting idea," Jame said.

"I was planning to have a special edition of the Carnival scrolls, painted in full color in a finely tooled leather case, for the opening of our shop here in Maymi." Jande rested brown eyes that looked as if they weren't accustomed to argument on Jame.

"Sounds like a good marketing idea," Jame said.

"Of course, it'd help to know if our shop here will actually be allowed to open," Jande said.

"That's just one of the gambles one takes when in business," Jame said. "These greens are really well cooked. The sauce is especially delicate."

"Thank you. We entertain quite a few Ingorans, so we acquired a cook who specializes in Ingoran cuisine," Jande said. "One of the ways of reducing the gamble in business is to engage in careful preparation before embarking on any new endeavor. We're thorough in our study of a possible location for a new scroll shop and up to now, we've never had a problem. That's because we never attempt to open a scroll shop in those cities we feel we wouldn't fit into. After several seasons of research, we felt confident that Maymi was a perfect location for one of our shops. We met with no opposition when we applied for the proper licenses, when we bought the property, when we made the announcement of intent to open our shop here. Under law, the citizens of Maymi had the chance to file their opposition at any point in this process."

"All the marketing projections pointed to the desperate need for a comprehensive scroll shop in this region," Enoc Kimer said with a knowing bob of her head. "The citizens showed a strong interest in having the kinds of products that only Jande and Rend can offer."

Tigh struggled to not roll her eyes at the sales pitch that came naturally to people in marketing.

"Then, all of a sudden, that young woman comes forth with a protest, the day before the city was to sign the papers to allow us to go ahead with establishing a shop here." Jande's attempts to keep her expression soft failed as it hardened into a displeased mask. "We think she's been forced into this by a group of disgruntled merchants in this city. From what we could gather, these merchants have spent years grumbling about the way certain businesses have been run in this city. They're blaming their own inability at running a business on the successful merchants. It's not the first time we've seen this kind of professional jealousy. Except this time they've been able to band together and force a novice merchant into this foolhardy challenge."

Jande paused, took a sip of tea, and watched Jame as if trying to gauge her reaction.

Jame swallowed a mouthful of greens. "Thank you for your concerns. I'll look into the matter."

"That's all we ask for," Jande said. "Our reports are available for your perusal and use. Cadryn seems like a reasonably competent young woman, but a mere apprenticeship is not enough for her to possess the experience needed to run a scroll shop. A good beginning job for her would be a part of the inventory staff, I think, so she can learn the inner workings of a well-run scroll shop."

"Are you saying there might be a position for her in your own shop here in Maymi?" Jame asked.

Jande shrugged. "She has the desired background for our entry level employees. We're always in need of people meeting our minimum requirements."

Tigh's temper flared, and she could tell Jame was working to keep her anger down.

"I'll keep your generous offer in mind as I determine this case," Jame said.

Jande allowed a smile to soften the hard planes of her face.

SPRAWLING WAS A good word to describe the Maymi Archives. The low-lying buildings stretched across a built-up piece of land like the web of a demented spider. Courtyards bordered patches of swamp, and cascades of gardens in wooden boxes on stilts filled the spaces between the numerous wings of the building.

Even with the rather natural setting, the atmosphere inside the building was a calm peace with a waterfall bubbling into a small shallow pool in the main hall of the archives.

"Which way?" Jame asked.

"She said down the corridor behind the waterfall," Tigh said, as she led the way around the pool that rippled with blue and yellow striped fish.

"I don't think I've ever seen fish like that before." Jame gazed at the playful darting creatures.

"I think they live in the Gulf which means this water must have salt in it," Tigh said.

Jame cast an amused glance at Tigh. "How do you know all this stuff?"

"Uh." Tigh glanced around. "I spent a lot of my time in the archives when we were in Ynit between campaigns."

Jame arched an eyebrow. "And why do I get the feeling this wasn't what all the other former archivists, librarians and scholars who made up the Guards did?"

"That was one of the paradoxes of our enhancements," Tigh said. "Not only did they lose their enjoyment of scholarship and learning, any scholarly pursuit was ridiculed."

"But you were still drawn to learning," Jame said.

"Yes. The impulse to learn was stronger than before I was enhanced," Tigh said. "I guess there was always something different about me, even with the enhancements. That's probably why the cleansing didn't work the same with me as with the others."

"I think Pendon may be interested in knowing about this," Jame said.

Tigh sighed and shook her head. "You're right. Maybe it'll help in their quest to completely heal the other Guards."

"Maybe we—"

The sound of running feet cut through the hushed peace of the long open-sided corridor that bridged a swampy patch of land. Two people wearing lightweight bird masks and armor-covered cloth tunics ran straight for Jame while four others focused on Tigh. Jame froze in her steps.

Tigh registered only one thing—Jame was in danger. She leapt in front of Jame in time to whack an assailant in the face, while tripping the second with a long, outstretched leg. She jumped back next to Jame and pulled her sword from its sheath with a satisfying hiss. Her cold glare froze the actions of the other four assailants.

Tigh flipped her sword. "Who sent you?"

"The person who paid us," the bravest of the group said.

"You're willing to die for someone you don't even know?" Tigh ran a thumb along the side of her blade.

The man scowled. "Not likely. We were told you may carry a sword, but you can't fight."

"Are you willing to test that rumor?" Tigh raised an eyebrow. "All you have to do is tell me who sent you, and I'll let you live."

The two assailants still sprawled on the floor pulled themselves back until they were next to their comrades.

"We got paid half already. That alone is more than we get for two jobs," one of them muttered to the man who appeared to be their leader.

"She could be bluffing," the man muttered back. "And the body of Tigh the Terrible is worth a lifetime of jobs to Tekl."

"He was drunk when he made that offer," a woman's voice breathed.

"And he had too many witnesses not to honor it," the man whispered back.

"I guess you won't have the chance to find out, will you?" Tigh said.

The six looked up, startled she had heard their whispered conversation. They gasped when they felt the pressure of steel against their necks.

"Let me introduce you to a few of my former comrades in arms," Tigh said.

Vorkin grinned and nodded to the other scholars who had snuck up on the assailants. "Thank you for your assistance. Could you kindly escort them to the main office and send word to the Chief Constable?"

Tigh sheathed her sword and Jame let out a long-held breath.

"Thank you, Vorkin," Jame said.

"I didn't think this was the best circumstance to test Tigh's fighting impulse," Vorkin said.

"I'm able to defend Jame without hesitation," Tigh said.

"But can you defend yourself?" Vorkin asked. "I think we'd better work on that before any more of these incidents happen."

Tigh nodded. "You're right. I won't be able to get away with bluffing forever."

Jame put a hand on Tigh's arm. "This is the perfect opportunity we were looking for. Who else can you fight without worrying about getting hurt? And who you won't worry about hurting?"

Tigh, falling as always into Jame's persuasive emerald eyes, nodded. She looked up at Vorkin. "Show us the maps, and then we'll go spar for a bit."

A HALF-DOZEN FORMER Guards whirled and struck at Tigh in blurring movements.

She felt lethargic and clumsy and was thankful of the Guards' skill to not injure her.

"All right, back off," Vorkin said as the Guards stepped away from the unresponsive Tigh. "This isn't working, and it won't help Tigh's credibility if we accidentally bruise or hurt her."

Iklas sauntered up to Tigh, tall enough to be eye to eye with her. "You used to be the floral language of an epic poem in motion. You could change your swings in mid-move with just a tightening of a muscle. Is all that gone, too?"

Tigh blinked Iklas. "I don't know. Outside my peace warrior training and working with a few village girls, I haven't really done any sword work."

"How did you pass the peace warrior's test?" Vorkin asked.

"I'll fight to defend Jame," Tigh said. "I learned to defend myself and to defend Jame, but I couldn't fight back with the intention of inflicting harm."

"Move for us," Iklas said as she backed away from Tigh. "Show us your sword drills."

Tigh sighed. "It's been a long time."

"Reacquaint yourself with how the movements feel," Iklas said.

The air in the warehouse seemed to thicken with anticipation.

Tigh turned to Jame, needing their connection to ground her unsettled reaction to such a simple request.

Jame approached Tigh from her safe place against the wall. "I'd love to see you do sword drills." She leaned closer to Tigh's ear. "You know how much I love to watch you."

Tigh's whole world focused on Jame's whispered words and the warmth of her closeness. She'd do it for Jame. She'd do anything that Jame requested.

"For you," Tigh breathed in Jame's ear.

"For us." Jame captured Tigh's eyes with her own.

Tigh read the unspoken words in Jame's eyes and nodded. She had to get past this barrier so they could live their dream without the constant shadow from Tigh's past threatening their safety.

Tigh brushed her lips against Jame's cheek. "You like to watch me move, huh?"

"Oh yeah," Jame said.

"All right." Tigh strolled to the middle of the wooden floor, and Jame went back to the wall with the other Guards.

Streaked by the bright sun sharply cutting through the broken planks in the wall, Tigh breathed in the quiet peace of the upper floor of the warehouse. She took a step forward and slashed the air with her sword, focusing on the satisfying pull of her shoulder muscles as she extended the sword to one side.

Her body, knowing this dance by heart, flowed around the briefly stationary sword. She pulled the sword to follow the momentum of her body and twisted into a graceful flip over the blade. She landed with the blade lifted upward, posed to strike.

Tigh stood for several heartbeats, sorting out what she felt and what she was supposed to be feeling at that moment.

A movement from the corner of her eye was enough to anticipate the body and the blade coming at her. She swung and the clash of steel rang through the silence. Iklas backed away to allow Tigh to continue her drills.

One by one, the former Guards interrupted Tigh's progress with quick strikes and retreats, getting her used to battle conditions. The length of the assaults increased as Tigh lost herself in the deadly dance that had always given her the sweetest satisfaction.

The Guards timed their movements so Tigh would have to push one of them away to stop another's attack. They seemed to gauge Tigh's reactions and experimented with how far they could push her while she felt her warrior soul become freer with each clash of swords.

Tigh relaxed into the exercise as she focused on what she was doing rather than what she was feeling. She could feel her body tingle with power as the assaults intensified.

She let out a shattering cry, and the Guards scattered in all directions, ready to retreat to the exposed beam rafters if need be.

Tigh stood in the middle of the floor, sword extended in front of her. She glanced around with a readiness to fight anyone who even looked as if they were going to move.

Several heartbeats of alert tenseness passed. The tension eased from Tigh's shoulders and arms as she lowered the blade. She took a deep breath and sheathed her sword.

"I think I found what I was looking for." Just the taste of what made Tigh the Terrible was enough to terrify her. What if they had undone the cleansing by pushing too far? What if she couldn't control it now that it was unleashed? She captured Jame's eyes and found the only truth that mattered. She'd have to learn to control it because she needed that part of herself to watch over and protect Jame.

CHIEF CONSTABLE BARY trailed Tigh and Jame as they walked out of the holding cells at the top of the Constabulary building.

"Did they tell you who sent them?" Bary asked. "Never in the history of Maymi has a peace arbiter been attacked."

"Strangers wearing masks," Jame said.

She and Tigh had agreed to keep the scattered details they had picked up to themselves until they had worked through them. Although they knew the Chief Constable had been honest with them to that point, they needed to be cautious with so much menace flowing just beneath the surface of the city.

"May we see the place where the hearing is to be held?" Tigh asked.

"Of course," Bary said.

He led them to a walkway corridor that bridged the third floors of the Constabulary and the Arbiters' Hall.

"Look at that." Jame stopped and stared out one of the small round windows that dotted the walls of the walkway.

The street below them was the main throughway that led to the long spits of sand that stretched away from the city. The walkway offered a clear view of the line of cauldrons that sat on fiery piles of wood. The revelers on boats pushed out of the surrounding swamps and dropped foodstuff into the cauldrons as the boats floated close to the spit.

"It always makes for interesting stew," Bary said.

Jame wrinkled her nose. "I bet."

They entered the nearly deserted Arbiter's Hall.

"Carnival's an official city holiday," Bary said. "Foreigners usually volunteer to work the cases that happen during the festivities. Because this is a high-profile case, the hearing will be in our largest chamber."

He led them down a winding central staircase to the main floor.

"We may have to change that," Tigh said.

Bary gave Tigh a wary look. "There has to be a very good reason to close a public hearing."

Jame knew he could feel this new edgy menace that seemed to emanate from Tigh. She truly was a different person from the gentle passive warrior he had met before.

Tigh swept her eyes over Bary. "I think protecting the life of the arbiter is a good enough reason."

"Uh. You're certainly right," Bary stammered and then hurried ahead.

Jame frowned as she gazed at Tigh. She refused to be unsettled by this frightening stranger in Tigh's body. She had to remember it was just another setback in Tigh's rehabilitation to work through. That's all.

"Tigh," Jame said.

Tigh turned, and Jame was relieved to see that she seemed just as confused about her actions.

"Try to keep it together long enough so we can talk about it," Jame said. "Alone."

Some of the tension flowed out of Tigh. "I think I'll be all right with it. I just need to adjust to feeling this way again."

Jame relaxed. "Try not to scare the locals too much then."

"I'll do my best not to," Tigh said.

Bary waited for them in front of a pair of opened doors.

"Tigh's still adjusting to the cleansing process," Jame said. "A part of the Guard mystique was the ability to give off a kind of menace. It still slips through sometimes. But you don't have to worry. Tigh only fights to defend me or herself."

Bary nodded as he eyed the now passive Tigh. "It must be a difficult adjustment to make."

BARY OPENED THE door and led them into a large square chamber. Tigh calculated it could seat several hundred people. What was worse from a security viewpoint was a balcony that hung over a good third of the lower chamber.

Soft footfalls from an opened door behind the Tribunal's bench at the front of the chamber captured Tigh's attention. A few heartbeats later, a man of medium height walked into the chamber and approached them. He had the typical look of an Arbiters' Hall administrator—nondescript, lacking any signs of enthusiasm for the job. Most people who held the position were the type who lasted long enough in the service of the city to work up through the ranks.

Not the type of person who, at first glance, would be considered Tigh's current prime suspect. Her incessant habit of picking up and reading anything that was at hand gave her in-depth knowledge of the city government of Maymi. The same name turned up in surprising ways sometimes.

"Ah. Here's the person who'll be able to help you with all your questions concerning the Hall." Bary smiled at the approaching man, who eyed Tigh and Jame with the bored expression of someone who was just doing his job and nothing more.

"Arbiter Jamelin." The man bowed his head. "We're pleased the Federation Council was able to get an arbiter to us so quickly. I'm Chief Administrator Tekl Hetler. Since this is a cross jurisdiction case, I'll be personally responsible for coordinating the hearing for you."

"Thank you, Chief Administrator," Jame said. "We're just getting a feel for the place right now."

"Then allow me to give you a tour," Tekl said.

Tigh sucked in her breath as she and Chief Constable Bary trailed Jame and Tekl. It gave her time to think about all the possible reasons why she wanted to grab Jame's hand and get them both out of the city, never to return. At least, thinking such thoughts kept her from reaching out and crushing the life out of the bland Chief Administrator.

Chapter 11

TIGH RAN A nervous hand through her hair as she wandered around their chamber in the safe house. They had spent the rest of the day visiting the site chosen for the Jande and Rend House of Scrolls and talking to the neighboring shopkeepers. The merchants of the town always took advantage of the day Carnival was celebrated in the surrounding swamps to tidy up their shops from being open day and night for several days in a row.

The merchants also spoke freer without the presence of masked festivalgoers all around them. What struck Tigh was the consensus that the location chosen by Jande and Rend wasn't considered particularly ideal for a scroll shop.

"These underground maps are really interesting," Jame said after a good quarter sandmark of just studying the detailed drawings. "Tigh?"

Tigh stopped kicking the logs in the cold fireplace and turned to Jame. "Sorry, I, uh . . ." She took a deep breath and shrugged her slumped shoulders.

Jame rushed to Tigh and looked into her eyes. "I'm so sorry to have gotten distracted." She pulled Tigh to the bed and sat down next to her. "Talk to me."

Tigh took a deep breath and studied her strong hands. "Is this going to change anything between us?"

"Why do you think it would change anything?" Jame asked.

Tigh swallowed, trying to push down what she knew were unreasonable thoughts. "I . . . I don't feel like the same person I was before. I got used to the passive Tigh and now she's suddenly gone."

"You said you'll be able to adjust to it," Jame said.

"I can, but what about you?" Tigh turned to Jame and captured her eyes. "Can you live with the knowledge that Tigh the Terrible is close to the surface now?"

"I don't think that's true," Jame said. "I think Tigh the warrior has finally broken through the last barrier. The ability to fight back wasn't what defined Tigh the Terrible. She was ruthless and cruel." Jame wrapped her hands around Tigh's hand. "If any part of Tigh the Terrible was lurking beneath the surface, we wouldn't be here having this discussion."

Tigh examined that thought. It was true. The Supreme Commander would have abandoned the peaceful arbiter without thought and without looking back. "I guess I don't want you to see that side of me."

"I grew up around warriors," Jame said. "I was a warrior-in-training myself. When you fight, it'll be for self-defense and to protect others."

"It just feels so different. In here." Tigh tapped her head.

"Different for bad or different for good?" Jame kissed Tigh on the cheek.

"Just different," Tigh said. "You saw how the other Guards backed away from me when they saw the change happen. You saw the Chief Constable's reaction when I felt the need to fight rising in me."

Jame smiled. "But that's a good thing. It'll warn people off from wanting to try to bribe or take advantage of me. The stronger you are as a formidable warrior, the better chance I have to do my job."

"I haven't actually fought yet," Tigh said. "We don't know what'll happen when I've actually engaged the enemy."

"If you faltered at all the what-ifs in your life, where would you be right now?" Jame asked.

Tigh stared into steady emerald eyes, knowing that only her uncertainties held her back. "And if I fight and I change for the worse?"

"Then we go back to Ynit and work on getting you better," Jame said. "I'm not going to abandon you or stop loving you just because you have to struggle with something beyond your control. Something that someone else had done to you in the first place."

"You have no idea how cruel I can be." Tigh tried to shut out the horrific memories of her past.

"And you have no idea how stubborn or persistent I can be." Jame sat up and held Tigh's head in her hands, forcing eye contact with her. "I'll not allow you to beat yourself up over things that may not even happen. We'll work through this one step at a time, but the important part will be that we'll do it together."

"I don't deserve you." Tears crept down Tigh's cheek as she gathered Jame into her arms. "You are my savior and my life."

Jame smiled. "I thank Laur in every breath I take that I'm able to share my life with you."

TIGH SIGHED AS she gently scooted out from beneath a sleeping Jame. Jame had such a wondrous contented expression on her face that Tigh was reluctant to disturb her. But she had to pull together a few loose ends of this puzzle masquerading as a straightforward civil case before she could determine who really controlled Jande and Rend.

Jame moaned a protest to the absence of the comfortable warmth of her bed mate. Tigh slipped her pillow into Jame's embrace.

"Not a good substitute," Jame mumbled.

Tigh brushed her lips on Jame's cheek. "What's a good substitute then?"

"There isn't one." Jame half-opened her eyes and grabbed Tigh's arm. "I know it's your job to do all the dirty work and keep me safe, but I have the right to worry about you."

Tigh grinned, then gently caressed Jame's lips with her own. "I'm always careful. I have everything to live for now."

Jame wrapped her arms around Tigh's neck and gave her an answering kiss that nearly dissuaded Tigh from leaving the cozy warmth of their bed.

"I know. You have to go snoop around while everyone is passed out in the swamps." Jame reluctantly released Tigh.

"I'll try to be as quick as possible." Tigh slid out of bed and pulled on her leathers and armor.

"You know I won't be able to sleep until you get back." Jame hitched up onto her elbows and looked at Tigh.

"I know." Tigh bent down for another kiss.

She went to the balcony and launched into a flip to the street below.

She landed with a muted thud onto the crushed shell and stone road. She caught a movement in a doorway and couldn't keep away a feral grin. She had counted three watchers outside the safe house and had no doubt there were more in the facing buildings. That meant at least one of them would be following her.

Tigh sauntered down the street and turned the corner in the direction of the future Jande and Rend Scroll Shop. As she strolled along in the moonlight-drenched street, she nodded in appreciation at the stealth with which her shadow followed her. Most likely not a Maymian, she mused as her ears caught only a whisper of footfalls behind her.

She rounded the corner to the street where Jande and Rend hoped to put their shop. With mountain cat skill, she jumped up and grabbed the iron holder of the dangling sign for the shop closest to the corner. She felt the presence of her shadow near the corner as she balanced on top of the sign.

The shadow peeked around the corner and after a few heartbeats, peeked again. Not stupid, Tigh thought as she looked above her. She silently thanked the Maymians for their wooden buildings with so many good places to put her hands and feet.

Tigh crawled to the roof and studied the person below. Something about the shadow's bearing shouted foreigner to her, even though the clothes were a nondescript brown. She dropped off the roof and landed cat-like behind her follower. She grabbed both arms of the shadow and pulled them behind its back.

"You know what I want to know," Tigh said in a low voice.

"I'll tell you everything I can, Dragonslayer," came a steady voice with a definite foreign tinge to it.

Tigh frowned in puzzlement. "Dragonslayer?"

"You defeated the Silver Dragon. For that my people are thankful," the woman said as she relaxed against Tigh's restraint.

"Why are you following me then?" Tigh asked.

"We didn't want to bring attention to ourselves."

Tigh spun the woman around. "Why?" She peered into earnest gray eyes.

"The people of the Silver Dragon conquered my people many generations ago," the woman said. "They terrorize us and capture us into slavery. A group of us have been working for many seasons to break the trade of slaves here, but of late we've become disheartened at our inability to free more than a few of those who've been enslaved. Then we heard news that the army of the Silver Dragon had been defeated in a single day. It sounded like an unbelievable miracle to us. When we found out the mastermind behind this defeat was here in Maymi, we couldn't believe our good luck. And when we found out you were here to arbitrate the scroll shop case, we hoped we finally had the means to break the slave trade."

Tigh nodded. "So, the two things are related."

"Yes," the woman said. "We hesitated to approach you because we weren't sure how you felt about slavery. Your ways are so foreign to us."

"Slavery was outlawed long ago." Tigh released the woman. "Where can we talk?"

"We'll let you know," the woman said. "I am Roseh."

"Tigh."

Roseh nodded. "Tigh the Dragonslayer."

It sounded better than Tigh the Terrible, Tigh mentally shrugged. "We've only five days before the hearing."

"You'll meet with us tomorrow. I'll send word by morning," Roseh said.

"We'll be waiting for it." Tigh watched as Roseh slipped into the shadows. She thought it strange how so many life threads overlapped. How a battle on the Ynitian desert could impact on a band of rebels on the Maymian Peninsula.

She shook out of her reverie and strode through the deserted streets back to her warm bed and Jame.

"DRAGONSLAYER." JAME IMPISHLY took a nibble of the word and rolled it around in her mouth to capture all the flavors of it. Tigh watched her with a wary expression. "Hmmm. Has a nice, noble sound to it."

"Can I convince you to forget you even heard it?" Tigh asked.

Jame stifled a smile at how cute Tigh looked when she was trying not to pout. "I think we might be able to come to some kind of settlement. But I anticipate lengthy negotiations. I like it too much just to give it up without a fight."

"Negotiations," Tigh said.

"Lengthy negotiations." Jame sat forward in the open-topped carriage.

Tigh's eyes twinkled. "Lengthy negotiations can be fun."

Before Jame had a chance to respond, the carriage slowed to a stop. "We'll continue this discussion later."

"Looking forward to it."

They jumped off the carriage and paid the driver. With Carnival finally over, Maymi felt less alien and more like the cities they were used to. The area they were in was known as the University District and had a different feel to it than the rest of the city. Knots of students sporting various colored scarves denoting their subject specialty were scattered about the street, in doorways, and on small greens. At the end of the street was the stone pillared entrance to the University grounds.

"There's Cadryn's shop." Jame nodded at the street corner closest to the stone pillars. "Nice location."

"Perfect location," Tigh said. "And Jande and Rend think they have the perfect location way over by the wharf district."

"I guess it depends on what they're really selling." Jame tucked that idea into the back of her mind.

The double doors on the corner of the block were wide open as workers both inside and out transformed what Cadryn had said was a rundown tavern into an inviting scroll shop.

"It's huge," Jame said as they crossed the threshold into a two-story chamber with a balcony lining the upper floor. Shelves for scrolls were being hammered into place on the walls. Stand-alone shelves haphazardly surrounded Cadryn who was intently studying the area she had to work with.

"That one should go over there." Cadryn directed the handful of young helpers, students by the looks of them. They went to the shelves in question and shuffled them according to Cadryn's instructions.

"What do you think?" Jame and Tigh turned as Vorkin stepped into the shop.

"It looks like it'll be a prosperous business," Jame said.

"She's put so much planning and work into it." Vorkin sighed. "It'd be a great injustice if an outsider takes it away."

"It looks wonderful," Jame said. "She's hiring students?"

Vorkin grinned. "They're volunteers. They've been showing up at the door offering to help ever since Jande and Rend filed the suit."

"Really?" Jame looked around and noted the cheerful enthusiasm of the young workers.

"The students have gone so far as to pass a petition around the university calling for a permanent boycott of the Jande and Rend shop, if they happen to win the suit," Vorkin said.

"Hmmm. There's nothing quite like the fervent protests of idealistic students," Jame said.

Vorkin laughed. "You're not that much removed from being one of those idealistic students."

"Gives me a clearer insight into this case," Jame said with a grin.

A handful of students walked into the shop. They stopped when they saw Jame and gasped and whispered to each other. Jame realized everyone had stopped what they were doing and were gazing at her as if Bal himself had paid a visit.

"You're something of a celebrity with the students," Vorkin said.

"Celebrity?" Jame asked.

"You've captured their imaginations," Tigh murmured into Jame's ear.

A young woman with big gray eyes timidly approached Jame. "Is it true you're an Emoran princess?"

Jame focused on the girl, seeing all the signs of a huge crush. She then glanced at the group huddled behind the girl, all wearing unmistakable expressions of worship. "Yes, it's true." She took a surprised step back at the sudden twittering response to her answer.

"We think you're beautiful," The girl said and then lost her nerve and retreated into the cluster of her excited friends.

A stunned Jame could only stare at the giggling young students. Tigh took Jame's arm and led her away from the hero worshippers.

Jame looked up at Tigh. "What are you grinning at?"

"You're cute when you're flustered," Tigh said, causing Vorkin, who trailed behind them, to snort a laugh.

"I'm sorry I teased you about those hero worshiping girls back in Artocia," Jame muttered.

"Welcome to my humble shop." Cadryn waved her hand around.

"It looks as if it's already popular with the students, and it's not even open yet," Jame said.

"They've been really supportive." Cadryn seemed to have a permanent expression of amazement. "Would you like a tour of the place?"

Jame smiled. "That would be nice, thank you."

She and Tigh followed Cadryn, who explained her vision for the shop as they wandered into the back chambers. Vorkin sauntered along behind the trio. Cadryn stopped at the top of a small staircase in one of the, as yet, unused storage rooms.

"The matter you asked about is down there," Cadryn said in a low voice, although there wasn't much chance of eavesdroppers wanting to do her harm close by.

"Thank you, Cadryn," Jame said.

"Anything to help the case," Cadryn said.

"I'll be your guide so Cadryn can get back to her work," Vorkin said, winking at Cadryn before leading the way down the steps.

Jame expected the damp cellars of the other shops she'd seen and was surprised to find a dry whitewashed corridor opening to an underground chamber with a door on the canal.

"The university area is on higher land," Vorkin said as she led them into the chamber.

Wooden crates were scattered about the room, and two women and a man, all dressed as common seafarers, were seated on a cluster of them in the corner.

Vorkin took her place at the door of the chamber as Jame and Tigh approached the group.

A relieved looking woman stood up and waited for them.

"This is Roseh," Tigh said.

"We're so honored that you agreed to meet with us," Roseh said to Jame.

"We're honored you can trust us enough to let us try to help you," Jame said, taking Roseh's hand in hers.

"The rumors are true," Roseh murmured.

Jame frowned. "Rumors?"

"You can charm the fur off a mountain cat with just a smile," Roseh said.

Tigh grinned. "She certainly can."

Jame gave Tigh a mock glare. "I don't understand how such rumors get started."

"I do," Roseh said. "Let me introduce my friends. This is Ktia. She's in charge of coordinating rescues. And this is Sefrin. He takes care of the safe house further up the coast."

"Sounds like you have a well thought out operation," Jame said.

"Well thought out but not as effective as we want it to be," Roseh said. "We almost got caught three moons ago, and they've been extra vigilant since then. We haven't been able to rescue anyone. We've still been able to keep track of what they're doing, though."

"Insiders?" Tigh asked.

Roseh nodded. "Three. They joined them a full season before we attempted anything.

That way no one could be suspicious of them as newcomers."

"Good thinking," Jame said.

She looked at the group's expectant eyes. Getting involved in their plight was way beyond her duties as an arbiter. But she was committed to making sure the settlement of this case was final. If Jande and Rend were truly involved in the horrible business of slaving, then she was going to stop them. Even if they weren't involved, Jame just couldn't turn her back on these victims of an oppressive regime. Her fervor to abolish injustice would probably get her into trouble someday.

She resolutely pushed down this thought. "So how can we help each other?"

TIGH CIRCLED IKLAS who sucked on her lower lip in concentration. The late afternoon sun streaked the upper chamber of the warehouse with intense fingers of light and dark. She moved in half light and half shadow following Iklas's movements like a mountain cat.

Tigh knew that Iklas was wondering why she had volunteered for this hapless task. But someone had to be the first to fight the former Tigh the Terrible. Someone had to test her ability to fight before too many lives depended on that skill.

It helped that a dozen former Guards were ready to distract her and rescue Iklas, if she lost control. Now she waited for Iklas to make that first . . . scary . . . move . . .

Iklas barely stopped herself from lunging when Tigh spun around and focused on the stairs. Heartbeats later, the rumble of heavy footfalls gave the others just enough time to get over their shock and have their swords ready as two dozen assailants in leather armor and wielding swords topped the stairs and attacked. The Guards moved between the assailants and Tigh, the crash of blades cutting through the silence.

Tigh, trying not to reel from the shock of battle around her, fought off the horrific images flashing through her mind as she lifted her sword to stop a blade flying toward her. She pushed away her attacker and ducked as the blade came at her again with ruthless force. Her senses could almost pick up the stench of blood and sweat, the cries of death, the blood that slicked her sword . . . She looked in shock at her shoulder, she saw that the blood was hers.

Anger exploded through her as the black-bladed sword followed a chilling war cry, and the attacker was suddenly the attacked, fighting off swift slashes and thrusts. Tigh disarmed the struggling woman and grabbed her arm. She spun her around and pressed her blade against her throat.

"Call the others off," Tigh said. "I know you're not getting paid enough to get yourselves killed."

"Stop," the woman stammered, careful of the blade against her throat. "Stop fighting. We can't beat them."

The attackers, seeing they had failed their mission, muttered words of surrender to the Guards. They dropped their weapons and the Guards corralled them into a corner.

"Why did you attack us?" Tigh pulled harder on the woman's arm.

"We were hired to capture you," the woman said.

Tigh frowned. "While I was surrounded by former Guards?"

"They thought it would be easier if your bodyguards were all in sight." The woman tried to catch her breath. "We hold them back and capture you."

"Didn't quite work out that way, did it?" Tigh looked up at the group of mercenaries.

"They said you lost the ability to fight," the woman said.

"Who are they?" Tigh pressed the blade a little harder against the woman's throat.

"Don't know," the woman gasped.

"You're going to be safely in jail, so you won't have to worry about them coming after you." Tigh grimaced at the pain in her shoulder. The leather around the wound was soaked with blood.

"You think it's safe in jail?" The woman laughed as best she could with a sword at her throat. "They have the Constabulary in their belt pouches. No one makes a move without them knowing it."

"Why did they want me captured?" When the woman didn't answer, Tigh threw down her sword and spun the woman around. She grabbed the stunned woman's tunic and thrust her up against the nearby wall, never letting go. Tigh then pressed her, several finger lengths off the floor, into the uneven wallboards. "Do I need to repeat the question?"

"To keep you away from the arbiter," the woman said.

Tigh released the woman who fell sprawled on the floor, scooped up her sword, and ran to the top of the stairs shouting, "Take care of our friends."

"Go after her," Vorkin said, and Iklas clattered down the stairs after Tigh.

Chapter 12

JAME LOOKED AT what she had just written with a sense of satisfaction. She thanked Laur that arbiters didn't need hard evidence to investigate suspicions and rumors. This privilege allowed her to send an appeal to the Federation Council to delay the hearing until it was certain that neither side of the case was involved in criminal activity.

Of course, she was too cautious to ever make an appeal unless she knew the rumors and suspicions were true. Given her reputation for only seeking the truth, and the ability of her companion to see the truth, the Federation Council would be inclined to believe criminal activity was indeed involved.

"This isn't as hard as I thought it would be," she said to her half-full mug of spiced tea. "I just have to do everything by the law and then there can't be any argument."

She looked out the window as the sun lowered enough to slash the room with intense fingers of light. Getting late. She tried to keep from thinking about what Tigh was doing, but that was impossible. She just had to trust the Guards and Tigh to work through the problem without anyone getting hurt.

Hurdles. It seemed sometimes that life was nothing but a series of hurdles. Just as one was successfully cleared, another popped up out of nowhere.

"But this is a major hurdle," she said aloud. "Our lives depend on her being able to clear it."

She folded several sheets of paper, melted wax on the fold, and applied her arbiter's seal. She then slipped her notes into her pack and returned it to its place on a small shelf behind a wall tapestry. The first lesson taught to student arbiters was to never leave any of their papers lying about or even in plain sight.

She hefted the packet and decided against putting it into the mail basket outside the door. Besides, she welcomed the opportunity to get out of the chamber a bit.

She wondered if she'd ever not feel a small tinge of nostalgic sadness every time she entered a safe house common room. The reminder she couldn't go home was always strongest when confronted by rooms full of Emoran tapestries and weapons. *Someday. Someday soon.*

Resde lounged next to the opening to the small corridor that led to the front door. The number of visitors had trickled down to normal since Carnival came to a close, and it was too early for the women who habitually haunted the establishment in the evening to wander in.

"Good afternoon, arbiter," Resde said.

"Good afternoon, Resde." Jame smiled as she glanced around the all but empty chamber. She lowered her voice a bit. "I need a packet taken to the Federation Council in Balderon. Do you know of any Emorans heading back home who might be able to drop it off there?"

Resde rubbed her chin. "I'll make sure your packet arrives safely at its destination. We have several scouts in training who we use as couriers."

Jame raised an eyebrow. "So, the Maymian post is a less than desirable choice for sending messages?"

"Yes," Resde said as she took possession of the packet.

"Thank you." Jame was relieved she had followed her instincts on this matter. "Could you send Olar over to the Ingoran place for our evening meal?"

"Of course, arbiter." Resde snapped her fingers at a girl who was seated at one of the tables, sorting through piles of eating utensils and plates.

"Thanks," Jame said.

She strode to the back stairs, wondering what she'd have done if she didn't have so many Emorans to help her, even so far away from home. The pain of the estrangement from her home hit her with an unexpected force. She paused at the top of the second flight of stairs and struggled to take in gulps of air, fighting a wave of profound sadness.

"I can't let it get to me." She held onto the railing for support of her physical reaction to the unhappiness she kept buried as deep as she possibly could. "Time. It will just take time." Uncertainty was her worse enemy and she knew it.

Her mind and body settled down. She drew a long breath and covered the short distance to the door of their chamber.

She opened the door and realized she had an unwelcome visitor. She sent a prayer to Laur to get Tigh to her side—without delay.

TIGH THANKED WHOEVER oversaw her destiny that the warehouse the former Guards used for sparring wasn't far from the Emoran safe house. She doubly thanked her somewhat fickle deities that the streets weren't full of Carnival revelers as her long legs carried her past curious pedestrians and she agilely dodged horses and carriages in the street. She had to admit Iklas was doing a good job of keeping up with her. Many of the Guard enhancements stayed intact after the cleansing, and the ability to run like a desert cat was one of those skills.

Tigh slowed and stopped around the corner from the street their room overlooked. She peeked into the street and spotted several watchers in shop doorways. They were all watching the balcony on the top floor across the street. Their presence told her they hadn't made their move yet. She owed her deities another prayer.

"How's your arm?" Iklas asked.

Tigh inspected the bloody mess on her upper arm. "I've had worse." Just to be on the safe side, she pulled her sweat rag from her pouch and tied it over the wound.

"Now what?"

"Make sure those watchers don't do anything foolish," Tigh said.

Iklas nodded and Tigh crossed the side street they were on and latched onto the side of the first carriage that passed by. About halfway down the next block, she dropped off the vehicle and recrossed the street. She ducked into the alley, pulled herself up on the first fire ladder she found, and climbed to the third story roof.

The humid climate made it impossible to control the vines that clung to the wooden buildings, so attempts were made to control the direction of the wild growth. The result was thick tangles of vegetation forced to grow around windows and balconies.

The third prayer Tigh sent to her often contrary deities was in thanks for the deep shadows that hid both the vegetation she climbed down and a part of the balcony in darkness. She crouched next to the partially pulled aside lattice screen and opened her ears to the noises inside the chamber.

After long heartbeats of silence, the door of the chamber opened and closed. The silence was tense until Jame finally spoke. "Cipronis Tangigar, isn't it? You're not allowed to be in here, you know."

"We didn't think it was enough of a matter to bother the proprietor with, so we found our own way in, so to speak."

Tigh grimaced at the oily-voiced smugness of the Ingoran arbiter.

"None-the-less, I'd feel better if we met according to the rules of the establishment." Jame sounded calm and steady, but Tigh detected a tightness. Jame knew she was in possible trouble. *Good instinct*, Tigh nodded with approval.

"My employers thought this more private meeting would be better," Cipronis said. "They're not very pleased with all the investigating you've been doing. So, they sent me to convince you to focus only on the particulars of their case."

"I *am* only focusing on the particulars of the case," Jame said.

Tigh could hear her moving further into the chamber.

"I apologize for disagreeing, arbiter, but you've been wandering far away from the focus of this case," Capronis continued in a smug tone.

Tigh grinned. So the overstuffed son of a mediocre merchant family thought he had the upper hand. Not quite.

"Then we'll just have to be in disagreement on this matter."

Tigh smiled with pride at Jame's refusal to be baited.

"It doesn't matter, anyway." Tigh pictured the pudgy man shrugging. "You'll be doing things Jande's way from now on."

"What makes you think that?" Jame asked. Tigh could hear a minute quaver in her voice.

Stay calm. Don't panic, Tigh mentally shouted.

"Because"—Cipronis paused to add a dramatic flair to his smugness— "we've captured your peace warrior."

Tigh, anticipating this revelation, scooted over a bit to look into the chamber and was pleased to see Jame facing the balcony. Jame caught a glimpse of her.

Jame raised an eyebrow. "You've captured Tigh?"

"Yes." Cipronis sounded puzzled. "We'll not harm her as long as you conduct the trial according to Jande's instructions."

Jame rubbed her chin. "Hmmm. Can I have some time to think about it?"

Tigh put her head in her hands and stifled a groan. She could only imagine Cipronis's expression.

"What?" Cipronis sputtered. "This isn't a game. We really do have your peace warrior."

"I believe you," Jame said. "I just need time to think about it. Is Jande offering anything else besides Tigh's safety?"

Tigh shook with silent laughter. She would have given her sword to see Cipronis's reaction.

"Anything else?" The smugness was gone from Cipronis's voice. "She's your life companion."

"I know. I remember the ceremony." Jame gave Cipronis a sweet smile. "By the way, if you have Tigh, who has the people who have Tigh?"

"Huh?"

Tigh vaulted into the chamber and pressed the black blade against Cipronis's throat.

"I asked, who has the people who are supposed to have Tigh?" Jame grinned at Tigh. "Could you entertain our guest while I go find Resde?"

"Love to," Tigh said in Cipronis's ear.

Jame ran out of the chamber, leaving the door open.

"Do you know what they do to men found in an Emoran safe house?"

"No," Cipronis managed to squeak.

"Let's just say, you'll be a guest in the jail in Emoria," Tigh said with feral relish.

"What?" Cipronis jerked against the blade. "They can't do that."

"Emoran law prevails over the safe houses." Tigh flattened the blade a bit to let the cold metal tickle Cipronis' skin. "As an arbiter, you should have known that."

"For how long?" Cipronis whimpered.

"Not long, if you show that kind of fear." Tigh kept her voice low and dangerous. "Emorans will think they're doing the world a favor by getting rid of a whimpering coward."

Cipronis was uncontrollably shaking by the time Jame returned with Resde and a pair of warriors-in-training. *Serves him right for threatening Jame*, Tigh thought as he was dragged out of the chamber.

"Could you tell Iklas across the street the situation has been taken care of?" Tigh asked Resde, who nodded and closed the door behind her.

Jame ran into Tigh's arms. "Every time I pray for a miracle, you show up."

"Must be a special skill," Tigh mumbled as she let relief wash over her that Jame was safe.

"You're hurt." Jame pulled back and inspected the bloody mess on Tigh's arm.

Tigh shrugged. "Just a minor cut."

Jame dragged Tigh to a chair next to the fire. She pulled Tigh's tunic and shirt off and took a closer look at the cut.

"I think we're going to need that medical kit Bcdc gave you," Jame said as she walked to their bags. "So, how did you know about my visitor? Cipronis seemed confident that you'd been captured."

Tigh took in a deep breath. "They thought it was a good idea to try to capture me when all the Guards were in one place." She flinched as Jame cleaned the wound.

"Sorry." Jame kissed Tigh's cheek.

Reveling in Jame's closeness, Tigh returned the kiss.

"How did they know about where the Guards do their sparring?"

"It's not that big of a secret," Tigh said. "We readily found out about it. Anyway, they tried to keep the other Guards back and one of them came for me."

"Only one?"

"They thought I couldn't fight," Tigh said. "Up to that moment they were right. It took this," she glanced at her wound, "to change that."

"So, you convinced them to tell you why they were attacking you?" Jame asked.

"Yes. Then I got here as fast as I could," Tigh whispered.

"I'm glad you did," Jame said as she covered Tigh's wound with a soft cloth and pulled a fresh shirt over her head. "I would've been really upset when Cipronis said you'd been captured."

Tigh pulled Jame into her lap, wrapped her arms around her, and let her presence sooth the unbearable fear that had clutched at her the moment she heard Jame was in danger.

"Cipronis works for Jande." Jame relaxed in Tigh's arms. "Did Jande really think she could get away with this trick?"

Tigh sighed. "It may have worked if I hadn't been able to fight back. But she underestimated how much your safety means to me."

"With your would-be kidnappers captured and Cipronis mysteriously disappearing, she now knows we foiled her plans," Jame said.

"We also know she's involved with the slaving because she doesn't want us to do any more investigating into Maymi's underground activities," Tigh said.

"I sent the appeal to the Federation Council." Jame traced a finger down Tigh's cheek. "But that will take several days to come through. What do you think Jande's next move will be?"

"If I were her," Tigh nuzzled Jame's soft hair, "I wouldn't bring attention to myself until the hearing. She has to realize she's in serious trouble right now. Not just with us, but with whoever's controlling her."

"You think Tekl or someone else is behind this?" Jame looked up at Tigh.

"No doubt. The slaving was here long before Jande and Rend showed up," Tigh said. "This is the time to keep alert because mistakes can be made out of frustration. So, we just wait for one of our spies to bring back something to us."

"Sounds like a good idea." Jame smiled. "I'd like to spend some time with a certain warrior this evening."

"Hmmm," Tigh purred in her ear. "I think that can be arranged."

TIGH HAD DISCOVERED something interesting when she made her trip across the roof of the Emoran safe house. The fourth floor, visible from the street, was actually a roofless chamber. More intriguing were the caches of staffs and wooden swords neatly hanging on the walls of the chamber. The Emorans in Maymi seemed to be closer to their traditions than the Emorans in Glaus.

The early morning sun tried to penetrate, without much success, the heavy gray clouds blanketing the city. Tigh welcomed the somber light because it reduced the distracting contrasts created by sharp sunlight. Of course, Jame's warm-up moves on the other side of the chamber were just as distracting but Tigh had to get used to seeing this side of Jame. She'd be hitting herself in the head with her own staff all the time, otherwise.

Jame wound down her exercises, then straightened and shook out her arms and legs. She took a deep breath and stepped to the middle of the chamber.

"Maybe we should have someone here, in case—" Tigh said.

"This is something we have to work out between us. I know with all my being that you'll not hurt me." Jame captured Tigh's uncertain eyes with a steady, serious gaze. "You're no longer Tigh the Terrible with the uncontrollable need to kill. You're Tigh the peace warrior, who cannot do harm unless threatened."

Tigh shook her head. "We don't know that for certain."

"I do. And so do you. In here." Jame tapped her chest. "Hold your staff out."

Tigh grasped the staff with both hands and held it out. Jame gently tapped it with her own staff.

"Now tap my staff." Jame held her staff out.

Tigh tentatively tapped her staff. They exchanged unhurried probing taps until Tigh allowed her body to relax a bit.

"How does it feel?" Jame asked.

"It feels . . . all right." Tigh analyzed all the signals shooting between her body and her mind and didn't find anything threatening or alarming. It felt . . . normal. The idea stole her breath away.

"What's wrong?" Jame stepped forward and put a hand on Tigh's arm.

"I just had the most incredible revelation," Tigh said. "I realized that my reactions to all this feels normal. Nothing enhanced, nothing extraordinary. Just normal."

"That's good then," Jame said. "That means you're in control of your actions."

"Yeah," Tigh said in wonderment.

"So, we just have to work to put it all together." Jame stepped back. "How about alternating a defensive move with an offensive one? I'll hit your staff and then you hit mine, until you get used to attacking without all the aggression you had when you were a Guard."

Tigh, still working through this new sensation, nodded and held up her staff.

Jame hit her staff against Tigh's and echo of the impact died out before Tigh swung at Jame's staff with equal force. Jame gave Tigh a few heartbeats to analyze her reaction to the minor act of aggression before giving Tigh's staff another hit.

They worked back and forth until it became a dance of sorts. Both controlled each move and didn't allow any of the edgy abandonment that helped sparring partners build up their fighting skills. That would come in time.

After a sandmark of intense concentration and control, they took a break.

"I'm not in as good a shape as I used to be," Jame said as she wiped the sweat from her face.

"It's been years since you've sparred like this." Tigh twirled her staff.

"Are you still all right with this?" Jame dipped a cup into the small cistern that collected rainwater for the establishment.

"I feel," Tigh searched for the proper words, "like there isn't a pressure to fight, yet all the skills are there. It's hard to explain, but my mind has always equated the need to fight and kill with the skills to do it. Now I realize they're separate. Have always been separate."

Jame wrapped her arms around Tigh. "I knew we could do it."

Rapid footfalls came from the stairwell. One of the young Emorans who worked around the establishment ran into the roofless chamber.

"Arbiter," the young woman said. "Something terrible has happened."

"What?" Jame asked.

"Several children of prominent families have been kidnapped," the young woman said. "By slavers."

"Kidnapped?" Jame frowned. "How do you know that slavers took them?"

"They sent a message to the Chief Constable," the young woman said. "They said they'd sell the children into slavery if their demands weren't met."

"What demands?" Tigh asked.

The young woman shrugged. "Only the Chief Constable knows."

Jame, brow creased in thought, took several steps around the chamber then stood still for several heartbeats with head bent. She took a deep breath and looked up. "I guess we need to pay Chief Constable Bary a visit then."

TIGH STOPPED THE young guard from opening the door to the Chief Constable's chamber. "Wait."

Jame just shrugged at the young man's questioning look.

Tigh thanked Bal for her enhanced hearing and listened to the voices coming from the chamber.

"You're what?" Chief Constable Bary said.

"Five thousand pieces of silver," Ofnal Dranderal said. "My grandchild and the children of my friends were kidnapped by an unsavory element that has been lurking on the undersides of this city for centuries."

"But five thousand pieces of silver—"

"Is enough to show that we're serious about wanting to stop this nefarious activity," Ofnal said.

"Now," Tigh said to the guard, who opened the door.

Ofnal turned as the door behind her opened, just keeping her eyes from narrowing as Jame, followed by Tigh, walked into the chamber.

"We came as soon as we heard," Jame said.

"Why would this concern you?" Ofnal asked.

"Actually it concerns Tigh," Jame said.

"Yes, yes, that's right," Bary exclaimed without trying to hide his relief.

Ofnal straightened. "What are you talking about?"

"Tigh will be in charge of finding the children and bringing the kidnappers to justice," Jame said.

"What?" Ofnal tried to laugh off her shock. "She's just a peace warrior."

"Who used to be the Supreme Commander," Jame said.

"Who lost her commission when she was rehabilitated," Ofnal said.

"Who was reinstated in the reserves when she became a peace warrior and who had her Supreme Commander rank returned when she saved Ynit from the army of the Silver Dragon," Jame said.

Tigh dug into her belt pouch and pulled out a bundle of folded parchment. She selected one of the sheets and presented it to Bary.

Bary scanned the document. He then stood and saluted a startled Tigh. "My Constables and all of my resources are at your disposal, Commander."

Ofnal opened and closed her mouth several times. "I think the people of this city should have a say in whether they want Tigh the Terrible in such a position of power."

"Tigh the Terrible is dead," Tigh said in a low voice. "She died peacefully at the hands of the healers in Ynit. Do you want to waste our time trying to resurrect her ghost when kidnappers are threatening to sell your grandchild into slavery?"

Ofnal glared at Tigh. "I think I have a say in who I believe is best suited to rescue my grandchild and the children of my fellow citizens."

"You may think you have a say, but you have no choice," Tigh said. "It'd look odd for you to waste time in protest while your grandchild may be suffering at the hands of these kidnappers."

Ofnal straightened. "I've offered five thousand pieces of silver to anyone who leads us to these kidnappers. I've offered my laborers and the extensive resources of the Dranderal holdings to aid in finding these children and capturing their abductors."

"And Tigh, a peace warrior for the state and former Supreme Commander of the Southern Armies, is offering her expertise and skills," Jame said. "You have every right to bring a protest against Tigh, like the one we faced in Glaus. But I must advise against it. Unlike the situation in Glaus, when Tigh was still being rehabilitated, she's now a free citizen and a warrior in good standing."

"But you give her back a little power—"

"That happened scarcely a moon ago," Jame said. "She was asked to take command to fight the invading army that had surrounded Ynit. She refused the command and acted only as an advisor. Her skill at seat-of-the-leggings strategy allowed us to defeat the army of the Silver Dragon in a single day, with hardly any fighting. It seems to me you'd be thankful to have the person who pulled together the people and resources of a city in a matter of sandmarks to defeat an army that had conquered half the territories on the eastern continent."

"Please forgive me, arbiter," Ofnel said. "The shock of having a grandchild stolen in such a way is making me a bit irrational. You're right, of course. We should be thankful Tigh is here to help us find these poor children."

Tigh concentrated on not rolling her eyes. She now understood the Maymian saying, "Beware when the alligator smiles."

Chapter 13

"WE AT JANDE and Rend Scroll Shops are outraged by the idea that this terrible kidnapping is somehow related to our civil case with Cadryn's Scroll Shop. We now see that the Federation Council made a grave mistake in appointing such a young, inexperienced person to the position of arbiter-at-large. We feel it's our duty to the Southern Territories to petition the Federation Council for the removal of Jamelin Ketlas from that post." Jande paused and scanned the Maymi Council on one side of the chamber and the over-packed spectators on the other.

"You may do what you think you must," Rasidid, a robust woman with dark hair and a shrewd eye, said from the mayor's seat. "But we're more concerned with getting our children back than by the possible catalyst for the action."

"But Jamelin Ketlas, who seems to see some kind of underground conspiracy in a simple business undertaking, may have brought on this kidnapping by digging into places that have nothing to do with the reason she's here," Jande said. "It's possible her over zealousness and inexperience has brought a potential tragedy to this community."

"That's something only a Federation Tribunal can determine," Rasidid said. "She doesn't know who the kidnappers are or where the children are being held and frankly, that's all we care about right now."

Jande straightened. "Of course, Mayor Rasidid. Please forgive me. I feel terrible that it may have been our case that set off this dreadful chain of events."

"We understand your frustration, Jande." Rasidid gazed her. "And it's up to you to do what you think you must do in regards to Arbiter Jamelin, but we need to focus all our energies into getting our children back."

"But you've put her life companion in charge of the rescue operation," Jande said.

"Unlike Arbiter Jamelin," Rasidid said in a steady, indulgent voice, "Tigh has the proper experience for rescuing our children and bringing their kidnappers to justice. We're at peace today because of her brilliant campaigns that ended the Wars."

Jande swallowed her frustration. "I thank the Council for letting me voice my concerns. I'd like to take this opportunity to offer Jande and Rend's employees and resources to aid you in this time of crisis."

"Thank you, Jande," Rasidid said. "We'll keep your offer in mind."

Jande stepped away from the speaker's box and quickly strolled out of the chamber through a side door. Even in the corridor, she felt the penetrating gaze of disapproval that had bored into her during her confrontation with the Council. She wished she'd never set foot in the city of Maymi.

"I'M GLAD I got my petition into the Federation Council." Jame sighed as she stared out the upper floor window of the mayor's office. The office boasted the best view of the Gulf, which was agitated from a storm scuttling in from the deep ocean.

Rasidid wandered around, carefully checking a variety of plants that decorated the chamber. "You know, I owe my current position to this civil suit against Jande and Rend. I'm the first Mayor in two centuries who hasn't had some kind of tie to the Dranderal Clan. We just got lucky the elections were held when Jande and Rend first showed an interest in moving into our city. For the first time, the citizens of Maymi saw a chance to finally break the Dranderals' hold."

Jame turned to Rasidid. "And we can break it. I know we can."

"Our hope truly began when we found out you were to be our arbiter and Tigh was your peace warrior." Rasidid smiled at Jame's puzzled frown. "You both have a reputation for working miracles."

Jame opened her mouth to respond to the absurd statement just as the chamber door opened and Tigh slipped in.

"Did you find out anything?" Jame asked.

"The children are on the top floor of the building Jande and Rend wants to use for their shop," Tigh said.

"Hiding them where no one would even suspect to look for them," Rasidid said.

"That's why we looked there first," Tigh said. "But we might have a problem."

"A problem," Jame said.

Tigh sighed. "We overheard the captors talking. They think they can get more money selling the children than what Dranderal will pay them for the kidnapping."

"Whoever said there was honor among thieves," Jame muttered.

"I've got every way in and out of that building covered," Tigh said. "If they try to move the children, we'll know it."

"So, what exactly did Dranderal think she could accomplish by staging this kidnapping?" Rasidid asked.

"I think the Dranderals want to be the ones to find and rescue the children," Jame said. "Restore their standing in the eyes of the citizens by becoming heroes."

Rasidid frowned. "What about all this talk of discrediting you?"

"I think Jande has her own agenda," Jame said. "We've a very strong case against Jande and Rend. I'm sure she's trying to get rid of me before we can start the hearing."

"So do you think Jande and Rend are involved in the slaving operation?" Rasidid asked.

"I think their association with the Dranderal Clan drew them into it," Jame said. "The fact they allowed the children to be held in their building is enough to implicate their involvement in the kidnapping."

Rasidid took a breath and looked at Tigh. "Now what?"

Tigh shrugged. "We wait."

"I was afraid you'd say that." Rasidid sighed. "Sometimes I wonder what ever possessed me to run for mayor."

Tigh grinned.

"DO YOU THINK Minchof will mind us doing this?" Renar, an earnest shaggy-haired young man, asked.

The three Wizard apprentices stood just inside the front door of Cadryn's Scroll Shop and could only stare at the activity around them. Dozens of students worked with an admirable focus as they made the most of their weekly day off from classes to help finish the Scroll Shop.

"She's always encouraged us to get involved in community activities," Yana said, as she pushed her wavy red hair out of her eyes.

"Do you think she'll think we're taking sides?" Renar asked. "I don't want to jeopardize my apprenticeship."

"If you really think about it, we're always taking a side in everything we do," Goodemer said.

"I don't think Minchof will mind in this case," Yana said. "She couldn't stop talking about how impressed she was by the arbiter and that former Guard in her last letter to us."

Goodemer had to keep herself from reacting to the offhand way her friend referred to her personal heroes. Tigh and Jame were a part of her own private world that she explored in obsessive secrecy. Only her intensive studies kept her from following them around Maymi as she had done in Ynit.

"Whoa." Renar's eyes widened as a small group of people entered the chamber through a back door. A young woman in a light tunic and leggings was flanked by four women dressed in black leather and wearing weapons and armor.

"I heard the Guards had been called back for temporary duty," Yana murmured.

A sensation tickled the back of Goodemer's mind. She glanced around, wondering why she was detecting more than the normal stray magic. Why would there be spells cast within the scroll shop? More importantly, what wizard would cast such spells without alerting the other members of their close society that they existed?

"This way," Yana said over her shoulder.

Goodemer followed her companions and couldn't understand why they weren't detecting the controlled magic somewhere in the structure. It could be a leftover spell, she tried to reason. Sometimes a wizard forgot to undo a spell. She cursed her inexperience at being able to do in-depth deciphering of magic. That skill only came with long practice.

A small bright-eyed woman in sturdy leathers gazed at them with a welcoming expression. "Here to help out?"

Yana smiled. "We're here to do what we can."

"Excellent, I'm Tret . . ." She stared at the front door.

Goodemer and her friends spun around.

Jande sauntered into the building and stopped to look around with the air of checking out the competition. Behind her were a handful of people wearing tunics embroidered with the Jande and Rend insignia.

Goodemer glanced across the chamber to see Cadryn's reaction to this intrusion. She was heartened to see the serious-faced young woman watch the unwanted visitors with a calm professional eye. The Guards' faces, on the other hand, had hardened into a menacing attitude.

Cadryn approached her adversary with a stocky Guard at her side. Goodemer realized the Guard was Vorkin, the quiet archivist who helped them in the archives.

"Good morning, Cadryn," Jande greeted in a well-practiced amiable voice. "I hope you don't mind us paying a little visit. I may spend much too much time in the office, but I still can't keep away from the reason I went into this business in the first place—the simple enjoyment of walking into a scroll shop and browsing up and down the aisles."

A sneer touched Vorkin's lips, and she made a show of looking Jande over.

"As you see, the shop isn't anywhere near finished." Cadryn spread out her arms.

Jande smiled. "Ah, but your design is very clear. Such originality in one so young. I've always admired youthful ambition. Willing to go ahead with untried ideas even though most drastic departures from tradition end in failure. I salute your confidence."

If the chamber had been quiet when Jande entered, it was now like Bal's Hall of Silence.

Goodemer could almost feel the students' indignation at Jande's unveiled condescension.

"This shop is patterned after the legendary library at Balderon founded by the great Hekolatis that stood for seven centuries before it was destroyed during the Kuntic Wars," Cadryn said. "The library was celebrated for its open inviting structure. That sounded like a good idea for a scroll shop."

Jande's smile never faltered. "Interesting. I think I remember having a look at those plans when we built our first shop. We looked at so many before deciding on, what we felt, was the best setting for selling scrolls. Isn't that right, Rend?"

All eyes shifted to the woman with a timid stoop, who looked as if she wanted to be swallowed into the floor she was reluctant to take her eyes away from.

"We looked at many plans," Rend said softly, raising her head but not making eye contact with anyone.

"But, as we all know, there's more than one way to do most anything." Jande glanced around as if making another assessment of the shop. "We can never truly predict what will be successful. We'd love to have a look around. At least you don't have to worry about us wanting to steal your design."

Cadryn and Vorkin exchanged quick bewildered looks.

Goodemer wondered what Jande was up to.

"It'd be a pleasure to show my humble establishment to the true giants in the scroll and book business," Cadryn said.

"THEY'RE TRYING TO keep us off guard." Jame kept her voice calm and reasonable, knowing Tigh would need time to cool down her agitation.

"Off guard," Tigh muttered as she stalked around the room in the Emoran safe house. "I don't think they're that clever. I think they want you out of the way. Period."

"All right," Jame said, willing to follow any path that would calm Tigh down. She reread the words on the sheet of paper. The kidnappers' demands were simple—the children in exchange for her. No wonder the slavers wanted to back out of the deal and sell the children. She wouldn't be worth anything to them—as long as they didn't find out she was an

Emoran princess. "Let's approach it from that angle. Slavers would never make this kind of demand. All they care about is making money. With the children of the rich families in their possession, they could ask for almost anything. It makes no sense to exchange the children for me."

Tigh stopped her pacing. "Go on."

"It doesn't make sense to us and it certainly won't make sense to the people of Maymi," Jame said. "So, this demand only confirms what they've been whispering about. The slavers are being controlled by someone else. Someone with both power and money."

"Why would these powerful people risk exposure by showing such a blatant motive behind the kidnapping?" Tigh asked.

"Because they're getting desperate." Jame nodded as the idea slipped puzzle pieces into place. "Everything they've tried, we've stopped, one way or another. They've gotten to the point where they don't care how it looks because it won't matter anyway. I'll be out of the way and won't be able to judge the case. But they made one important mistake."

"They thought the slavers would just go along with the plan," Tigh said.

"They underestimated the slavers' greed." Jame pounded a fist into her hand, her mind on the brink of completing the puzzle. "They forgot that the slavers don't need Maymi for their operations. They can always move on to another place."

"And that's exactly what they're planning to do." Tigh dropped cross-legged before the hearth of the fireplace. Jame sucked in a relieved breath. That was Tigh's favorite position for thinking through problems. "They're going to take the children away before the exchange is to happen."

"So, there won't be an exchange because no one will be there," Jame said. "But Jande and the Dranderals don't know that."

"Our first duty is to save the children, even if it means not being able to make the connection to the Dranderals," Tigh said. "We can, at least, imply Jande's involvement because the children are being held in the building for her scroll shop."

"Remember, once we have the slavers in custody, we can use their confessions as evidence against whoever hired them." With a clear plan in her head, Jame felt less overwhelmed. They just had to remove all the obstacles in their way to reach justice.

A gentle rap on the door brought Tigh to her feet. She approached the door and opened it a crack before letting a grim-faced Iklas enter.

"It seems the slavers were waiting for the demands to be announced," Iklas said as a greeting. "They're getting ready to move the children."

Tigh turned to Jame. "We have to move fast."

"I know, I know." Jame held up her hands. "Go down to the common room and stay in plain sight."

"There's something else," Iklas said. "The slavers holding the children have been doing a lot of complaining and grumbling. They'd been given orders to move the children to a chamber below Cadryn's shop tonight."

"What?" Jame let this new information permeate her mind. "If they want to frame Cadryn with kidnapping the children, they'd have to stage a way to find them before Cadryn does. Jande wants to be the hero in this little drama. But there are people working day and night on that shop. How do they expect to hide children there? The open architecture has removed the smaller chambers and all that's below the shop are the docks. I don't remember any other chambers."

"If they want to frame Cadryn, then the demands and the arrangement for the exchange is a ruse." Tigh ran a hand through her hair. "It's like the hilt of the sword doesn't know what the blade is doing."

Jame straightened as the nagging final piece of the puzzle fell into place with a satisfying clink. "That's it. That's it." She pulled a baffled Tigh into a quick hug and then paced around the chamber.

Iklas raised a sympathetic eyebrow at Tigh.

"What's it?" Tigh asked.

"I just figured out why this isn't making any sense." Jame stopped pacing and faced her waiting audience. "What happens when plans of deception start to go wrong? There's a desperate scramble to salvage the plans. Now what happens when too many different parties with their own agendas are involved in these plans of deception? Squabbling, finger-pointing, and everyone suddenly not quite as loyal to the idea of meeting all their agendas with a single simple plan. Their own agendas take over, and each tries to achieve what they want before the others take away their means of succeeding."

"So, the Dranderals, Jande, and the slavers entered into some kind of business agreement, and we got in the way of it," Tigh said. "The only way an outside business can come into Maymi is to enter into an agreement with one of the local clans. I'm sure Jande was quite shocked when she finally discovered the full extent of the Dranderals' underground activities and ruthless style of business."

"So, who is doing what?" Iklas asked.

"Jande doesn't want to waste time with a hearing so her solution is to discredit Cadryn," Jame said. "So, she has probably offered the slavers more money to go against the Dranderals and move the children to Cadryn's, where she'll stage a dramatic rescue. She discredits Cadryn and becomes a hero at the same time. Dranderal wants me to stop digging into the underground activities, so she has arranged the exchange. And the slavers want to collect all the money they can from both Jande and Dranderal before taking off with the children to sell into slavery."

"Which means, we still have to rescue the children first," Tigh said.

Jame walked up to Tigh and slipped her arms around her. "Be careful."

"Always." Tigh affirmed the word with a gentle kiss. "Walk us down to the common room."

"JANDE PANICKED," VORKIN announced as she ran up to Tigh and Iklas on the almost deserted street to Jande and Rend's shop. "We have to get to Cadryn's shop."

"Where do you think they're planning to hide the children there?" Tigh asked as they turned in the direction of Cadryn's shop and walked quickly, but careful not to bring too much attention to themselves. Too many eyes watched their movements.

"There just isn't any good place." Vorkin shook her head. "Cadryn really opened up all the space in imitation of the old libraries. They believed that large chambers helped preserve the scrolls. The smallest chamber is her office."

"What was Jande's visit all about?" Tigh asked as they went through the gates of Old Maymi, where the University and the supporting establishments and residences dominated the original foundations of the city.

"Hard to tell," Vorkin said as they ducked into a narrow lane that proved to be a shortcut to the scroll shop. "She just walked around with her little entourage and made cutting comments. Whatever the purpose, it wasn't to entice customers to her shop. The student volunteers were ready to kill her by the time she left."

"I don't think Jande would pull something like this if she didn't think she could get away with it," Tigh muttered, not liking to go into a situation without all the facts.

They rushed through the front door of Cadryn's shop, then stopped to focus on the task at hand—finding a group of slavers and children.

Cadryn, directing the placement of shelves, watched them with curiosity as they approached her.

"We need to explore the lower chambers," Vorkin said.

"Trouble?" Cadryn asked.

"Is there anyone working down there?" Tigh asked.

"There are people everywhere," Cadryn said.

"Jande's up to something," Vorkin said. "I'll explain it when we have time."

Cadryn nodded as Tigh and the two former Guards hurried into the back chamber to the stairs.

They stood at the bottom of the stairs and took a puzzled look around the large chamber filled with stacks of lumber and crates of scrolls. Tigh opened up her enhanced hearing for any sounds beyond the group of students gathering wood for new shelving.

"If they took the canals, they'd be here by now," Vorkin said.

"This is the only chamber down here?" Tigh walked several steps away from the stairs, focusing every sense to her surroundings.

"Yes, except for the landing through those double doors," Vorkin said.

"There's another chamber." A wide-eyed Goodemer, staring at three sword points, froze at the bottom of the stairs.

The Guards relaxed their stance and sheathed their swords. Tigh would try to figure out later how this girl was able to follow them without their knowledge.

"Another chamber," Tigh said. This girl looked familiar.

"It's hidden by magic," Goodemer said.

"Magic?" Tigh frowned. "How do you know this?"

"I'm a student at the School of Mages," Goodemer said. "I detected magic when I came to volunteer this morning and discovered an empty chamber over there." She pointed to the wall where the double doors stood open.

Tigh and the Guards went to the place in question. "The dock is on the other side of that wall. There isn't any room for another chamber."

"It's at the top of the wall," Goodemer said, pointing at the two-story high ceiling. "There's a set of steps right here." She indicated an empty space hugging the wall.

"But how could someone get to the stairs without being seen?" Vorkin asked.

"The magic spreads all the way to the waters around the dock. A boat can come up from around the corner unseen." They walked through the opened doors and observed how close the dock was to an intersection of two canals.

"This means a wizard is involved." Tigh had never realized the use of wizards was so widespread. Their influence had never been strong in the western part of the Southern Territories.

"Only a rogue wizard would do something like this," Goodemer said.

"Can you tell if anyone is in the chamber?" Tigh asked as she re-entered the chamber and looked up into the empty air above them.

"No one," Goodemer said. "I don't think the spell's been disturbed since it was cast."

Vorkin nodded. "So, we wait for them."

Shouts and rapid footfalls exploded on the floorboards above them. Tigh put her fingers to her lips to the students working with the lumber and took cover behind the stacks of crates with Vorkin and Iklas.

Jande and a thin man in a light robe appeared on the stairs followed by Cadryn, a handful of Constables, and a grim-faced Chief Constable Bary.

"Thank Bal Ofnal thought to engage a wizard to help track down those poor children." Jande's smug tones echoed in the chamber. "You can imagine our shock when he discovered this chamber when we visited here this morning. I was stunned when he revealed he could hear the voices of small children, cleverly hidden in plain sight."

"The magic is here," the thin man said.

He dramatically held his amulet toward the blank wall and muttered several words that sounded like nonsense. The air shimmered into a solid wood staircase leading to a small chamber hanging from the ceiling. The Constables and the students working in the chamber gasped at the revelation. Cadryn could only stare at it in shock.

"Check it out," Bary said.

The Constables hesitantly climbed the stairs of magic. They slid open the outside bolt and pulled the door outward. Silence. One of the Constables poked her head into the chamber.

"It's empty," she said.

"What?" Jande reacted then quickly recovered herself. "She must have moved them." She gave Cadryn an accusing look.

"You said yourself you had every way in and out of this place watched since this morning," Bary said. "When I mentioned the comings and goings could be hidden by magic, you assured me your wizard would detect any magic."

"But the chamber," Jande said.

"Is nothing more than that," Bary said. "A magic chamber. Merchants have been known to use similar things to keep precious merchandise safe. For all we know, this could have belonged to the previous owner. Taverns take in a lot of money and have reason to keep their stock of expensive spirits locked away."

"Perhaps you're right," Jande said.

"We'll make a full investigation, just in case," Bary said.

The group disappeared back up the stairs and Tigh and the Guards emerged from their hiding places and took a look at the wizard's handiwork.

"We need to find Roseh," Tigh said. "Thank you for your help." She clasped Goodemer's shoulder then slipped through the door to the dock with Vorkin and Iklas.

Chapter 14

WHEN THE DRANDERAL carriage clattered through the city at such an abandoned pace, people knew to get out of the way without complaint. No one had ever won a case against the Dranderals' definition of an emergency—the only legal reason for such reckless driving. The carriage finally pulled up in front of the simple door of the Emoran safe house.

A stone-faced Ofnal slammed the door of the carriage open and hopped out, leaving the driver to climb down from his seat and reclose the door. She stomped to the door engraved with a crossed sword and bow and pounded her metal-headed walking stick against the heavy wood. When the door didn't open within two heartbeats, she pounded again. No one made her wait.

A small head-high panel slid open and passive eyes studied her for several heartbeats.

"Let me in," Ofnal demanded. No one left her to wait in the streets.

The eyes studied her for several more heartbeats. "What is your business here?" came a steady, clearly unintimidated voice.

"My business is with the arbiter, Jamelin Ketlas," Ofnal said. "Who else would I want to see in this uncivilized establishment?"

The expression in the passive eyes never wavered. "Do you have an appointment with her?" the Bal-be-cursed woman asked.

"Are you the owner of this establishment?" Ofnal demanded.

"Yes, my name is Resde," came the calm response.

"I'll have your license for this treatment," Ofnal said.

"For asking questions that I ask all visitors to the safe house?" Resde asked.

Ofnal fumed. "I am not any visitor."

"Yes, you are. At least as far as Jamelin Ketlas is concerned," Resde said. "You've come to an Emoran safe house, where the laws and customs of Emoria are upheld, and have demanded to see our princess. This is not showing the proper respect, and we take great offense when someone doesn't give a member of our royal family basic courtesy and honor."

"Your territory is hardly large enough for a princess, much less a queen," Dranderal said. "I have twice the population of Emoria working for me."

Resde's eyes glinted with amusement. "Yes, but we have a bigger army."

"Now that was a threat," Ofnal said.

Resde shrugged. "Just a comparison of Emoria with your work force."

Ofnal, knowing she had to play the Emoran's petty game to gain access to Jame, calmed her anger into a focused thought of revenge on this Bal-forsaken establishment. No one treated her this way. "I'm sorry if I sounded a bit put out. The worry over getting my grandchild back, coupled with the knowledge that slavers are doing their dirty business right beneath our eyes, has put me on edge."

Resde opened the door.

Ofnal stomped in and started down the narrow corridor without pause, Resde grabbed her arm.

Ofnal reared around and glared her. "Let go of my arm."

"Not until you demonstrate you are worthy to be in Emoran territory," Resde said.

Ofnal took in the tall, muscular woman who possessed a steady eye and even steadier hand. She was used to people being afraid of her and who were willing to do anything to stay on her good side. She had to, at least, pretend to play by these mountain savages' rules. Her entourage of protectors wasn't around her. *Why did I think I wouldn't need them for this little visit?*

"How do I do that?" Ofnal asked.

"You can start by acting as if you don't own the place," Resde said with a hint of a feral smile. "Follow me."

Ofnal swallowed her anger by mentally listing the different ways she could rid Maymi of this establishment.

THE COMMON ROOM was surprisingly full for the middle of the afternoon, something Jame gave thanks to Laur for. She watched out of the corner of her eye as Resde led Ofnal around the tables to her place against the back wall. The Emorans on either side of her wrapped themselves in a casual menace as they ate and chatted.

Jame kept her attention on bowls and plates of vegetables and sauces.

"My princess," Resde said. Jame looked up. "Please forgive the intrusion. Ofnal Dranderal would like to speak to you."

Jame rested calm eyes on Ofnal, who seemed to be struggling to keep her temper under control. "Please be seated." She indicated the chair across from her with a hand. "Could you please bring our guest some spiced ale and a plate of tidbits, Resde?"

"At once, my princess." Resde bowed her head. She glanced at Ofnal and rolled her eyes, much to Jame's amusement.

"Now what can I do for you?" Jame asked as she returned to her meal.

"I wish to have a few words with you. In private." Ofnal glanced at the seemingly disinterested Emorans on either side of Jame.

"I've been ordered by the Federation Council not to be without a guard during my stay in Maymi. All private words will have to be given to me in writing." Jame wished Tigh was there to see Ofnal struggle to keep from squirming. She wished Tigh was there with her, period.

Ofnal looked at the bench with distaste, but sat down. "I thought the Federation Council had better things to do than to think about a minor civil case in out of the way Maymi." She took a sip of the ale Resde put in front of her.

"They've taken offense to their arbiter-at-large being threatened and nearly kidnapped," Jame said as she speared a bit of green and dipped it in a light orange sauce.

"Threatened? Kidnapped?" Ofnal sounded so surprised that Jame truly wished Tigh were there to determine if this woman was acting or not. "When did this happen?"

"During the course of my stay here." Jame raised an eyebrow. "The circumstances also made it an Emoran case, so I'm not at liberty to discuss it." She had spent several sandmarks convincing Resde to only charge Cipronis with unlawful trespass and not for trying to threaten and kidnap an Emoran princess. The last thing she wanted was for her aunt, the queen, to get wind of what she was trying to do in Maymi.

"Then perhaps we could talk in the corner there," Ofnal said, nodding at the private two-person corner table.

"While I'm under Federation protection, I can only receive messages of a private nature in writing. It is the law," Jame said before taking a sip of tea. "It'll only be viewed by my eyes and promptly destroyed by fire."

Ofnal picked up a small pocket of bread filled with fruit and took a bite as she studied Jame. "I've had all my resources trying to find these slavers and possibly rescue my grandchild and the other children before this exchange tomorrow. It hurts my sense of honor that Maymi would have succeeded in saving the children but letting the slavers get away with an arbiter."

"I appreciate your concern but your worries are unnecessary." Jame shrugged and caught a fleeting startled look in Ofnal's eye.

"That's very brave of you, but I don't think your people would be too happy if we let you be sold as a slave," Ofnal said.

Jame smiled and returned to her food.

"With all respect, I think it'd be a foolish move to not allow my clan to help in bringing these slavers to justice," Ofnal said. "Our involvement would have an honorable reflection of Maymi in the eyes of the Federation Council."

"Thank you for your offer, but we have things under control," Jame said with another smile.

"You're not from around here, so you don't have a true understanding of my clan's position in this city," Ofnal said. "I don't want your youthfulness and inexperience to contribute to what could be a serious mistake with calamitous consequences."

"Again, thank you for your concern." Jame looked into Ofnal's eyes. "But we have the combined knowledge and resources of the Southern Territories government behind us. Believe me, we have everything well in control."

Ofnal stared hard at Jame. "You've just begun your career, but you already have a reputation for taking gutsy gambles. Let this be a friendly warning. You're way over your head in this situation."

"I have a reputation for making what looks to be gutsy gambles but are really carefully worked out sure bets," Jame said. "I'd never take a gamble when the well-being of children is involved."

"But slavers are lowly dishonorable creatures," Ofnal said.

"Yes, that's true," Jame said. "It also makes them the easiest to deal with because there is little imagination in greed."

"I think your cockiness is going to get you into trouble someday," Ofnal said.

"What you perceive as cockiness is nothing but confidence in the execution of the plans put together by the woman who served as the Supreme Commander of the Southern Territories armies," Jame said. "If you can offer an expertise equal to that, I'm willing to listen."

Ofnal's temper flared. "If you don't accept my offer to help you, I won't be able to keep you from harm."

"What would this offer of help entail?" Jame asked, as she tore off a piece of bread and dipped it into a pale green sauce.

"We've evidence against Jande and Rend that will greatly impact their case against Cadryn," Ofnal said.

Jame raised steady eyes. "Offer me something I don't already have."

Ofnal looked as if Jame had just slapped her. "I'm not talking about irregularities in the filing of forms or in acquiring the building for her shop."

"Neither am I." Jame lifted an amused eyebrow. "Let me give you a friendly word of advice. You're way over your head in the matters of cross-jurisdiction legal proceedings and Federation control of criminal activity.

I wouldn't want your inexperience in these matters to have calamitous results."

Ofnal lunged over the table and wrapped her hands around Jame's throat.

Resde pressed a knife blade against Ofnal's neck. "Let her go," she said in Ofnal's ear, "or you die right here."

Ofnal released Jame. The women beside Jame held onto her as she coughed and gasped for air. Resde pulled Ofnal away from the table and bound her hands behind her back.

Jame cleared her throat and nodded to the warriors that she was all right. She stood, straightened, and studied Ofnal. Probably for the first time in her life, fear sparked in Ofnal's eyes.

"The jails in Emoria are getting rather full," Jame said. "For now, you're a prisoner of Emoria until I have all the evidence gathered against you for assorted criminal activity here in Maymi."

"I demand to see my counsel," Ofnal said.

"In attacking a member of the Emoran royal family in the presence of witnesses, you've forfeited your right to counsel," Jame said. "You currently have the penalty of death hanging over you. In other words, you've given your rights and your life to Emoria. Take her away." She dismissed Ofnal with a wave of her hand.

"You can't do this," Ofnal said as she was dragged from the chamber. "My family, my business."

"You made your choices, now you have to live with them," Jame said.

When the matriarch of the Dranderal clan was out of the room, Jame sank back onto the bench.

"Well done, princess." Resde grinned as she sauntered back into the chamber.

Jame nodded. "One down. Three to go."

THE NARROW CATWALK that soared above the canal, hanging from the beams that supported the street above, squeaked in protest as Tigh, Vorkin, and Iklas ran down its length.

A wiry former Guard, crouched at an intersection of walkways, popped up when she saw her comrades rushing toward her.

"What's the word?" Vorkin asked in a soft voice.

"It looks like they're heading for the cliffs," the former Guard said.

"Cliffs?" Tigh asked.

"The eastern cliffs start to rise just north of here, on the edge of the swamps," Vorkin said. "They're covered with caves and hidden coves. Maymians have used them for centuries as hideouts and cover for less than legal activities."

"We need to find Roseh, fast," Tigh muttered, frustrated that the children and the slavers had slipped through their fingers.

The former Guard straightened. "We've already sent someone to warn her."

"I have directions to their hideout," Vorkin added.

Tigh nodded as she mentally pulled together the scattered ruins of her plan. "I need someone to tell Jame what's happened."

"I'll do that," the wiry former Guard said.

"Tell her we're investigating the best way of getting the children back," Tigh said, knowing that Jame was going to worry no matter what.

"INVESTIGATING," JAME MUTTERED as she watched the former Guard rush out of the common room back to the excitement of tracking down the slavers.

"This is too complicated." Resde plopped down on the bench across from Jame. "It's making me dizzy."

"I've got to think this through," Jame mumbled as she rubbed her finger over the crossed sword and bow design on her mug. "The slavers have decided to pull out of the games here in Maymi and they know Tigh and her company of Guards are after them. Why would they go to these cliffs instead of boarding a ship and getting away from here as fast as possible?"

"They can't risk having their ships anywhere near the city, so they hide them in the coves further north," Resde said. "Their hideout in the cliffs is very well hidden and well protected. They'll be ready for anyone following them."

Jame pushed down the quick rise of fear for Tigh. She had to keep reminding herself that Tigh had been the master of the skirmish. But that didn't mean she couldn't use some help. "How well do you know this cliff area?"

Resde exchanged glances with the young warriors gathered on either side of Jame. "We use it as a training ground."

Jame chuckled. "Which means you know it better than the birds and beasts who live there. Do you know where the slavers' camp is?"

"Yes," Resde said. "It has the same kind of protection as Emoria. Only two narrow ways in and out." She arranged empty bowls and utensils on the table into a rough map. "One entrance is through what we presume is a narrow cave on the south and the other entrance is an opening, about a person and a half high, on a cliff overlooking the harbor where their ships are. They drop a ramp from it to get in and out."

Jame studied Resde's handiwork. "So, Tigh will follow them to the south entrance."

"Yes," Resde said.

"As I see it, the slavers are expecting Tigh at their south door, but I seriously doubt they'll be expecting Emorans at their north door," Jame said.

Resde nodded. "It sounds like it could work. Ghet here could lead—"

"I'll lead," Jame said.

"You know you can't do that," Resde said.

"Not as an arbiter, but I can as an Emoran princess," Jame said with a grin. "Now before you argue. I'll be as safe surrounded by a group of Emoran warriors as I am in this establishment."

"But it's still too much of a risk," Resde said.

Jame held up a hand and paused to compose her words. "This just isn't about catching a group of slavers who have kidnapped children. This is about breaking the underground criminal activity in Maymi once and for all. That means your actions have to be legally sanctioned to hold up before a Tribunal."

"Couldn't you just order us to do it?" Ghet, an eager-faced young warrior, asked.

"Do any of you have warrior's braids?" Jame asked, already knowing the answer. A warrior from Emoria visited in the summer to train them, but they had to serve time in Emoria to earn a braid. Most Emorans who went to their homeland made the decision to settle there.

"That doesn't make us any less as warriors," Ghet said.

"No, but the Federation laws are very strict about this," Jame said. "You have to be led by someone with the clear authority as a leader. In this case, that would be me."

"Can't we send for one of the Guards?" Resde asked.

"We don't have time and we don't want to risk the element of surprise," Jame said. "We have a good chance of stopping these slavers and getting the children back by catching them off guard."

"Tell you the truth, we don't want Tigh angry with us," Ghet said.

"If we succeed, she won't have any reason to be angry with any of us," Jame said. "Besides, she knows you were only following my orders as your princess."

Ghet glanced at the Emorans around her and faced Jame. "We'd be honored to follow you on this mission."

THE GROUP OF eleven former Guards stood on a spit of sand that hugged the southernmost edge of the cliffs that characterized the seacoast to the north of Maymi. Tigh looked ahead and eastward and could barely make out the higher cliff that jutted out to form the partially swampy cove they were in.

"Now what?" she asked, watching the thickly bunched trees rising up from the shallow black waters.

A soft rattle of leaves above them answered Tigh's question. Sefrin climbed down a tree a pace from the edge of the sandy spit and jumped to solid ground.

"The children are in the slavers' hideaway," he announced as a greeting.

"Then we don't have much time," Tigh said.

"Come with me." Sefrin leapt to the tree, grabbed an overhanging branch, pulled himself up, and disappeared around the other side of the thick trunk.

Tigh followed with the others behind her. She was surprised to find herself on a bridge of rope and vines that ran through the thick foliage of the water-strengthened trees. This clever trackway allowed them to delve undetected into the naturally darkened patch of swamp.

The safe house for rescued slaves was ironically within sight of the tunnel the slavers used to enter their own domain. Halfway up the cliff wall facing the swamp and the sea, the opening was hidden behind a craggy mass of rock that had split from the bluff and stood several paces out into the swamp.

"Not bad," Tigh muttered as they followed the rope bridge around the freestanding rock and entered the cave.

The rock chamber was large and well settled by the people who called themselves the Adars. The space was divided into eating, sleeping, and meeting areas with the orderliness of a well-run military camp. A handful of people in the same earth-toned leathers as Sefrin were gathered around a small fire pit, deep in discussion.

Tigh and Vorkin followed Sefrin to the group, while the other Guards waited by the cave opening.

Roseh looked up. "Welcome. It appears the slavers have double-crossed everyone."

"So, we just have to make sure they don't get away with it," Tigh said.

"We got a signal from our people on the inside that their ship hasn't come back from taking away their last group of slaves," Roseh said. "They're rather unsettled, arguing amongst themselves. The only thing they can agree on is they have to hide the children. They fear the Dranderals' wrath. We have to be careful of the Dranderals, too. They'll be swarming all over this place to get those children back."

"If the Dranderals are waiting for a signal from their matriarch before taking action, then we won't have to worry about them." Tigh was still filled with wonder about the brief message the young Guard brought back to her. Jame took out one of their formidable opponents using only words as her weapon. If she could burst with pride, she would have been in a thousand proud pieces at that moment.

"What?" Roseh asked.

Tigh grinned. "Jame has taken Ofnal into custody for the crime of assaulting an Emoran princess in an Emoran safe house."

The group around the fire pit twittered at this near miraculous news.

"This is wonderful," Roseh said with relief. "The Dranderals have always been in the way of our efforts."

"So where do you think the slavers will hide the children?" Tigh asked.

"There's a place where they've hidden slaves before," Roseh said. "This isn't the first time the slavers have gone against the Dranderals. That outcropping is sacred to the Maymians. Only the acolytes of Unher are allowed past the ancient stone gates where the land juts outward to the sea. The slavers are careful not to be seen violating this by keeping their activities to the caves inside the outcropping, but they've used the temple to hide slaves in on occasion."

"What about the acolytes?" Tigh asked.

"They're only there one night out of every moon," Roseh said.

"And lucky for the slavers, tonight is not the night," Tigh said.

Roseh nodded. "The acolytes were there three nights ago, so the slavers can hide the children in the temple for almost a full moon."

"Looks like that's their only choice of action," Tigh said. "Once the children are hidden, we go into this temple and get them out. The slavers won't be expecting it, so we shouldn't have a problem catching them off guard."

"We can get you there going overland," Roseh said. "The back tunnel leads to the forest above."

A young woman burst into the chamber from the opening in the back wall. "Roseh." She stopped and stared at the group of black-clad warriors.

"It's all right, Sera," Roseh said. "They're here to help us."

Sera nodded. "The children are being moved to the temple."

"They didn't waste any time," Tigh said. "The sooner we get up there, the sooner we can end this little drama."

Chapter 15

"WHAT?" JAME STOPPED at the threshold of the common room as fifteen sets of eyes stared at her in wide-eyed wonderment. "What?"

Her band of Emoran warriors blinked out of their stunned surprise.

Our apologies, Princess," Resde said. "The Emoran leathers fit you well, as they should for our future queen."

Jame glanced down at herself, still a little confused by their reaction. "Thank you, Resde.

I thought I'd blend in more if I was dressed like the rest of you."

"Wise thinking." Resde nodded.

Jame hefted a borrowed staff and looked around at the now expectant eyes. "Is everyone ready?"

The young warriors gave her eager nods.

She led the way to a small passage that connected the safe house with the sword and knife shop next door. Below the shop was a landing for the underground canal and three long narrow flat boats waited for them.

"Good luck to you," Resde called after the boats as they slipped away from the landing.

The flat boats glided through the canal, deserted during the time of the evening meal.

Jame tried not to clutch the sides of the boat or show her extreme discomfort at the thought of the city above her supported by very thin-looking wooden beams. She let out a relieved sigh when the boats floated through a gate into the swamplands.

"We have a camp in a river gorge not far from here," Ghet said as they paddled through watery paths that seemed to appear at the last moment in the thick stand of trees.

Red knobbed knees stood sentinel around the trees they were attached to. The dying sun turned the water into the color of ink. Jame could understand why so many frightening legends had grown up around the swamplands of Maymi.

A subdued wolf howl brought Jame out of her reverie. *A wolf?*

Ghet smiled and pointed through the shadow-deepened trees. Jame squinted and made out a figure on a solid bit of land. As they got closer,

Jame saw that the figure was an Emoran, and she stood in front of a rocky bluff that overlooked the swamp.

The young Emoran grinned at them and raised her hand in greeting.

"Good evening, young wolf." Ghet returned the grin.

The young woman laughed. "Nice night for a hunt."

They maneuvered the three boats alongside the narrow strip of land until they faced sheer rock rising out of the water. Before Jame could voice her question, Ghet thrust her staff against the rock, and it pivoted around until there was an opening, wide enough for a flat boat, on either side of it.

"We stay with the old ways of keeping our domains out of sight," Ghet said as they eased the boats into a cavern.

Jame couldn't hide her shock and delight. The water formed a pool in the middle of the cavern. On all sides, but the mouth side, was almost a tiny Emor. The floor level held a temple to Laur, a tavern, a weapons shop and blacksmith. Above them, narrow paths led to the openings for residences. Everything needed for a well-run camp for warriors and scouts. She had heard about the Maymian camp—Emorans from the southeastern cities went to train there—but she had never imagined it to be like this. Like home.

This sudden reminder of home blindsided her and pulled up all the emotions surrounding her estrangement from Emoria. As her boatmates tossed ropes to waiting women on the wooden landing, she struggled to push down the one great shadow in her life.

"Amazing, isn't it?" Ghet asked. "It's been here for centuries. We even have a little palace in case any of the royal family visits."

Jame recovered her first shock in time to react to the second one. "Palace?"

"It's actually three chambers," Ghet said, "but it has a gallery lined with quartz windows like the palace in Emor."

Jame climbed out of the boat and gazed at the replica of the doors of the palace in Emor. "I can't believe it." What an amazing surprise. She had to show this place to Tigh. "Has anyone here seen Tigh and the Guards?"

"If they're around here, someone has seen them." Ghet grinned as she hopped out of the boat. "We'll get news in the tavern."

Jame couldn't believe how closely the tavern resembled the one in Emor. She realized that, unlike other cultures, Emoria had clung tightly to its traditions and customs that the Maymi settlement didn't stray very far from what had been conceived centuries before.

A half-dozen women stumbled to their feet, ready to offer their bench place to Jame.

Ghet laughed at the warriors' behavior. "Come, let's sit and find out what everyone knows." She indicated a table in the center of the chamber, hastily vacated by a half-dozen warriors.

As she sipped a mug of spiced tea, Jame was able to piece together Tigh's activities up to the last message from a scout. "They're in the Adars' hideout now?"

The young scout nodded. "Yes, princess."

Jame sighed. "We can't make our move until we know what they're going to do."

"We're watching both entrances to the Adars' hideout," the scout said.

Another scout ran into the chamber and nearly crashed into a table as she tried to stop. Panting, she straightened and focused on Jame. "The Guards left the hideout through the way on top of the cliffs. They're hiding at the edge of Unher's Crag, watching the slavers move the children up to the temple on the Crag."

Jame took in this information with some relief. No longer were they going to work blindly on opposite sides of the little crag. "All we have to do is watch their backs while they get the children out."

"LOOKS LIKE ONLY two slavers to guard them," Vorkin said as she and Tigh watched the six-sided temple balanced on the farthest point of the small peninsula.

"They must have them locked in a chamber of some kind," Tigh said as she studied the structure in the waning daylight. "I think only two of us should go in to free them. The rest can spread out and keep watch."

Vorkin shook her head in agreement as a chill touched the air with the disappearance of the last rays of the sun.

A vague whisper of something indefinable tickled the back of Tigh's mind as she opened her senses to the area around them. She couldn't latch onto anything specific to cause her to be uneasy. Maybe it was stray spiritual energy from the temple.

They waited a half sandmark longer for the sun to completely sink behind them. Tigh signaled the group to spread out so they could observe both sides of the small peninsula. When Tigh felt the Guards had enough time to get into place, she nodded to Vorkin, and they dashed between the pillars of Unher . . . not expecting to be chased by shadow bolts shooting from the stone sentinels. They dove and twisted away from the black weapons of magic. Tigh was thankful for their Guard enhanced hearing.

"Now we know why the temple's such a good hiding place," Vorkin muttered as she crashed to the ground and rolled away from the dark streak that impacted and lit the ground next to her.

"Why would a deity guard their temple with earthly magic?" Tigh flipped over one bolt and pushed sideways to avoid its close companion.

The shadow bolts continued to pursue them with the same single-minded intensity as they ran. With the exception of scattered small boulders, Unher's Crag was flat grassland, with no shields for Tigh and Vorkin as they focused all their attention on not getting struck by one of magic's darkest weapons.

"The slavers seem to have discovered the bolts are only set off by going between the pillars," Tigh said as she scrambled to her feet while a bolt hissed past her ear.

"Hopefully they'll stop once we get to the temple." Vorkin bounced into a contorted twist.

"I hope so . . ."

A rumble shook the ground . . . the earth opened up beneath them.

"Go with it," Tigh yelled and tumbled into the sinking earth. "Must have been one shadow bolt too many," she muttered as she slid into the earth.

"BLESSED LAUR. NO!" Jame cried.

Ghet held Jame down as she tried to jump from their hiding place overlooking the northern side of Unher's Crag.

"Sink hole," Ghet said.

"A sink hole with Tigh in it," Jame said.

"We can save them when we get the children," Ghet said.

"We must hurry then." Jame looked around at her little band of warriors. All eyes were on her for guidance. Tigh was doing her job and so must she. No matter how much she wanted to rush to the sink hole and get Tigh out of there. "We'll have to climb up the side closest to the temple, I think, so we don't set off those shadow bolts." She worked to keep her mind steady. They'd get to Tigh soon.

"Archers." Ghet glanced at five eager-faced warriors. "Keep your arrows trained on the slavers' entrance. Don't hit a Guard. The rest come with us. I think the Guards have the area pretty well covered."

"What if they think we're slavers?" a compact warrior asked.

"That's why we're in our Emoran leathers," Jame said. "There will be no mistaking who we are."

"Any other questions?" Ghet looked around. "Let's go."

They followed a centuries old half-hidden trail cut into the cliff down to the thin, rocky strip that ran along the shoreline. Soft Emoran boots barely crunched on the rocks as they hurried in the shadows of Unher's

Crag. A black-clad Guard materialized in front of them as they picked around a field of cracked boulders.

"What happened up there?" the Guard asked.

"Shadow bolts from the pillars of Unher caused the ground to collapse," Jame said. "What of Tigh and Vorkin?"

"They were caught in the collapse." Jame's mouth dried around the words.

"The Guards above signaled they were going in for a rescue," the Guard said. "I thought they meant for the children but now I know they meant Tigh and Vorkin."

Jame relaxed with relief. "If they save Tigh and Vorkin, we'll get the children."

The former Guard nodded and turned to look up the cliff behind them. She voiced a series of noises that sounded like rocks or wood being hit together. A heartbeat later, similar noises came from high above them.

"Word is being passed of what you're doing," the Guard said. "Good luck."

"Thanks." Jame allowed a grim smile before the band of Emorans continued to the sea end of Unher's Crag.

They heard alarmed shouts and movement as they passed below the northern entrance of the slavers' domain. It sounded as though the cave-in had penetrated the caverns. Jame sent a silent prayer to Laur, thanking her that the children weren't in the caves. Then she added an equally fervent prayer for Tigh to be all right. *Please, let her be all right.* Jame swallowed a rising despair and concentrated on locating the bottom part of the trail the slavers used to climb the cliff face.

"Here it is," a younger warrior whispered.

Jame took a step up the trail and Ghet stopped her with a hand on her shoulder.

"I'll go first," Ghet said, both gentle and firm. "Tigh would kill us if we weren't in the position to protect you."

Jame held Ghet's steady eyes for several heartbeats then nodded. She didn't want to belabor the fact that Tigh wasn't going to be pleased with any of them for being out there in the first place. *Please, Laur. She has to be all right.*

Jame and the rest of the young warriors, scrambled up the narrow trail behind Ghet, living up to the boast that Emorans had the blood of mountain goats in them. They took advantage of the chaos coming from the cave entrance fifty paces away and climbed undetected.

As a precaution, they crawled off the path into the knee-high grass and lay flat. Jame opened her senses and could hear the voices rising up from within the sinkhole. The smell of freshly disturbed dirt and rock tickled her nose and rock dust stung her eyes.

They caught their collective breaths at a crunching sound on the grass on the other side of the Crag. Ghet and Jame eased their heads up and saw the shadowy figures of the former Guards darting to the sinkhole.

"Guards," Ghet breathed. "It might be best to follow the cliff line until we're closer to the temple."

Jame nodded, relieved the Guards were getting to Tigh so quickly.

The small band of Emorans slithered through the grass to the narrowest point of the Crag where the temple stood. Jame raised her head and studied the six-sided structure. The walls were partially open, like most rural temples. Behind the building were two supply carts that looked in good repair, though Jame couldn't think of a use for them. Since no horses were stabled on the Crag, the carts were the sort that could be pulled by hand or beast.

She knew at least two slavers stayed with the children, so they had to be cautious in their approach.

"Pick two of your best warriors," Jame said to Ghet.

"Tita. Edye," Ghet said.

The pair slithered up to them.

"I want you to secure the temple," Jame said as she observed a combination of excitement, nervousness, and a touch of fear in the young warriors' eyes. An expected reaction for warriors on their first true dangerous mission. "Be cautious and methodical. No heroics." She waited for their solemn nods. "Good luck."

Tita and Edye slithered away in the shadows of the temple.

A noise in the grass from the end point of the Crag caught Jame's attention and she squinted into the deepening darkness. The strange noise she had heard the Guard make earlier reached her ears. A heartbeat later the grass whispered, and a Guard appeared like a black leather clad snake.

"Iklas sent me to tell you that Tigh and Vorkin seem to have more lives than a cat," the former Guard whispered, but Jame could hear the amusement in her voice. "They landed on a rather opulent bed of one of the slaver leaders and are down there creating more havoc for them than the blasted sinkhole did. Some of the Guards are down there helping them, the rest of us are keeping watch out here."

Jame put her head in her hands as relief swept over her. Tigh was still far from safe, but at least she had a fighting chance. "Thank you for the news. We have archers watching the northern side."

"Good," the Guard said. "I'd better get back in case there have been more developments. Good luck." The whispered words were almost lost in the swish of moving grass.

"Thank Laur, she's not badly hurt." A movement in the temple caught Jame's attention. "That was quick."

Tita and Edye stood within the opening of the temple and gave them the all-secure signal.

"They're good warriors," Ghet said.

"All right." Jame took a deep breath. "Let's do what we came to do."

TIGH AND VORKIN bounced a few times and then blinked around the darkened cavern in surprise.

"Interesting place for a bed," Tigh said as they crawled off the soft surface covered with splintery white rocks, soil, and uprooted grass.

She didn't have time to think about her good fortune as a group of slavers, responding to the echoing rumbles of the cave-in, appeared at the entrance of the cavern's tunnel. Tigh unsheathed her sword. This wasn't quite the plan, but it would do. They just had to get all the slavers' attention to keep them from going up top and escaping with the children.

The ring of her sword, as it smashed against a slaver's blade, sent a feral joy through Tigh. This feeling had consumed her when she'd been a Guard, but now it simply filled her with the satisfaction that she was able to give in to the delicious ecstasy of fighting and not turn into Tigh the Terrible.

They fought off a handful of slavers and hid behind some rubble to evaluate their sudden presence below ground. Shouts and excited voices sounded from unseen caverns all around, telling Tigh that the cave-in caused more damage further in.

"Should we create some havoc down here and leave it to the others to rescue the children?" Vorkin asked, squinting into the gloom. A few recessed lamps were still valiantly burning in their niches in the partially collapsed wall.

"Iklas knows the children come first." Tigh shrugged. "Which means we can play with these scum-filled excuses for human beings."

"I like the way you think." Vorkin grinned as she followed Tigh toward the chaotic voices.

GHET AND JAME joined Tita and Edye, and they slipped into the small building. They stopped to listen for the sounds of children.

"There're two ways down," Edye said. "The slavers were up here playing sticks and rocks, so they weren't actually guarding a door or anything."

"All right." Jame nodded as she glanced at the brooding stone around them.

Each deity's temples had a unique feel to them, and this temple to Unher was no different. She found the atmosphere unsettling, reflecting the fact that Unher was not a benevolent deity like Bal or Laur. *Why would a people worship such an ageless soul as this?* Jame shook herself away from her thoughts and focused on why they were there.

"You two go down that way," she pointed to a partially hidden staircase, "and we'll take this way. And be careful, the lower chambers could have been damaged by the cave-in."

Tita and Edye hurried across the temple to the far staircase as Ghet led the way down the well-worn steps next to them. As with most temples, the lamps set into the walls were lit with a perennial flame, so they didn't have to be hampered with carrying a lamp.

Halfway down the stairs, they stopped and stared at the chamber, at least two stories high and many times larger than the temple above them. Tall stone walls created a complex maze that covered the floor. Parts of the maze were opened at the top and other parts were covered.

"Why can't anything be easy?" Jame muttered as she studied the chaotic placement of walls.

Across the chamber, Edye and Tita paused on the steps and looked to Jame for guidance.

"I bet the maze is controlled by the deity," Jame said, "which means we'll never be able to find our way around it. But something tells me the slavers wouldn't be allowed to use the maze either."

"So where are the children?" Ghet asked looking around.

"We're here," distant voices called.

Jame and Ghet blinked at each other. "Did you hear that?"

"Yes. Sounds like it came from . . ." Ghet turned and stared at a covered part of the maze.

"Where are you?" Jame called out.

"We're right in front of you," came a voice.

"Are you being hidden by magic?" Jame asked, remembering the report from the Guard about the magic chamber at Cadryn's shop.

"Yes," came the weak voice. "We're on top of the maze. The slavers used an amulet to put us here."

"Amulet." Jame looked up at Edye and Tita. They nodded and ran up the steps.

Several heartbeats later, the young warriors rushed down the steps above Jame and Ghet. "This is all we could find." Tita gave Jame a pair of wood tokens roughly carved to resemble the temple.

"Thanks," Jame said. She rolled the tokens over in her hands, as if something about them would reveal how they worked. She turned to the children. "Do you know how they work?"

"They held the amulets out and said the words, 'hiding place,'" the weak voice said.

Jame raised an amused eyebrow at Ghet, who shrugged.

"Slavers aren't known for their soaring intelligence," Ghet said.

Jame gave one of the amulets to Ghet and they pointed them in the direction of the voice.

"Hiding place," they said together.

A solid-looking wooden walkway with rope banisters materialized in front of them, leading to an equally solid structure on top of a maze tunnel.

"By the waterfalls of Laur," Edye said.

Jame took a step onto the walkway, only to be stopped by Ghet. She looked down at the hand on her arm and then up at the earnest warrior.

"Me first," Ghet said, giving Jame a steady look.

Knowing that Ghet would have to answer to Queen Jyac if she came to any harm, Jame swallowed her initial defensive reaction and moved aside. Ghet stepped onto the walkway. When she was satisfied it was indeed solid and safe, she walked, followed by Jame, the thirty or so paces to the magic chamber.

The door was small and round, just big enough for a child to slip through. More frustrating, there wasn't any lock or knob or any indication of how to open it.

"How did they open the door?" Jame asked.

After a few heartbeats of mutterings from several children's voices, the one child said, "It was open when we were put in here."

Jame sighed, and Ghet kicked at the small door in frustration. Jame stared at the door as she put all the pieces she had so far together. She grinned.

"You figured it out?" Ghet asked.

"We've determined the slavers didn't have to memorize anything too difficult to make the magic work," Jame said. "So how about," she held out the amulet, "open door."

The door silently and obediently slid open.

"You're going to make a great queen," Ghet said.

Jame chuckled and poked her head into the dark chamber and just made out a half-dozen children huddled against the far wall. "Are you unbound?"

"Our hands are bound," a young girl squeaked.

Jame, being smaller than Ghet, squeezed through the small door and moved down the row of wide-eyed children as she cut their ropes with her knife.

"Now one at a time, go through the door and walk carefully to the steps." She helped the first child stand. The young boy startled her with a relieved hug. What an ordeal these children must have been through. "Now go."

With the last child out of the chamber, Jame crawled through the door and hurried back across the walkway with Ghet. By the time they got to the steps, Tita and Edye had led the children up into the temple proper.

"Now what?" Edye asked, when Jame and Ghet joined them next to a small altar. Jame shrugged. "Back the way we came. But be careful."

Keeping her eyes and ears attuned to everything around them, Jame led the group out of the temple and into the tall grass. She could hear shouts and voices coming up from beneath them, but the top of the crag was quiet.

With Ghet leading the way, they walked toward the trail that wound down to the shoreline. Ghet froze twenty paces from the edge of the bluff and held up a hand. The others stopped behind her, tensely waiting.

A head popped up, followed by a body, as the unmistakable figure of a slaver climbed onto the crag. Within heartbeats, a dozen slavers stood in front of the Emoran rescue team and a half-dozen terrified children.

Chapter 16

ALL IKLAS AND the handful of Guards with her had to do was follow the sounds of blades clashing together. They slipped past wounded and unconscious slavers. She marveled at how much damage Tigh and Vorkin had done in a short bit of time. Rocky dust settled around them, adding another layer to an already unreal underground world.

The dust created ghostly streams in the flickering torchlight making it difficult for Iklas to tell people from shadows. The noises were real enough, as shouts of anger and surprise rented the air.

"What are you doing here?" came a whisper from a pair of shadows in front of them.

"Making sure you don't have all the fun," Iklas said, as she looked at the slumped and wounded slavers around them.

"You're supposed to be saving the children," Tigh said.

"A group of Emorans have taken over that chore." Iklas studied Tigh and Vorkin. They were covered with dirt and rock dust. Their leathers were ripped, and she could only imagine the collection of scratches and bruises covering their bodies.

"Emorans?" Tigh frowned. "Jame sent them out here?"

"We got the impression they came out to keep an eye on the north entrance to these caves," Iklas said.

Tigh nodded. "And they're rescuing the children."

"As we speak," Iklas said.

"So, we still have to keep these slavers from going above ground," Tigh said. "We need to split up to cover both exits."

JAME STUDIED THE slavers' smug expressions as they glowed in the light of the torches they held. *Emorans don't panic. They make quick revisions to the original plans.* They used to laugh at their Weapon Master's dry words, but Jame now understood what she'd been talking about.

"This just turned into our lucky day," a slaver, with curly black hair and an unpleasant grin, said. "Not only do we have children to sell, but we have strong warriors. Let's get them and get out of here before this whole rock collapses."

The dozen slavers stepped forward and the Emorans backed away, keeping the children behind them. They couldn't just turn and run because they didn't know where the other way down was, and they didn't want to risk setting off the shadow bolts.

Jame glanced around for anything to help them as they went to the backside of the temple. Trapped. Tigh was going to kill her for getting into such a mess.

A few of the slavers circled around to the other side of them, laughing and making sport of them. Edye growled.

"Don't let them get to you," Jame whispered. "Just concentrate on where they are and attack any that get too close."

"You may as well give up," the curly-haired slaver said. "You can't get away."

Desperate, Jame looked around, taking in the brooding temple, the chaotic noises from below ground, the dark waving grasses . . .

"Let's get them into the wagons and take them out overland," one of the slavers said. "The shadow bolts only try to stop people from entering, not leaving."

"Good idea." The curly-haired slaver nodded. "Then no one else will know what happened to them and we can get all the profits."

Jame mentally rolled her eyes at their terminal greediness. The dozen slavers moved forward with purpose.

"Wait," Jame said and, surprisingly, they stopped. "I can't believe you think you'd make more money off of us than off these wagons."

The Emorans gave her puzzled looks.

"Wagons?" The slaver laughed. "We have no time for games."

"You mean, you don't know?" Jame asked.

"Know what?" the slaver asked.

"About the temple wagons of Unher," Jame said.

"What about them?" the slaver demanded.

"They bring unlimited silver to whoever can harness their special magic." Jame put on her best arbiter's face and mentally squared her shoulders to present the most convincing argument possible for what was going to be an absurd story at best.

"Unlimited silver." The slaver narrowed his eyes in half suspicion and half interest.

"It just so happens the Maymi branch of Emorans was entrusted with the secret long ago when they were chosen to act as silent guardians of this temple," Jame said.

"Why would Unher entrust her temple to the followers of Laur?" the slaver asked, crossing his arms.

"She did it at a time when her followers split into two factions who were fighting for dominance over the temple," Jame said. "She decided the best way to protect the temple was to put it in the protective hands of outsiders."

"And you know this special magic?"

"Yes." Jame nodded. "And I'll give it to you in exchange for our freedom. Unlimited silver. Unimaginable riches for the rest of your life."

The dozen slavers exchanged greedy-eyed looks. Jame thanked Laur that silver seemed to have the loudest thread in their thought patterns.

"Show us this magic," the curly-haired slaver said.

Jame shrugged and sauntered up to the pair of wagons. "They must be in a specific place for the magic to work."

She gave the slavers an expectant look. A half-dozen stepped forward, and Jame instructed them to pull the wagons to near the edge of the cliff behind the temple. She was pleased to note the ground slanted ever so subtly toward the cliff.

"What exactly does this special magic do?" the curly-haired slaver asked as he studied the wagons lined up facing the sea.

Jame lowered her voice to a conspiratorial whisper. "It makes the wagons fly to the place where the deities hide their silver."

"Fly?" Several slavers eyed the wagons with skepticism.

"Yes." Jame walked up to a wagon and patted it. "Haven't you ever wondered why every temple to every deity has two wagons such as these in the back? I mean, has anyone actually seen these wagons being used?"

The slavers pondered this for a heartbeat and shook their heads. Jame hid her amusement.

Most people wouldn't know a temple wagon, away from the temple, if it ran over them.

"So, only the deities use them to get to their silver?" the curly-haired slaver asked.

For reasons unknown to Jame, it seemed to make some kind of sense to him. He probably related to the devious aspect of the story.

"Right," Jame said. "They can fly off to the silver, fill the wagons, and fly back without anyone being the wiser."

"That explains how they can build these temples." The slaver grinned. "I never believed they were built on contributions from the followers."

"You want to learn how to work the magic?" Jame asked.

"You think we're fools?" the slaver roared. "Of course, we want to know how the magic works."

The Emorans and children alike let out long slow breaths in relief.

"First off, everyone who wants to go to where the silver is, has to get into the wagons," Jame said.

The slavers exchanged wary looks. A short argument resulted in all of them deciding to go.

Anxious to get to the riches, the slavers piled into the wagons.

While the slavers were engaged in their discussion, Jame whispered instructions to her small band, and they positioned themselves, awaiting Jame's signal.

"This is all you have to do to make the magic work," Jame said. "Face forward toward the sea."

The slavers shifted until they were all facing away from Jame, who bit back a grin.

"Raise your hands and clasp them out and above your head."

The spectacle was almost too much for Edye and Tita, and they received a sharp warning glare from Ghet.

"Now here's the important part. You must ask Bal to push the wagons into the heavens."

The fervent prayers to Bal drowned out the crunch of grass as the Emorans and the children ran forward and gave the wagons enough of a push for them to fly off the cliff. The Emorans grabbed and pulled the children back so they wouldn't witness the end of the short-lived flight into the watery rocks below.

Silence overtook the little crag for all of two heartbeats. They were startled by the sound of whopping and cheering behind them. They spun around, and Jame was relieved to see a group of Guards.

"Why didn't you help?" Jame asked.

One of the Guards laughed. "And spoil a perfectly good story?"

JAME HAD NEVER seen quite so many scratches and bruises collected together on one human being before. The black leathers, piled on the stone floor, weren't much better off.

"You look awful," Jame said.

Tigh gave Jame a sheepish look.

"Let me help you into the water." Jame led Tigh to a pool that had been fashioned and smoothed by Emorans many centuries earlier to take advantage of a warm spring bubbling within the caverns. The chamber was a miniature tribute to the palace at Emor with towering walls and long quartz windows that refracted the torchlight from the main cavern.

Tigh winced when the water washed over her, then relaxed as the warmth soothed the bruises and scratches. Jame stripped out of her leathers and eased into the pool next to Tigh.

"So," Jame said as she swam around to face Tigh, "how mad are you at me?"

"I'm not mad at you at all," Tigh said. "I'm a little upset you put yourself in danger. But that's only natural. I understand why you decided to help and, the truth is, your presence was the only reason we succeeded." She took Jame's hand in both of hers. "I'm so proud of you. You're a born leader. And your inventiveness and ability to convince anyone of just about anything leaves me in awe."

Jame stared dumbstruck at Tigh. "I think you might be a little biased in your opinion."

"I mean it," Tigh said as she lifted Jame's hand to her lips. "You're the most incredible person I've ever met, and I thank Bal every day that I have you in my life."

"You're the incredible one," Jame whispered as she wrapped her arms around Tigh's neck. "Laur knows I'll never leave you. She also knows I'll choose you over Emoria. I already have."

Tigh shook her head. "You're meant to be queen. You'll make a magnificent queen." "Only if you're by my side." Jame pulled her head back and captured Tigh's eyes with hers. "I'll be queen and you'll be my consort. Nothing more than hurt Emoran pride stands in our way."

Tigh nodded as she gently turned Jame around and pulled her close. Sighing, Jame settled back against her. Tigh's arms were her paradise.

"You know your people better than I do," Tigh murmured in Jame's ear. "The Emorans I've seen have shown you great respect. Even the ones representing your queen and council. I believe time will heal this rift between you and your country. Perhaps stories like what you did tonight will help persuade your aunt."

Jame stiffened, then turned around in a panic. "Oh no. Jyac mustn't hear word of this."

"Why?" Tigh asked.

"Because, when I cut myself off from Emoria, I lost all the rights that go with the title of princess," Jame said. "I led these Emorans as their princess when I really didn't have the right to."

"But you are their princess," Tigh said.

"It's complicated." Jame sighed. "But this story can't be let out. The warriors who helped me can receive braids for their involvement, but my name must not be mentioned. Let's say that they assisted the local Constabulary in saving the children and breaking up the slaving operation."

"Someday you're going to tell Jyac the story of what happened tonight." Tigh raised an eyebrow at Jame.

"Only if you're there to hear me tell it to her."

TIGH BARELY HAD a chance to slip through the door of their room at the safe house, when an impatient Jame grabbed her, pulled her to the table, and pushed her into a chair.

"Well?" Jame asked as she sat in the chair adjacent to Tigh.

Tigh rubbed her chin. "Hmmm. Where to begin?"

"Begin by telling me everything," Jame said, beyond frustrated.

"I'll tell you the conclusion first," Tigh said. "Since that'll answer all your questions at once."

Jame rolled her eyes in exasperation. "All right. What's the conclusion?"

"You're to judge the case of Rend versus Jande the day after tomorrow." Tigh sat back and crossed her arms.

Jame let the statement sink in. "That's it?"

"That's it." Tigh grinned. "And the only reason you're involved in that one is because both parties are not from Maymi, and it involves the less than legal activities that Jande had gotten mixed up in here in Maymi."

"What about Tekl?" Jame asked.

"The slavers were very enthusiastic in naming him as their leader," Tigh said.

"Did he work for the Dranderals?" Jame asked.

Tigh nodded. "Not only that, he's obscurely related to them."

"So Cadryn is free to open her shop?" Jame saw the answer in Tigh's twinkling eyes and finally relaxed. "We actually did it."

"Yep," Tigh said. "You created an environment where justice can be handed down without fear. By eliminating the underlying problem, you eliminated the reasons for the case that brought us here in the first place. Cadryn is free to open her shop and the people of Maymi don't have to worry about the illegal underground activities that have made them uneasy for centuries."

"I'm just glad it's over with," Jame said. "Please tell me all our cases won't be like this one."

"I hope not."

They looked at each other and laughed. The tension Jame had worn like a second skin from the moment they had entered Maymi fell away.

A gentle rap on the door pulled them back to reality.

"Now what?" Jame sighed dramatically. "Come in."

The door opened and Resde peeked in before stepping into the chamber.

"My princess." Resde approached them with a scroll. "This just arrived from the mayor."

Jame gave the scroll, with its blue and yellow tassels hanging from a large wax seal, a puzzled look and took it. "Thank you, Resde."

"My princess," Resde hesitated then straightened, "it's been my honor to have you and Tigh stay in our establishment. You reminded us of what it's like to be truly Emoran, and for that, we'll send prayers to Laur every day in thanks that you'll someday be our queen."

"Thanks," Jame said, a little stunned by the fervent words. When Resde was gone, she turned to Tigh, not surprised to see that knowing grin. "They're Emorans."

"But they're right," Tigh said.

Jame shook her head at Tigh's obvious blindness in this matter. She broke the seal on the scroll and read through the brief message. "Oh, no."

"What?"

"The mayor wants to have some kind of ceremony in our honor. For saving the children and ridding the city of the slavers." Jame walked to the table and sank onto the chair.

"Us?" Tigh wrinkled her nose.

"Yes, us." Jame leveled a knowing gaze at Tigh. "You led the Guards against the slavers."

"And you led the Emorans to save the children," Tigh said. "I guess there isn't any way we can gracefully decline the honor."

"I guess not." Jame sighed. "I don't remember hearing about any other arbiters getting into these kinds of fixes."

"But the other arbiters are ordinary people living ordinary lives," Tigh said. "You're an Emoran princess, so your approach to life is completely different from everyone else's. You aren't an arbiter because you have to make a living. You chose to be an arbiter because of a desire to pursue justice according to your own ideals."

Jame frowned. "I don't feel like I'm doing anything different."

"That's because you are different." Tigh placed her hand on top of Jame's. "A wonderful kind of difference that brings me to my knees just looking at you."

Jame stared into Tigh's tender and sincere eyes. "And you're the only person who can leave me speechless."

Tigh brushed her lips against Jame's. "Let's celebrate a job well done."

CADRYN WALKED INTO her shop and stopped so suddenly Vorkin nearly crashed into her. She couldn't believe the sight before her.

Cadryn surveyed the work of dozens of volunteers from students to Guards to shop keepers to citizens off the street who had worked all night. The volunteers stood in the circular open area in front of the first ranges of scrolls and waited for her reaction to their efforts.

"I can't believe it." Cadryn scanned shelf after shelf of neatly arranged scrolls. The shop was cleared of the clutter from construction, and every bit of wood was so polished it caught the morning sun streaking through the lowest tier of windows.

"Everyone thought you'd waited long enough for your shop to open," Vorkin said.

Cadryn turned to her. "I wonder how they all got in here after I locked the doors last night."

"Just one of those little mysteries, I guess." Vorkin shrugged but couldn't keep the twinkle from her eyes.

"So, when do I get to buy a scroll?" a voice behind them asked.

Cadryn spun around to find Jame, sporting an impish grin, and Tigh, standing in the doorway.

"As soon as you've picked one out," Cadryn said as a deep sense of satisfaction filled her soul.

The chamber echoed with whoops and cheers as the volunteers pulled jugs of spiced tea and platters of tidbits from behind the service counters.

"You mean as soon as the celebration is over," Jame said.

Cadryn looked around at the beaming faces of the people who had given up a night's sleep for this wonderful unexpected surprise. "After the celebration."

Jame led Cadryn to the spiced tea.

VORKIN PULLED TIGH away from the group, then hesitated on what she wanted to say. She kept glancing at Cadryn.

"Uh, I kind of need your advice," Vorkin said.

Tigh raised an eyebrow. "Advice?"

"Uh, since you're already joined." Vorkin looked down at her boots. The former Guards still wore their black leathers and armor with pride, at least for this last day of celebration.

"Advice on being joined?" Tigh asked.

"How did you, I mean, how did you tell her you loved her?" Vorkin asked.

"It was kind of something that happened over time, as we got to know each other," Tigh said.

"But what setting did you actually profess your love to her?" Vorkin asked.

"You mean, like the first time we kissed?" Tigh asked.

"Yes." Vorkin nodded vigorously.

Tigh laughed. "We were in the sculpture garden in Ynit during the Summer Solstice. Jame suddenly had this predatory look in her eye, and

I started to take a step backward and tripped over the big toe of the foot sculpture. Jame was on top of me in a heartbeat. I didn't even have a chance to defend myself."

Vorkin stared at Tigh in disbelief. "That was your first kiss?"

Tigh nodded. "Yes."

"Somehow I don't see Cadryn and myself in that situation," Vorkin said.

"If you're meant to be together, the perfect situation for the first kiss and the first words of love will present themselves," Tigh said.

"I guess you're right." Vorkin sighed. "But I don't even know how she feels."

Tigh put a hand on Vorkin's shoulder. "She feels." Then she strolled away as Vorkin worked on that idea for a while.

"WHAT WAS THAT all about?" Jame asked in a low voice as she handed Tigh a mug of tea.

"Vorkin is trying to figure out how to approach Cadryn," Tigh said.

Jame grinned. "She should just kiss her. I know there won't be any protest from Cadryn."

"Not everyone is as forward as you are," Tigh said.

They turned at the sudden silence around them.

Rend stood like a timid mouse in the doorway. It looked as if her courage was failing her, and she was ready to turn and rush away. Jame stepped forward and held a hand out to her.

"Please come in," Jame said as she took a gentle hold of Rend's arm and led her to Cadryn.

"Welcome to my shop," Cadryn said.

"Thank you," Rend murmured, not raising her eyes from the floor. "I'm sorry to have interrupted your party."

"That's all right," Cadryn said. "Would you like some spiced tea?"

Rend lifted startled eyes and looked at Cadryn. "Thank you, no. I just . . ." She took a breath. "I just wanted to make an offer."

"An offer?" Cadryn asked.

"I'm suddenly the sole proprietor of sixteen scroll shops. And I'm in need of a business partner to run them." Rend found a spot on the floor and studied it as Cadryn stared at her in bewilderment.

"You think Cadryn might be suitable for the job?" Jame asked, as Cadryn gave her a startled look.

"Yes." Rend nodded and raised sincere eyes to Cadryn.

Cadryn exchanged surprised and intrigued glances with Vorkin, who shrugged. "Perhaps we can go to my office and talk a bit about it."

Rend, let out the breath she held, nodded, and followed Cadryn and Vorkin across the shop.

"That was an unexpected development," Jame said.

"But a good move on Rend's part," Tigh said.

"Cadryn and Rend's House of Scrolls. I like the sound of that." Jame grinned. She was delighted her persistence in making sure justice prevailed led to this new and promising partnership.

Chapter 17

IT WAS BAD enough Tigh spent the whole day teasing her about it, but the smirk on her face as she slept was too much for Jame.

Jame looked around the tidy room in the sprawling inn that overlooked the dramatic cliffs of the southern coast and took a deep satisfying breath of arid, cool air. She was more than relieved to be away from Maymi and well on the way home.

"Laur's waterfalls. I'll never be able to set foot in that city again." A chuckle bubbled up from the lump under the covers next to her. She glared at the lump. "Remember the promise I made about never mentioning you fainting at our joining ceremony?"

Tigh rolled over and sat up. She blinked sleepy but suspicious eyes at Jame.

"I think our friends back in Ynit would enjoy hearing about it," Jame said.

Tigh's sleepy eyes narrowed. "What do you want?"

"I was just thinking about how they would find the story entertaining . . ."

Jame found herself pinned to the bed with Tigh peering down at her through wary eyes.

Tigh slowly lowered her head until Jame felt her warm breath in her ear. "What do you want?"

"Don't ever mention anything about the statue." Jame was having problems concentrating on the discussion with Tigh on top of her.

"You forget there's one difference between the statue and my fainting." Tigh placed soft kisses around Jame's ear.

Jame struggled to suck air into her lungs. She wasn't going to let Tigh distract her away from this very important subject. "What's that?"

"Only a handful of people witnessed my fainting." Tigh explored the tender skin below Jame's ear. "Anyone who visits the Gardens of Trinagol in Maymi is going to see the statue of you with the children."

"Why?" Jame gasped, then pulled away from Tigh, who raised her head and an eyebrow at the same time. "Why didn't they make a statue of you?"

"Because I was just doing my job." Tender affection danced in Tigh's eyes. "You were being a hero."

"I wasn't—"

Tigh put a finger to Jame's lips. "Yes, you were. And I'm so proud of you."

Jame blinked in surprise. "You are? You have a funny way of showing it."

"You're so fun to tease." Tigh grinned, earning a playful smack on her arm.

"You're—" A cacophony of clanging metal interrupted Jame's retort.

"What the—?"

Tigh rolled out of the bed and threw back the closed shutters of the window overlooking the sea. Hundreds of pale lights bobbed where there should have been unrelenting black.

Jame walked up next to Tigh. "What's that?"

"Ships," Tigh said as lamps lit up like a nest of disturbed fireflies in the small village sprawled below the cliff they were on. "Unexpected ships."

IT SEEMED ALL the inhabitants of the small resort town of Tanders were out on the expansive white beaches that drew visitors to the area in the first place. After all the noise they made, they at least had enough sense not to set the torches used for nightly entertainment ablaze, Tigh thought as she and Jame pushed through the crowds.

Tigh scanned the shadowed masses of people and structures on the beach and spotted what looked to be the village leaders clustered in a heated discussion on the musicians' platform near the drinking pavilion.

"This way," she murmured as she altered her course and snaked around knots of people until they came to the steps on the side of the pavilion.

"You're crazy to think it's a large joining party," an exasperated voice wafted down to them.

"Why else would they be hovering out there?" another voice asked. "They probably got delayed somewhere and are disoriented in the dark. We should light the torches to guide them in."

"There are too many boats to be a joining party or any kind of party for that matter," the first voice said. "Besides we'd have been notified if such a large group was planning to come here."

Jame grasped Tigh's arm. "Let's just go set them straight, all right?"

Tigh nodded, and they walked up the steps to the sizable wooden platform.

"Who else could it be, if not a large party?" A small man waved his hands.

"A very large invasion force from across the ocean," Tigh said.

The six men and women turned to Tigh and stared at her.

"What do you mean? That's ridiculous. Who'd want to invade us?" the small man sputtered.

Tigh opened her mouth to utter an inappropriate response and closed it at Jame's meaningful look. She sighed and mentally stepped aside to let Jame handle these idiots in a diplomatic manner.

"The Southern Territories has been the target of an aggressive campaign by the people of the Silver Dragon, who live on the East Continent," Jame said. "We've already defeated an advance force that attempted to capture Ynit."

One of the women nodded. "We heard about that."

"We also have reason to believe the leaders of this campaign wouldn't back away from continuing their invasion, even after the defeat at Ynit," Jame said. "They're a proud people who've always been successful in their campaigns."

"But why are they off our shore?" the small man asked.

"The beaches, most likely," Tigh said. "They can make an easy landing and move inland quickly."

"But what about us?" another man squeaked.

Tigh shrugged. "They don't seem to care what's in their way."

"What can we do? We can't possibly stop them." A woman stepped forward. "I'm Pijhon, Mayor of Tandor."

"I'm Jame, peace-arbiter-at-large for the Southern Territories, and this is Tigh, my peace warrior," Jame said. "We arrived too late last night to check in with your office."

"How can an invasion force of that size just appear out of nowhere?" Pijhon asked.

Jame and Tigh exchanged knowing looks.

"There wasn't any sign of it yesterday?" Jame asked.

Pijhon shook her head. "We got a report that a fleet of fishing vessels were coming in from way offshore. That's a common sight this time of year. But those ships out there are not a part of a fishing fleet. They're too large."

The southern sky lit up in an eerie violet, illuminating a line of sails puffed out from a seemingly enchanted wind that didn't have the power to actually propel the ships forward. The image of the Silver Dragon almost leapt off the sails.

The people on the beach gasped and many fell to their knees.

Jame shook her head and Tigh rolled her eyes.

"They need to work on their maritime magic," Jame muttered.

"At least that confirms who we're up against," Tigh said. "We need to send word to Ynit. Just in case all those ships are real."

"What do you mean, in case they're real?" Pijhon asked.

"They've been known to enhance their presence with magic," Tigh said.

As suddenly as the illumination had appeared, it flashed out, replaced by thick darkness dotted by pale bobbing lights.

Tigh sighed. It was going to be a long night.

TIGH KNEW SHE had to think of something to give these hapless villagers a chance against the invading force. It didn't matter whether this armada was the size it appeared to be or a fraction of that size; the village had no way of defending itself. From where she sat, on the outermost tip of a high crag of land, she saw only what the army of the Silver Dragon wanted her to see.

Jame stirred a bit in her sleep and tightened her hold around Tigh. Jame had insisted on staying with her as she sat out in the breeze-cooled night air, keeping an eye on the bobbing ships . . . and thinking.

The country of the Silver Dragon had been built on the foundations of endless conquests and Tigh had the feeling these invaders fed on the fears of the people they perceived to be weaker than themselves. Why else would they engage in continual conquest? They had no pressing need for land and resources. No. They thrived on a combination of greed and an inbred desire to see conquered people suffer.

She remembered feeling that way once. She pondered that thought. Was the mind set of the battle leaders of the Silver Dragon the same as when she had been an artificially enhanced Supreme Commander? Did her enhancements make her thoughts work differently? What would she do if she commanded a fleet of vessels with a resort village inhabiting the perfect place to land her army? If she were bent on conquering everything in her path, she'd conquer the village and continue on, without a thought that they had senselessly ruined the villagers' lives. The ones that survived, that was.

The people of the Silver Dragon conquered for the sake of conquest, nothing more. Tigh choked back a surprising sob at the worthless violence of this endeavor. She used to engage in that kind of worthless violence. But that was war. That was different.

Her mind told her war, for all its horrific bloodshed, was necessary for the protection of life and land from ruthless invaders. The panic stole her breath away and finally loosened as she focused on a single important word—defense. She kept forgetting about that simple word. Fighting had always meant being the aggressor. She had to work on the idea that fighting could also mean not being the aggressor.

It meant not figuring out how to get these villagers to fight off the invading army but how to protect them. Not standing to fight. Running away. Hiding. She struggled with keeping the intense disgust down as she convinced herself it was the residue of her enhancements and cleansing that gave her that reaction, not what was truly inside her soul.

Tigh studied the bobbing lights and the crowds milling on the beach below her. Her heart knew what she had to do. What she was obligated to do as a part of her duties to the state. It was her duty to save the lives of these villagers—any way she could.

She glanced at the sleeping Jame under her arm. Her duty was to keep Jame safe no matter what. She had an obligation to the state, to Emoria, and most importantly, to herself. She gently squeezed the shoulder under her hand and let Jame wake up.

"It's not morning yet," Jame mumbled as she raised her head and gazed blurry-eyed at Tigh.

"Morning will be too late," Tigh said.

Jame sat up. "Too late for what?"

Tigh sighed. "To get everyone off the beach and out of the village."

"Where will they go?"

Tigh blinked at Jame. "Out of sight somewhere."

Jame pulled herself up and scooted around so she faced Tigh. "Tell me what you think needs to be done."

Tigh ran a hand through her hair as she pulled together the threads of her idea. "The people of the Silver Dragon conquer just for the sake of conquering. A part of that is feeding a sick satisfaction of watching people suffer. If we remove the people from the village, it'll deny them the opportunity to fulfill this need. Leaving them frustrated and, hopefully, put them off guard."

Jame nodded. "Do you think you can convince the villagers to leave their homes and possessions?"

"If they stay, they'll lose everything anyway, including their lives for some of them." Tigh felt a greater conviction in her plan but became distracted by a fleeting thought.

"What?" Jame asked.

"I just remembered a story I read about this army." Tigh took Jame's hand. "I remember thinking when I read it, it was too strange to be really true because an army wouldn't act that way. But after seeing them up close and hearing Roseh talk about them, I think there might be some truth to it."

"What's the story?" Jame asked.

Tigh climbed to her feet, pulling Jame up with her. "We need to find the mayor. I'll tell you on the way."

"DO YOU HAVE somewhere for the people to go?" Jame asked Pijhon after Tigh had presented her plan.

"We have those shelters we built during the war," Pijhon said.

Tigh pinned Pijhon with steady eyes. "This is the reason why they're there. Did you also work out an evacuation plan?"

"Yes. But that was years ago," Pijhon said.

"Refresh everyone's memory," Tigh said. "The village has to look deserted by sunrise."

"But what about the people's possessions and property?" Pijhon asked.

"Do they value that over their own lives?" Tigh arched an eyebrow. "You have to convince them that possessions and property aren't much use to someone who's been taken into slavery or killed."

Pijhon jerked her head back. "Slavery?"

"We just broke up a major slaving ring. Slaves for the people of the Silver Dragon," Jame said. "These people don't live by the same rules we do."

"Slaves," Pijhon said with a shiver of disgust.

The ghostly sails looming in the now misty sea glowed green and then yellow before returning to silver, causing a new rise of noise from the villagers on the beach.

"I can't guarantee this army won't do much damage to the village," Tigh said. "But if my guess is right, they'll be more interested in hunting the villagers down first. They're into showing their power and that needs an audience."

"I'll call for an evacuation," Pijhon said. "I'll emphasize that anyone left will risk being killed or taken into slavery."

"That ought to do it," Tigh said. "Jame and I will secure the village as much as we can before we join you in the shelters."

Jame turned to Tigh with a raised eyebrow. "We'll what?"

"We're going to secure the village," Tigh said.

Jame gave Tigh a sidelong look and then turned to Pijhon. "Don't worry, Tigh knows what she's doing. You just make sure everyone gets to the shelters. By the way, where are the shelters?"

"Follow the westbound road until you get to the first farm lane, go north past the second farm cottage then follow the dirt road just north of that around two hills," Pijhon said. "We'll have someone looking out for you."

"We'll be there as soon as we can," Jame said.

Pijhon rushed off the pavilion.

"Secure the village?" Jame asked.

Tigh stared at the silver sails lining the horizon. "We have to figure out a way of stopping that army. Reinforcements from Ynit will come too late."

"How can we stop that?" Jame waved at the bobbing ships.

"I don't know." Tigh sank down cross-legged on the pavilion.

PIJHON ALLOWED THE villagers a sandmark to put their most treasured belongings into the hidden rooms that were fashioned for each resident during the Grappian Wars. She reminded them they all learned what to do in the face of an invading army, and this situation was no different just because they weren't officially at war.

"Tigh thinks the army is more interested in people than things," Pijhon said as she stared down Hicom, a sputtering little man with more possessions than sense. "If your collection of carved turtles is more important than your life, then you can stay and protect it and everything else you hold precious."

Hicom's scowl was contradicted by a nervous laugh. "They wouldn't actually hurt us. We're civilians."

"This army doesn't fight other armies unless it has to," Tigh said in Hicom's ear. He jumped and spun around to find her steely blue eyes boring into him. "They like to prey on innocent people. Take them as slaves. Kill them for sport. They especially like to see particularly vain and foolish people suffer where it hurts them the most. Let's just say, if you want a chance of keeping your collections intact, hide them away and escape the village before that army sees you."

Hicom's eyes were so wide they seemed to engulf his thin face. Without a word, he turned, sprinted across the beach, and disappeared into the mass of people rushing to their homes.

"Nicely put." Jame gave Tigh an amused look.

Tigh raised an eyebrow. "Words can be very powerful tools."

"Thank you. I'll see you later, then." Pijhon gave them an uncertain look.

"We'll get there when we can," Jame said.

Pijhon nodded and ran off to save her own possessions.

Tigh stepped to the edge of the lapping sea and stared at the line of Silver Dragon sails.

"Surely they know the villagers are being evacuated," Jame said.

"They probably look forward to chasing them through the countryside," Tigh said through clenched teeth.

"I can't bring myself to believe that anyone could be that ruthless," Jame said.

Tigh turned cold eyes to her.

"Not even you."

"Not me." Tigh sighed and dug the toe of her boot into the sand. "Patch was that ruthless."

"How do we have any chance against them?" Jame asked.

"Our only hope is to give them something outside of their narrow scope of expectations." Tigh turned around and gave the beach a speculative look. She then looked at the shadowy cliffs looming over the long, wide strip of sand. A mist rose off the sea. "Let's take a little walk."

Jame padded alongside Tigh as they climbed the steps carved into the cliff back up to the village proper. Tigh led the way down the narrow main road and into the tight rolling barren hills of the countryside.

"I thought we were going to secure the village," Jame said.

"We are." Tigh stopped at the base of a low hill and looked up its slope into the darkness. "Let's go up here."

Jame followed Tigh to the rounded top of the hill. Tigh stopped and looked down into what appeared to be a mist-filled valley in the night darkness.

"What?" Jame asked as she peered into the shrouded landscape.

"Stay here for a moment." Tigh shuffled down the hill and disappeared into the mist.

Jame sighed and plopped down on one of the rock outcroppings that revealed the volcanic origins of the soft rounded hills. She was going to have to work with Tigh on communicating what ran around in that complicated mind of hers.

She didn't have to wait long for Tigh to reappear out of the mist.

Tigh held out a hand. "Let's walk this way."

Jame took the hand, and Tigh pulled her to her feet. "Do you finally have a plan?"

"Yes." Tigh didn't offer anything more as she trudged down the spine of the hill.

"Care to fill me in?" Jame tried to keep her voice light as she fought back her growing frustration.

"Maybe." Tigh flashed her an impish look.

Jame relaxed a bit. Tigh must feel confident enough with her plan to play with her.

"Am I supposed to guess what it is?" Jame asked.

Tigh cast her an amused look. "I'd like to see you try."

Jame laughed. "Knowing you, it could be anything."

They followed the hill until they met the mist on the lower slope. Several steps into the mist took them to an unexpected drop off. A cliff revealing an inland harbor.

"You don't think they know about this?" Jame asked.

"They've probably seen the mouth to it and most likely dismissed it as a large river," Tigh said. "Nothing that could possibly stop them."

"It's an interesting plan but I have one little question." Jame crossed her arms and sauntered around Tigh. "How are you going to convince them to climb this particular hill?"

Tigh turned to look at the distance ships shrouded in thick white mist. "There are a couple of details I haven't worked out yet."

Chapter 18

COMMANDER DRUTHE SPENT the night on the bow of the lead ship staring at the place Commander Nerlon had confidently chosen as the perfect place to land her invasion force. She got a good look at the long wide beach when the alarm had sounded in the village, and all the villagers jumped out of their cozy beds to see what was off their shoreline. They made enough noise and lit enough torches to betray an innocence that only came with living without armed conflict.

Commander Nerlon stood beside her and laughed at how naive these villagers who lived on the frivolity of others were. Druthe made no comment. She was there to be ridiculed for botching a simple straightforward siege. Her punishment for bringing defeat and dishonor upon her people was for this invading army to use her knowledge of the land and show her how easy it was to defeat the soft and weak inhabitants of the Southern Territories.

Druthe watched the villagers evacuate the beach and wondered if they thought hiding in their homes would protect them. More slaves to ship back to the homeland. She scrunched her nose in distaste. She found little sport in the capture of pampered villagers who were used to having everything they needed.

Someone down there had the sense to evacuate the villagers from the beach. The fact the people had gone to the beach to look at the fleet in the first place caused Nerlon to think the people of the Southern Territories had the mentality of a herd of cows.

"They even let men into their armies," Nerlon bellowed, holding her sides from laughter. "Any woman who would trust a man's ability to guard her back is an idiot."

Druthe kept her comments to herself. The men in the Southern Territories weren't the weak creatures found on their home continent. Some were even in surprisingly skilled jobs.

She stared across the low mist at the beach and the tumble of buildings on the hills above the cliffs. Quiet. Not the restless with anticipation kind of quiet. An eerie silence like she felt after they'd rounded up all the inhabitants of a village. Nerlon would most likely laugh at her. Nerlon had as much sensitivity to her surroundings as a cabbage, maybe less.

Muffled splashes alerted her that the small boats were being lowered. Nerlon was eager to get on with the first major campaign of her career. *Too eager?* Druthe mused. *Time will tell.*

Landing magic-enhanced troops by boat was a lot trickier than marching across land. The number of small boats needed was absurdly large for the number of actual troops, considering two-thirds of the inhabitants of any given boat were illusions.

Druthe's impression of the quiet only intensified once she stood on the silver sand in the gray before the dawn. A smirking Commander Nerlon strode up to her.

"The fools. They think they can hide from us." Nerlon made of show of studying the soldiers as they lined up in their Regiments and looking up at the buildings on top of the cliff. "I think all we have to do is fill the streets with soldiers and ask for a peaceful surrender. Resort villagers don't make good enough sport to waste extra effort on."

Druthe merely nodded and followed after Nerlon as she took her position at the head of the column of troops. Her feeling about the place didn't improve as she stood alongside Nerlon on one of the decorative towers used for watching the ocean. The view also took in a good portion of the village.

When all the troops were in place, Nerlon raised an amulet in front of her mouth. "We'll not harm anyone if you come out and peacefully surrender. If you don't come out, we'll torch the town. It matters not to us which one you choose. Your village is of no consequence to us."

Silence swallowed the last echoes of Nerlon's projected voice. Heartbeats passed and the silence was broken by the call of sea birds and the breeze playing with the ornaments on the buildings.

Nerlon let out an incredulous growl. "Are they such fools that they think we're bluffing?"

"I don't think anyone's here," Druthe said.

"Not here?" Nerlon spun around and scowled at Druthe. "They wouldn't have left their village for the wind to defend."

"They aren't from our continent," Druthe said, trying to keep her voice reasonable. "We can't think we know them, because we don't."

Nerlon glared at Druthe. "Rhoy!"

Several heartbeats later, a woman with gray streaked hair and impossibly smooth skin on her face climbed to the top of the tower. The edges of the brown cloth wrapped around her body fluttered in the stiff sea breeze.

"Do you detect any people in this village?" Nerlon asked, keeping an eye on Druthe.

Rhoy casually waved her hand and shrugged. "Only the troops."

"What?" Nerlon stiffened. "Where are the villagers?"

Rhoy sighed and waved a hand again. "Over that hill." She pointed to a sizable mound that rose from the edge of the village. "Behind where that person is standing." She raised an amused eyebrow.

Druthe and Nerlon spun around and stared hard at the hill.

Half-illuminated in an intense finger of orange from the rising sun and half in shadow, a solitary figure stood dead center on top of the hill.

Druthe put her pocket spyglass to her eyes, studied the person, and then slowly lowered the instrument.

Nerlon glared through her own spyglass. "What an idiot. Must be a battle-addled soldier with a death wish."

You got it half right, Druthe thought as the figure blazed in the light of the rising sun.

"I WASN'T EXPECTING all this exercise," Jame said as she put her shoulder to a round bale of hay that was half her size in height.

"Staging a battle can be hard work." Tigh pressed her shoulder to another bale and rolled it down the hill.

"I don't remember the chapter on hay bales as weapons in military history class." Jame pushed her bale until it rolled on its own.

"We'll be writing that chapter if this works." Tigh worked her bale into position, then wobbled Jame's bale next to it.

Eight bales now stood as a divider on the little strip of land that separated the hill from the rest of the continent.

"You really think this will work?" Jame asked as she hopped on top of a bale.

Tigh raised an eyebrow. "It either works or we have an army chasing after us."

Jame, towering over Tigh for a change, crossed her arms and raised her own eyebrow. "Then we'd better make sure it works."

Tigh grinned and pulled Jame down into her arms. "It'll work."

Jame looked into Tigh's night-darkened eyes. "Be careful."

"I'll be careful."

"No, really." Jame put her hands on Tigh's cheeks. "It would kill me if anything happened to you."

"I wouldn't survive if . . ." Tigh faltered, unable to even voice the unthinkable.

Jame wrapped her arms around Tigh. "I want to live long enough to become Queen of Emoria with you as my consort."

"Sounds like a simple enough goal," Tigh said.

Jame straightened and touched her lips to Tigh's.

"If we want that as our goal, I think we'd better work on not getting into situations like this," Jame said.

Tigh could only nod as she pulled Jame closer, allowing that sensation to imprint on her soul. Everything she had desired in life had been tied to fighting. She had craved the feel of the sword in her hand like she now craved Jame in her arms. "I promise you'll rule Emoria with me at your side."

Jame pulled back and studied Tigh. "I promise to hold you to that promise."

They stood in a wheat field in the sandmark before dawn with an invading army dropping small boats into the sea intent upon invasion and Tigh felt a confident strength from the words of a simple promise.

"You need to go tell the villagers to stay put," Tigh murmured in Jame's ear.

Jame nodded. "I'll be back as quickly as possible."

Tigh scanned the ships bobbing in the gray light of the false dawn before the sun restored color to the land. "I think we have about two sandmarks. It takes a while to land an army of that size."

Jame sucked in a breath and pulled Tigh down for another heartfelt kiss. "Remember our promise."

"It's engraved on my heart," Tigh said as she released Jame.

Jame took several steps backwards. She pulled her eyes away from Tigh, jumped over the hay bales, and jogged down the narrow dirt trail to the shelters.

Tigh sighed as she watched until Jame disappeared around a hill. The promise may have been outrageously impossible to keep, given their tendency to get mixed up in dangerous situations, but it calmed her. It helped her focus on the sole purpose of her life, which was to keep Jame safe and happy. This meant keeping herself safe and happy.

She trudged up the hill and found a boulder to sit on that allowed a clear view of the Silver Dragon fleet and the village. As the small boats kicked up small white splashes alongside the ships and crept to the long shoreline of sand, her mind meandered around what they had truly promised to each other.

She stared at the silver and bronze uniforms lining up on the beach with enviable efficiency and was possessed with the determination to stop this army no matter what it took—short of sacrificing her own life to do it. The concept was new to her warrior heart. Elite Guards had been trained to always put victory above their own lives. Now victory came with even a greater price—fashioning a strategy she had the best chance of surviving.

Facing down an army single-handed didn't fit into this new strategic outlook. Tigh sighed as the orderly troops marched into the deserted streets of Tanders. *We should have had that little chat earlier.*

NERLON SNEERED. "I take it you know who this madwoman is."

"She's the one the people call Dragonslayer," Druthe said as she watched Tigh with both curiosity and an earned respect. "She was the one who masterminded the Siege of Operal."

"So that's Tigh the Terrible," Nerlon said. "What's she doing here? How could she have known we were here? Until last night, we were nothing more than a dozen fishing fleets out at sea."

"She was working with a wizard before," Druthe said.

"There's no wizard here," Rhoy cut in with confidence.

Druthe leveled cold eyes at her. "That's what Rinra said."

"Rinra had always been too cocky," Rhoy muttered but her eyes betrayed her uncertainty.

"Why else would she stand alone up there like a mad person if she didn't have a wizard behind her?" Nerlon asked.

Rhoy shrugged. "She could be bluffing."

"That's what Rinra thought." Druthe couldn't help but rub it in.

"Rinra made a mistake." Rhoy straightened and pressed her spyglass to her eye in a show of confidently studying the tall black-clad figure. "She's alone on that hill, and somewhere behind her are the villagers, hiding from us like scared rabbits."

Nerlon strutted around the platform in agitated thought. "If there isn't a wizard, and if the only people around are those cowardly villagers, then she's going to try to bluff us into stepping down. You may have allowed it to happen, Druthe, but I'm not going to. It's only fitting that our first action upon invading this new land is to cut down their hero from the Grappian Wars."

Druthe kept her opinion to herself. A part of her was too interested in seeing Nerlon put in her place by the warrior standing calmly on the hill.

"Assemble the troops." Nerlon's magic enhanced voice echoed throughout the village.

The figure on the hill unsheathed her sword and casually flipped it over her hand.

THE EARLY MORNING mist didn't drift across the land but hovered over the surrounding water in bloated winter-touched clouds.

Time to get home to Ynit, Tigh mused, as the focused fingers of sunlight touching her did little to take away the chill from the air. But first she had to ensure they had a home to go to. This army of the Silver Dragon was making a pest of itself.

She observed that a good two-thirds of the troops remained on the beach. She guessed these were illusions. It's what she would do.

Tigh cocked her head as she observed the troops stomping up the hill toward her. The precise rhythm of their march sounded incongruent with the number of soldiers. Another illusion. Only an army used to getting their way would rely so much on magic.

The soldiers fell into long lines that followed the irregular undulations of the hill of dry remnants of wheat plants and then snapped into rigid silent statues in the windy dawn air. Something stopped them from just coming at her and removing her as an obstacle.

Ah, now things were making some sense. Tigh casually flipped her sword over her shoulder as the Commander and a wizard, trailed by an expressionless Druthe, pushed through the middle of the line of soldiers to stand fifty paces from her. Of course, they could have gone up the next hill and not bothered with her at all. But these were a people who couldn't resist an easy conquest.

"One thing I never tolerated in my army was the inability to make sensible decisions. Especially when they could turn into life or death decisions." Tigh rested her sword on her shoulder as she eyed the bristling young Commander with disinterest. "You don't look as much of a challenge as Commander Druthe had been."

The commander lunged forward a pace and then looked as if she realized she shouldn't react like that in front of her troops. She straightened and glared at Tigh. "Looks can be deceiving. You haven't felt the sting of the command of Nerlon."

"Hmmm." Tigh swept casual eyes over Nerlon. "I think you'll have to convince me."

Nerlon tensed in anger. "I don't think you're in much of a position to be making comments like that."

Tigh allowed a feral grin. "Looks can be deceiving."

Nerlon glanced back at the wizard, who shrugged. "You cannot defeat us. You have no army and you have no magic."

Tigh swept a glance to either side of her. "I have all the army and all the magic I need to defeat your puny army."

"You cannot weave an army out of nothing," Nerlon said.

Tigh laughed. "Why not? You've woven an army out of a handful of nothing soldiers." The wizard glanced around at the line of soldiers behind her. "Don't worry. Your rather primitive illusion is still in place."

The wizard glared at Tigh. She grabbed her amulet and squeezed it. The smirk on her face turned into frustrated puzzlement. She muttered a few words and squeezed her amulet again.

Tigh frowned a bit at the wizard's actions and waited for them to make the next move.

"Things are not what they appear," the wizard muttered to Nerlon.

"What?" An angry Nerlon spun around and glared at the wizard.

"Magic is at work here," the wizard said in a low tone.

"Then stop it," Nerlon said. "That's your job, isn't it?"

"It's a complicated magic," the wizard said.

"Complicated?" Nerlon sneered. "The magic here is of a minor sort. How can it be complicated?"

"There are obviously some things we don't understand about this magic." The wizard eyed Tigh.

"Are you saying there's an army stashed in these hills somewhere?" Nerlon asked.

"I'm saying it's possible," the wizard said.

Nerlon straightened and cast an arrogant look at Tigh. "I think the wizards in this army have faced the dragon's fire one too many times and have become cowards. We don't need any magic to rid the world of this so-called dragonslayer."

Tigh raised her hand to stifle a yawn. "Sounds fine with me. I could use the exercise. Do you want me to fight one at a time or all at once?"

Druthe snorted her amusement. Nerlon unsheathed her sword and ran toward Tigh.

"I don't need any help to wipe that arrogant smirk from your face." Nerlon swept her sword at Tigh who checked her progress with the black blade flashing in the long morning sun.

Tigh pushed Nerlon away, flipped over her head, and gave her a booted shove down the hill away from the army. A muffled splash was heard a few heartbeats later.

Tigh turned around and sheathed her sword. "Next?"

Druthe drew in a deep breath and took a step forward. "Nerlon was a hot-headed fool. But even you can't defeat a whole army."

Tigh crossed her arms. "Are you so positive you're willing to risk a more humiliating defeat than at Ynit?"

Druthe studied Tigh. "Why all this playing? Why not just bring your army out into the open and face us in a fair fight?"

Tigh shrugged. "You like to play with illusionary soldiers, we like to play with fire."

A hiss cut through the mist-shrouded air, and Druthe and the wizard turned toward the direction of the sound. Jame stood on a hay bale that blocked the narrow entrance to the hill. She held up a blazing torch.

"You may not have noticed, but we're standing in a newly harvested wheat field," Tigh said. "We're also in the dry south where there's very little rainfall this time of year. Any little spark has been known to consume one of these fields when the wind is blowing just right." She held up her belt rag and nodded in satisfaction as the breeze vigorously pushed it away from Jame's direction. "I think we have the perfect conditions for a little field fire, don't you?"

"Do you think a fire will stop us?" Druthe straightened. "Rhoy here will stop the fire as soon as it starts."

Tigh nodded as she bent down to pick up an unlit torch. "The funny thing about fire is that it takes on a life of its own once it starts and even a wizard can't devise continuous spells to put it all out." She struck a flint against the stick of the torch and lit a taper. She lifted the taper to the tip of the torch and set it ablaze.

"You'll burn yourselves," Rhoy said.

Tigh shrugged. "We're protected by magic. And so is our fire."

The wizard reached for her amulet but was stopped by a mind jangling blow to her head.

Tigh flashed a grin at Jame, who flipped her slingshot back onto her belt. She then sprinted toward the bales of hay while running the tip of the torch along the broken and dry wheat stalks.

The field in her wake and took no time to pass the flame across the field with a speed that startled the army enough to force them to flee back to the village. As soon as Tigh leapt onto a bale of hay, Jame set the stalks in front of them aflame.

Without a conscious wizard to maintain the illusion, the ranks of soldiers dissolved until there were maybe two or three hundred troops fleeing the now out of control fire.

"There are hardly any real soldiers at all," Jame said as they watched the fleeing army of the Silver Dragon.

"The confidence that comes from too much success can conquer an army faster than any enemy," Tigh said.

A distant rhythmic pounding from behind pulled their attention away from the blazing field.

"I think Commander Maure needs to thank you for another sash on her shoulder," Jame said as the Reserves for the Southern Territory rounded the top of a distant hill.

"I think I'll let her earn her own sashes from now on," Tigh said.

Chapter 19

THE SOUND OF a happy and contented whistling reached Jame's ears before Tigh strolled around the corner into their tiny lane. Tigh carried a sizable wooden box on her shoulder.

Jame straightened from her stooped position in front of an artful arrangement of newly planted cactus. She never imagined she would get so much satisfaction from puttering in her small garden patches.

"What's that?" Jame asked as Tigh stopped in the lane in front of her.

Tigh raised an eyebrow. "A trunk."

Jame gave Tigh a good-natured slap on the arm. "Let me re-phrase that. Why are you carrying a trunk?"

"Because it can't walk on its own," Tigh said.

"And why would it need a reason to walk about?" Jame couldn't help but revel in Tigh's playful mood.

"So it can inhabit a corner of our bedroom," Tigh said. "It was most insistent about that."

"That sounds like the kind of excuse an obsessive shopper would make," Jame said in amusement. "And you may be a lot of things, but a shopper you're not."

"Sometimes I make an exception for special things," Tigh said as she turned to the little path that led to their front door.

"Special things." Jame intercepted Tigh at the door.

"Very special things." Tigh shuffled around Jame to get through the doorway.

A curious Jame followed Tigh into the bedroom, where she lowered the trunk to the one empty corner. Tigh knelt down, unlatched the top, and pushed it open. Jame looked over Tigh's shoulder and was surprised to see that the trunk was lined with a soft gray cloth.

She cocked her head at Tigh. "What are you planning to put it there?"

Tigh's face creased in an impish grin. "Things that are very, very special."

Trying not to laugh, Jame put her hands on her hips in a stern pose. Tigh walked to a shapeless leather pouch hanging from a peg on the wall. "I thought you didn't put much importance on that sort of thing."

Tigh looked down at the neatly swept floor. "I, uh, thought we should keep these things safe for, uh . . ." She took a deep breath and exhaled. "For our descendants."

Jame bit her lip at Tigh's shyness around the subject of children. She knew it was a difficult idea for a non-Emoran to grasp. "That's very thoughtful of you." She took the pouch from Tigh. "I think the Emoran people would also want to have these things kept in the archives."

Tigh nodded, and they knelt in front of the trunk. The first thing Jame pulled from the pouch was a stone plaque. Tigh took it from her and studied the words etched on it.

"I'm so proud of you," Tigh said.

"Really?"

"Of course." Tigh brushed her lips against Jame's cheek. "You saved those children and got rid of the underground activity in Maymi."

"You did as much to help," Jame said.

"You got a plaque because you went beyond the call of duty to do your job," Tigh said. "I got this scroll of commendation because I was just doing my job." She placed the scroll on top of the plaque and put them in the trunk.

Jame gazed at the items cushioned in the soft gray cloth and felt a tingle at the thought that their child or children would open this trunk of cherished memories. She raised her head and captured blue eyes. "Thanks for thinking of this." She pressed her lips against Tigh's, feeling thankful at that moment for everything in her life. Feeling that a future in which she could pursue her dream and do her duty to her people was, not only possible, but a wondrous journey as long as Tigh was by her side.

Tigh grinned and pulled another scroll from the pouch and put it into the trunk.

"I have the feeling you're going to be collecting a lot of those," Jame said.

"I don't even know why Maure did this," Tigh muttered.

"If she could have done more she would have," Jame said. "Your guidance allowed her to stop the army of the Silver Dragon. That's something she's not about to forget."

"I was just following her orders." Tigh shrugged as she reached back into the pouch and pulled out a pair of scrolls tied together with a ribbon imprinted with the seal of the village of Tanders.

"I like this one the best because we both received equal thanks," Jame said.

Tigh wrapped her arm around Jame and gave her a squeeze. "We'll have to work on doing that more often."

"Even if it means a big military ceremony in front of everyone in Ynit?" Jame asked.

Tigh groaned and laid the double-scroll into the trunk. "Maybe we can just sneak away. We can visit my family."

"I think Maure has invited them to attend. She sent an invitation to Emoria, too." Jame sighed. "I don't expect anyone to show up."

"They might." Tigh lifted Jame's chin with a finger and looked into her eyes. "They have to be proud of you."

Jame nodded. "They can't show what's in their hearts though. Not while I'm estranged from them."

"If I could make it right with them, I would," Tigh said.

"That would mean us not being together, so that wouldn't make it right with me," Jame said. "I'll go back on my own terms, not theirs. Until then, my life is complete and content with you as my family."

Tigh dropped the empty pouch and pulled Jame into her arms. "I can now lift a sword without fear of losing who I am now. You've completed my soul."

"WHOA, THAT'S AN imposing look for you, sis," Juon greeted as he and the twins, Pandon and Patlin, entered the billowing tent tucked behind the ceremonial platform on the plaza.

A puzzled Tigh looked down at herself and shrugged. Pandon and Patlin walked cautiously up to their big sister.

Tigh had added her full set of armor plating to her usual black leathers. The metal, polished to a proud shine, seemed to sparkle from its own light source. Several purple sashes dangled from the armor plate molded to her left shoulder. One for each victory she brought home during the Grappian Wars. Ceremonies such as the one she and Jame were about to participate in had not existed for the Elite Guards during the Wars. The Guards had been too wild and unruly to control, so their sashes were kept for them until after they were cleansed.

"We're very proud of you," Pandon said as she kissed Tigh on the cheek. "Even Mother's been bragging to the other Guild members about how you saved us from another war."

Tigh rolled her eyes and accepted a kiss on the cheek from her brother and other sister. "We were only doing our job."

"Facing down an army alone?" Juon exclaimed. "I've never seen a peace warrior do anything like that."

Tigh shook her head as she carefully re-wrapped Jame's braid onto her belt. Much to Jame's delight, Tigh not only kept the braid given her for the Summer Solstice, she always had it tied to her belt.

"Of course, there's never been a peace warrior quite like Tigh," Jame said from behind them.

The Tigis siblings turned as Jame slipped into the tent. Their jaws dropped open at the sight of her dressed in full Emoran warrior leathers and armor. The hilt of a sword even peeked over her shoulder.

"Wow," was all Patlin could utter.

"I'm only wearing this because it was the only way to get Tigh to wear her full-dress uniform," Jame said.

"Besides, I really like you in those leathers," Tigh said.

"Really?"

"Oh yeah," Tigh said.

"What a coincidence." Jame sauntered up to Tigh. "I really like you in all that leather and armor."

"It's good to see you two still like each other," Pandon said as Juon and Patlin stifled a laugh.

"Oh yeah." Tigh gave Jame a silly grin.

Jame laughed and wrapped her arms around Tigh's waist. "We've decided to keep each other around."

"That's good to hear," Paldon said from behind them. She and Joul stepped into the tent. "We're very proud of both of you."

"Thank you," Tigh said. Never did she think the day would come when her family could feel nothing but pride for her deeds as a warrior.

"We should get to our places in the stands. We'll see you after the ceremony." Paldon gazed at Tigh with proud eyes and an understanding passed between them. Paldon was ready to accept Tigh's chosen life.

"The party's at our place," Jame said as the Tigis clan tromped out of the tent.

Tigh went back to adjusting her armor, allowing the strange feeling of peace to drape over her. Up to that moment, she hadn't realized how much uncertainty she had about her parents' true acceptance of her life as a warrior.

"You know," Jame said, as she helped Tigh with a stubborn clasp on the armor covering an arm brace, "something about how we beat that army has been bothering me."

"The wizard?" Tigh asked.

Jame looked up at her. "Yeah. That's it. Why didn't that wizard just cast a spell on you?"

"She seemed to be uncertain about what happened to the wizard Minchof destroyed," Tigh said. "I have the feeling those wizards are considered indestructible."

"So, she feared we had a wizard more powerful than herself on our side." Jame nodded. "That makes sense."

"It's the only answer I can figure out," Tigh said. "I thought she was trying to cast a spell at one point, but maybe she was just probing around for the other wizard."

"Thank Laur something stopped her, or we'd have a full-scale war on our hands right now," Jame said.

They looked up as the noise from the plaza died away, leaving an almost unsettling quiet in its wake. Several pairs of footfalls approached the tent, and Maure, smartly decked out in her brown dress leathers, stepped into the tent. She froze and stared at them for a several heartbeats, then took a deep breath and nodded.

"Ready?" she asked.

Tigh and Jame nodded in return as they followed Maure out into the intense afternoon sun. An honor guard of six soldiers fell into place beside them. They walked along the back of the platform to the side, but instead of going up the platform steps, Maure led them around to the front.

Tigh's legs stopped before her brain fully comprehended what she was seeing. Before them was not only the full complement of the soldiers stationed at Ynit, but lined in front of these troops were several regiments of black-clad Guards at proud attention.

Jame blinked at the Guards and looked up at Tigh.

Tigh labored to suck in enough air as images from her past and present collided in her mind before settling on the deathly quiet review grounds on that day of peace and celebration.

"We didn't invite them," Maure said. "They just showed up wanting to pay tribute to their former Supreme Commander. It'd be a great honor for them if you reviewed your troops one last time."

Tigh swallowed down the rush of emotion that threatened to envelop her. She nodded, then strode to the Guard standing in front of the first black-clad regiment, and was face to face with Iklas, who straightened and saluted.

"Show your troops," Tigh ordered quietly.

Iklas spun on her heel to front the stone-faced Guards behind her. The sound of her sword sliding against the leather sheath cut through the air. Three hundred black-bladed swords hissed in unison and whipped into a precise salute. The menace that once flowed off the Guards was no longer present, but the memories of the feeling sent shivers through the spectators.

Iklas gave a sharp whistle, and the troops dropped to one knee and laid their swords on the adobe brick ground. Iklas blew two sharp whistles, and hundreds of black gloved hands slapped the ground. The Guards then jumped to their feet.

Iklas turned, dropped to one knee, and laid her sword on the ground in front of Tigh. She then stood. "We give our swords to you, Supreme Commander. We'll stand behind you in peace as we did in war. All we need is your call to arms and we'll be there."

The pledge was too much for Tigh to take in at once. How could these women give that kind of loyalty to her? How could they ever be certain that Tigh the Terrible wouldn't return one day?

She took in the expectant faces of the women who lived through the same personal nightmare as she had and knew any bit of dignity was better than none. If pledging their swords to her gave them that dignity, then she certainly wasn't going to deny it to them.

"I accept your swords."

The Guards dropped to their knees, scooped up their swords, and held them in a salute.

"Instruct your troops to stand and be at ease," Tigh said.

A grinning Iklas held her sword aloft and the Guards rose to their feet, sheathed their swords, and clasped their hands behind their backs. The sounds from their precise movements striking the air died quickly away.

The stunned spectators filled the air with cheers as Tigh stepped back to a beaming Jame.

"They love you," Jame whispered, "and so do I."

Captured by the only words that meant anything to her, Tigh finally relaxed and gave Jame a tentative smile.

Maure led them up onto the platform where representatives of the Federal Council, in their robes of the colors of Ingor, Ynit, and Tanders, stood waiting.

The Council member from Ynit stepped forward and waited for the crowds huddled around the edges of the plaza to be silent.

"I'm pleased to announce we're here to declare that all is at peace in the Southern Territories rather than at war." The strong voice of the Ynitsian Council member was a legacy of the warrior she once was. "We can thank Jamelin Ketlas, peace arbiter and Princess of Emoria, and Paldar Tigis, peace warrior and Reserve Supreme Commander for this miracle. Because it's truly nothing short of a miracle that we're gathered here in peace. The first time the army of the Silver Dragon tried to invade our Territories, we had our brave peacetime army led by Commander Maure and the wise counsel of Tigh to stop them. The second time the army of the Silver Dragon attempted to invade, we had only the wits and resourcefulness of Tigh and Jame." The Council member smiled and turned to them. "They're not ones to brag, and we may never know exactly how they persuaded that army to leave our shores without a fight. We'll just have to settle for the eyewitness account of Commander Maure, who saw them standing up on a hill above the village of Tanders with the mighty army of the Silver Dragon fleeing these two as if they were an army of twenty thousand."

The Council members from Tanders and Ingor, with purple slashes draped over one hand and a plaque in the other, stepped next to their colleague.

"Come accept our tokens of thanks for your acts of bravery in facing down the army of the Silver Dragon as they attempted, once again, to invade our continent," the Council member from Ynit said.

Tigh and Jame gave each other reassuring looks that this ordeal was almost over and approached the three members of the Federation Council.

The proud old warrior took the purple slashes and hooked them on Tigh's and Jame's shoulder armor.

"You make this warrior's heart pound with pride," the Council member said as she handed them their plaques.

Tigh read the words on the plaque as the thunderous cheers beat against her ears. The old warrior gently turned them to face the jubilant crowd.

"This is too strange," Tigh muttered, blinking back unexpected tears.

"Yes," Jame said with tears in her own eyes. "But it's a good kind of strange."

Tigh turned to Jame and then looked back out at the joyous faces. "I think I can live with this."

T.J. Mindancer may be a figment of someone's imagination or just someone who likes to imagine she's a figment while she creates worlds for her characters to inhabit. She has spent her life working with books as an academic librarian and as an editor for two publishing companies and has had some of her scribbled words published under a couple of pen names—at least one, not a figment. Her work includes the *Tales of Emoria* series of books and shorter tales set in the Emoria world. She also likes to make up places in the real world and write about them. She lives in her Tiny House of the Dragons in Northern California.

L. M... has been a former of... and a magazine of... software... she has worked as a... writer... and... She has been learning... with... and... she... author for two... consulting companies and has... since... she... been a freelance published... author... writer... of... software... and... During her... career... she holds... of... and... she... ... in the... world. She also lives in... She... lives in... in... the... of... the... Sonoran... desert... in... California.

www.ingramcontent.com/pod-product-compliance
Lightning Source LLC
Chambersburg PA
CBHW022153260626
47155CB00017B/1863